Advance Praise for

LEASE ON LOVE

"A hopeful, heartwarming debut. With a relatable disaster of a protagonist and an adorably nerdy hero, this opposites-attract, roommates-to-lovers romance is a true delight."

—Rachel Lynn Solomon, author of *The Ex Talk*

"*Lease on Love* is a delight on every level. Ballard delivers a soft, sweet story with enough shadows to make the happily ever after feel that much more earned. Jack and Sadie together are real in the best ways, and the cast of characters shows the abiding love of friends and found family. This is a beautiful love story about finding something precious that seems out of reach. *Lease on Love* is one of my new favorite romance novels!"

—Denise Williams, author of *How to Fail at Flirting*

"Sadie is a firecracker of a protagonist who's very aware of her flaws, and Jack is her perfect counterpart, embracing all of her rough edges with softness and understanding. *Lease on Love* warmly and wittily underscores that none of us are perfect, but we are all worthy, we are all enough; we all deserve to be loved, not just by others, but by ourselves too."

—Sarah Hogle, author of *Twice Shy* and *You Deserve Each Other*

"*Lease on Love* is a crackling, compulsively readable debut about forging new career and romantic paths, finding strength in found family, and discovering what it truly means to be 'home.' I enjoyed every minute of it!"

—Suzanne Park, author of *Loathe at First Sight* and *So We Meet Again*

LEASE
on
LOVE

LEASE on LOVE

a novel

FALON BALLARD

G. P. Putnam's Sons
New York

PUTNAM
— EST. 1838 —
G. P. PUTNAM'S SONS
Publishers Since 1838
An imprint of Penguin Random House LLC
penguinrandomhouse.com

Copyright © 2022 by Falon Ballard
Penguin supports copyright. Copyright fuels creativity, encourages diverse voices, promotes free speech, and creates a vibrant culture. Thank you for buying an authorized edition of this book and for complying with copyright laws by not reproducing, scanning, or distributing any part of it in any form without permission. You are supporting writers and allowing Penguin to continue to publish books for every reader.

Library of Congress Cataloging-in-Publication Data

Names: Ballard, Falon, author.
Title: Lease on love : a novel / Falon Ballard.
Description: New York : G. P. Putnam's Sons, [2022] |
Identifiers: LCCN 2021048793 (print) | LCCN 2021048794 (ebook) |
ISBN 9780593419915 (trade paperback) | ISBN 9780593419922 (ebook)
Subjects: LCGFT: Romance fiction. | Novels.
Classification: LCC PS3602.A621125 L43 2022 (print) |
LCC PS3602.A621125 (ebook) |
DDC 813/.6—dc23/eng/20211008
LC record available at https://lccn.loc.gov/2021048793
LC ebook record available at https://lccn.loc.gov/2021048794

Printed in the United States of America
2nd Printing

Book design by Alison Cnockaert

This is a work of fiction. Names, characters, places, and incidents either are the product of the author's imagination or are used fictitiously, and any resemblance to actual persons, living or dead, businesses, companies, events, or locales is entirely coincidental.

To Matt, for showing me the meaning of happily ever after

LEASE
on
LOVE

ONE

I *PLUG THE FINAL* numbers into my Get That Promotion, Bitch spreadsheet. Even though I've done enough mental calculations to know the end result will be positive, I still hold my breath, crossing my fingers as I hit enter.

"This could be it. The chance to finally pay off those damn student loans and live comfortably." There's no one else actually in my office, but as usual, I hold a one-sided conversation with the air plant sitting on my desk, housed in a concrete planter dipped in bright pink paint. Neither the plant nor its neon home is finance-firm approved, but it's the only spark of joy in my tiny office.

When I finally force myself to look at the computer screen, my suspicions are confirmed. There it is, beaming through thousands of harmful blue-light rays: A complete budget. A budget based on the salary increase I'm about to earn. A budget allowing me to pay rent on my Kips Bay apartment while also paying off my student loans. In

other words, shining down on me in my cramped office in this towering skyscraper is the Holy Grail of millennial life: a chance to be debt-
free. I just barely manage to hold back a shriek of joy.

Now all that's left is to actually secure said promotion.

I *will* get this promotion. And I will walk into that meeting with
confidence.

Once I get a little reinforcement. Pushing my chair back and standing, I grab my phone, tapping on the screen and pulling up FaceTime.
Our group chat is preset, so I hit call, checking my makeup as I wait
for my best friends, Gemma and Harley, to pick up.

Other than a tiny zit brewing under the would-be-pasty-were-it-
not-for-bronzer skin of my forehead, my face looks flawless. I touch
up my matte pale pink lip anyway and fluff out my light-brown-but
highlighted-within-an-inch-of-its-life hair.

Gemma answers first. "Okay, I've got ten minutes until my room is
flooded with twelve-year-olds and their post-lunch sweaty hormones.
Hit me."

"First, did not need that visual. Second, where's Harley? I only have
time to do this once."

"I'm here, I'm here." Harley's face pops up on my screen, and judging by her slightly breathless greeting, she had to duck out of her own
office before answering my call. "Are we waiting for Nick?"

"Like he'd step away from his desk for a pep talk." Gemma snorts.
"Sadie, stop touching your face."

I glare at her but also heed her advice. "First things first, appearance check." I hold the phone as far away from my body as I can, turning slowly from one side to the other, like I'm a ballerina in a music
box. Or a chicken on a spit. I learned very early on what a perfect

appearance could do for a woman, and I work hard to maintain mine. Confidence in my above-average looks often helps mask the self-doubt in my brain.

"You look fine." Gemma's not even looking at me, currently scribbling something on her whiteboard instead of bothering to glance my way.

Harley jumps in before I can snap at Gemma. "You look perfect as always, Sadie. You got this."

I push my shoulders back, my non-phone hand clenched in a tight fist, resting on my hip. "I am a strong warrior goddess."

"You are a strong warrior goddess," they both chant along with me, Harley mustering much more enthusiasm than Gemma.

The outward confidence seeps inward, drowning out my pesky negative inner thoughts. "I am going to get that promotion and show these motherfuckers who's boss."

"Yeah, I'm not saying that in the middle of my classroom when a kid could walk in any minute. But yes." Gemma plops down at her desk and shoves a chip in her mouth. The loud crunching travels through the phone, making my shoulders tense up.

I drop the mask for a brief second. "Guys."

"Sadie, seriously. You've got this. You've earned that promotion three times over, and it's going to be yours." Harley flashes me a calm smile and a thumbs-up. "You look beautiful, but more important, you know your shit, inside and out." Harley rarely swears, so she must really mean it, and her words give me a much-needed boost.

Gemma moves the phone closer to her face so her eyes dominate my screen. "You got this in the bag, bitch." She lowers her voice on her term of endearment, then anxiously checks to make sure no little ears

3

heard her utter a grown-up word, though lord knows her middle schoolers have heard way worse. And probably said way worse.

"Text us as soon as it's official." Harley gives me a through-the-screen high five.

"You're so buying drinks this weekend." Gemma shoots me a finger gun.

"Love you guys." I blow both a kiss and hang up after their chorus of "I love you too."

Badass-bitch mask firmly in place and bolstered by my friends' confidence in me, I resume my superhero pose, this time tilting my head up and thrusting my chest out for the full effect, both hands firmly planted on my waist. I've never been more thankful to have zero windows in my office.

After sixty seconds of power posing, I peek in the mirror I keep hidden in my desk drawer. I adjust my gray pin-striped pencil skirt and fluff the sleeves of my white silk shirt. "You got this," I tell my reflection before stuffing the mirror back in its hiding space. "I got this," I repeat to my air plant. After one last deep breath, I put on my work face—one slight step up from resting bitch face. A face that says, *I know what I'm doing but I'm also totally approachable!* A woman-at-work-in-finance face.

My phone dings with a text as I pull open my office door.

NICK: Show those motherfuckers who's boss, baby!

Oh, I plan to.

I full-on strut down the hallway of the high-rise building, making my way toward the conference room.

I am an accounting badass. I make spreadsheets my bitch. I'm going to kick this promotion's ass.

The mantra runs on repeat through my mind as I stride through the open conference room door. Most of the team is already here, lounging in high-backed rolly chairs around a long glass-topped table.

I slip into a seat next to my best work friend, Veronica. Other than Veronica and myself, there's only one other woman in the room, my supervisor and mentor, Margo. She hired me right out of college and has guided me through the ranks of the financial analyst world ever since. I give her a small smile, but she doesn't meet my eyes. Shit. My stomach goes for a ride on the Tilt-a-Whirl.

Why won't she look at me? Margo always acknowledges me, even if it's with a simple head nod. This can't be good. Holy fuck.

Any confidence built up by my friends slips right out of me.

No. I'm not going to do that. There could be plenty of reasons Margo doesn't want to look at me. She probably doesn't want to show favoritism. Or spoil the big reveal. I've got this promotion in the bag. I've been working my ass off—I'm talking unpaid overtime, weekends, and holidays—for the past six years, and it's finally about to pay off.

The thought of not living paycheck to paycheck, something I'll be able to do for the first time in my life with the raise accompanying my new job title, almost brings me to tears. But I sure as fuck am not going to blow this promotion by crying in the middle of the conference room.

So I paste on my easygoing-girl smile and clasp my hands together on the table.

The men in the room, a.k.a. the majority of the room, straighten up in their seats when we see our senior partner walking down the hallway. Bill Stevens reminds me of my grandfather, and I know how lucky

I am to work with a manager who actually gives a shit about his employees and hasn't ever once hit on me. Just the fact that I think of it as working *with* him and not *for* him puts him leagues ahead of every other boss I've ever had, and I've been working since I was fourteen. Bill is joined by a guy in his midthirties whom I've never seen before, dressed in an expensive tailored suit and a Yale School of Management tie. Gag.

Veronica pinches my elbow, but I don't turn her way, my eyes glued to Bill as he takes his seat at the head of the table, gesturing for the newcomer to fill the seat on his right.

"Thank you all for coming." Bill takes a minute to look around the room. "I know you're all anxious for the big announcement, and I promise to not keep you in suspense. But before I make anything official, I want to say a few words about one of our rising stars, Ms. Sadie Green."

Veronica pinches my elbow again, and out of the corner of my eye, I see Margo's lips purse tightly together, like she's trying to contain her glee. Or keep from vomiting. One or the other.

"Sadie has been with the company for more than six years now, and I know I'm not the only one who has noticed how often she goes above and beyond the call of duty." Bill makes direct eye contact with me, a warm smile on his face. "And while she has succeeded in all of her previous endeavors, it's now time for her to manage her biggest project yet . . ."

I take in a long breath and just for a second close my eyes, hearing my new title before it actually comes out of Bill's mouth.

". . . training our brand-new senior financial analyst, Chad Thompson."

The room goes silent, and my stomach bottoms out like I'm in a free-falling elevator. Which, frankly, would be preferable to sitting in this very room at this very moment. My hands clench the armrests of my chair like I might actually be plummeting.

Nobody speaks for at least a minute. It's like we're in an episode of *Saved by the Bell* and Zack Morris has called for a time-out. My chest aches because I'm pretty sure I've stopped breathing altogether.

"Who the fuck is Chad Thompson?" The words come blurting out of my mouth in a rush of air before I have time to fully comprehend what I'm saying. All I know is this has to be some kind of sick joke.

Bill stares at me like he's never seen me before. "Chad is my future son-in-law. He just graduated from Yale with his MBA, and I think he's going to be a terrific asset to the company. With your help and guidance, I have no doubt he'll be a great leader."

My mouth drops open, my brain struggling to process the words coming out of Bill's stupid, stupid mouth. "With my help and guidance?" My voice is low and rumbly, one octave above full-blown Exorcist. "You seriously want me to train the man who's straight-up stealing my job?"

Veronica tugs on my elbow, surreptitiously trying to calm me down, but I am having absolutely none of that.

"Sadie. You're a very hard worker and a smart girl, but you aren't ready for senior-level responsibility." Bill's voice drips with condescension, and I mentally take back every nice thing I've ever said about him.

"But some guy who hasn't stepped foot in the building until today is? His major qualification being that he fucks your daughter?"

The room inhales a collective gasp. Veronica rolls her chair away from me, as if no longer willing to claim association.

My cheeks burn and oh my god I said that out loud.

"Everyone out," Bill commands, his quiet pitch more terrifying than if he screamed the words.

I clasp my hands together tightly, focusing on my perfectly manicured fingers, taking slow, deep breaths. I can't believe I just lost my shit in a room full of my colleagues. In front of my boss. In six years, I've never once so much as raised my voice, knowing it only takes one outburst to be labeled *emotional*. And in five minutes I blew right past emotional and straight into irrational and aggressive.

I remain as still as one of those painted statue guys in Times Square, not moving until the rush of suits brushes past me, the room emptying within seconds. I push back my own chair and start to rise, but Bill stops me.

"Sit down."

Closing my eyes for the briefest of seconds, I pull myself together. Sit up straight. Bright smile. Confident eye contact. Cool. Calm. Collected. I can fix this. "When would you like me to start working with Chad, sir?" If I pretend hard enough, he'll forget all about this, right?

Bill steeples his fingers together, tapping his chin thoughtfully. "Of all the girls in this office, I never expected you to react in such an unseemly manner."

"Oh?" I just manage to keep my voice from cracking. Or from firing back how I never expected to fall victim to his straight-up nepotism. "I apologize for my language. I'm not going to lie, I was expecting this promotion. Given my years of service to the company, and the many, many unpaid hours and tasks I've not only willingly taken on but have accomplished successfully."

"Coordinating a few spreadsheets doesn't mean you are ready for senior-level management." His eyes narrow. "And one of your greatest selling points up until today has been your attitude, never pushing back or making a fuss."

My shoulders start to creep up around my ears, my body shrinking in on itself, my anger and disbelief morphing into something far more sinister, a repeated refrain that's been on a constant loop in my mind since I was a kid.

Why would you think you're good enough? You know you'll never be good enough.

"I apologize for my outburst. It won't happen again." My voice is as small as I feel. I push my chair back from the table.

"I'm afraid it's too late for that." Bill stacks his papers before standing. "I'm going to have to let you go, Sadie. That kind of behavior is unacceptable in a place of business. Gather your things, and make sure you stop by HR to sign the paperwork."

My blood chills, freezing the breath caught in my lungs. "You're firing me?"

He strides to the door, not even looking over his shoulder to speak to me directly. "It didn't have to be this way. You should've kept those emotions in check." He pushes out the door, letting it swing shut behind him with a thud.

I sit for less than a minute before I rush out of the conference room. Scurrying as quickly as possible down the hallway I strutted through less than an hour before, I duck into my office without meeting any eavesdropper's looks. The few personal items I keep on my desk—a color-coded planner, my college diploma—get hastily tossed into my purse. I lovingly cradle my air plant in my arms, attempting to gain even a breath of solace from my spiky green friend.

The door to my office opens before I have the chance to escape back out into the hallway.

For a minute, I just look at Margo. My mentor, the woman who took me under her wing and has always had my back—until today. I hold my stuffed purse in front of me like a shield. "Did you know?"

She sighs and tugs on the cuff of her right sleeve, her nervous tic. "I heard a rumor, but I didn't think it was actually true."

I wait for her to say something, anything, to offer a small word of comfort, even though I know comfort isn't her style. "Why didn't you say anything in there? You hung me out to dry, Margo."

She bristles at the accusation. "You hung yourself out to dry with your inexcusable outburst, Sadie. Do you know how bad you made me look? Did you even think about how your behavior would reflect on me as your mentor? How selfish are you?"

I almost laugh because I know exactly how selfish I am. Margo sure as hell isn't the first person in my life to tell me.

But selfish or not, I know I just got screwed over. "I watched a man who hasn't been here for five minutes take the position I rightfully earned over the past six years. But my words were inexcusable?" I move to push past her, beyond ready to be free of this place.

She blocks my path. "Sometimes you have to take what you're given and make the best of it."

I stare at her for a second, not fully believing what I'm hearing. Shaking my head, I pull open the door to my office for the last time. "Fuck that."

I practically run to the elevator, my finger hovering over the button for the lobby before I think better of it and hit the one for the next floor up, where the HR office lives. The chances of my scraping a reference out of this are slim, but I'll at least have to try if I have any hope of finding another job in finance.

The HR representative doesn't waste any time, walking me through the termination contract I have to sign. I should probably have Harley, who moonlights as my personal lawyer, look it over first, but I don't want to be in this building for a second longer than necessary. I scrawl my signature at the bottom of the page and sprint back to the elevator.

As soon as the doors open at the lobby floor, I run as fast as my heels allow to the exit of the building, pushing outside and sucking in a big breath of fresh New York City air. I purchase a pretzel from a nearby cart and sink down at one of the bistro tables dotting the courtyard of the building next door. Fishing my phone from a pocket of my purse, I pull up our group text chain.

ME: Blueprint at 7:00.

HARLEY: Perfect place to celebrate!

ME: I think you mean commiserate.

NICK: Fuck. What happened? And do we really need to trek to Brooklyn?

ME: I'll tell you guys tonight. And yes. I can't go out and be surrounded by whiny finance bros tonight.

ME: No offense, Nicky.

HARLEY: *hugs*

GEMMA: Shit, just seeing this. WTF, Sadie? Also, Nick, kindly remember the actual hardworking half of us live in Brooklyn.

NICK: 😩

I don't bother to respond. After inhaling my pretzel, I manage to make my commute home, moving on autopilot, proceeding straight to my neighborhood liquor store as soon as I climb the subway stairs at my stop. Grabbing two bottles of wine, I head to the cashier before doubling back for a third and fourth. I pick up a basket, also tossing in a bag of Cheetos and a supersized pack of M&M's.

My apartment is just a block away from the store, but lugging home all my loot makes it feel much farther. I trudge up the five flights of stairs in my nondescript brick building, my reusable tote full of booze and junk food hitting the back of my leg with each step, the smacks punctuating the negative thoughts racing through my brain.

Of course you got fired.

Who would want you to work for them?

It's not like you work that *hard.*

Why do you think you're so much better than everyone else?

Pausing on a landing to catch my breath, I shut my eyes and attempt to push the voice to the back corner of my brain.

I've lived in this building for almost a year, one of my longer residences since I moved to New York for college ten years ago. It's the first time I've lived by myself, which is low-key my favorite feature of the space. The apartment itself is clean and boring, nothing even close to Instagram worthy. I have a kitchen and a bathroom and a bedroom with a door, more than I've ever had to myself before. But I have zero outside space, not even a tiny balcony, and since I've always been a seriously dedicated, bordering-on-overzealous plant enthusiast, it's a major downside.

So I filled the interior with plants that don't require a ton of sunlight, and I spend more than I'd like to admit on fresh flowers from the farmers' market each week. But my soul still itches for a backyard, or even a patio. Growing up in Southern California, outdoor space was plentiful and I always found solace in the garden of my parents' home. It's one of the only things I've missed since I moved to the East Coast.

"Now you'll never be able to afford anything with a yard," I mutter to myself as I finally reach my front door, sweaty and out of breath. You'd think after climbing these stairs every day for a year, I'd be in better shape. You would think.

I place my bottles of wine in the fridge, tearing into both the Cheetos and M&M's, alternating handfuls of each in some disgusting sort of salty/sweet, cheese/chocolate rotation. Kicking off my shoes, I unzip my skirt and flop onto my sofa.

Really, as far as New York City living situations go, it could be a hell of a lot worse. Shit, I've been in a hell of a lot worse. But when I moved into this apartment, a guaranteed promotion was on the horizon. So while it was a bit of a stretch budget-wise, I thought it'd be a short-term stretch. Now even if I find a new job, I have no idea how I'll continue to afford this place.

I swing my feet up onto the coffee table, wishing I'd thought to pour myself a glass of wine before sitting down. Technically, my lease is up in a couple of weeks. And technically, if I want to get out of student loan debt any time before retirement, I should probably move. Again. But the thought of packing up another apartment, lugging boxes down five flights of stairs to a double-parked rented van, makes me want to puke up my stomach full of sugar and processed cheese. I unlock my phone and re-download the roommate-finding app I've used in the past. But even the simple act of logging in to my dormant account makes me want to curl up in a ball and take up permanent residence on this couch.

"Fuck it. I'll just have to settle for being poor." Though I do stop and wonder if investing in a roommate might keep me from talking to my plants.

My phone chirps with an email notification, and I automatically swipe to open it, despite the fact that said chirp is likely spam and not an urgent client email. Since I no longer have clients. Or a work email.

"No!" I declare to my fiddle-leaf fig, tossing my phone to the opposite side of the couch. "I am no longer tied to my phone." And since the opposite side of the couch means only a foot away from me, I reach over and pick up the phone again, turning off all my email notifications. I've been jumping at the first trill of that stupid email chirp for the past six years, like a millennial Pavlov's dog. It's interrupted dates and time with my friends and countless hours of sleep. No more.

It's Thursday night. I'm going to give myself a nice long three-day weekend to grieve and gripe and moan. And then on Monday, I'll hit the pavement. I'll be hired somewhere new and fabulous in no time.

"Now," I say to my tiny room full of plants, "let's get drunk!"

TWO

*B*LUEPRINT IS PACKED when I step out of my Lyft two hours later. Should I have taken the subway? Yes. Did I pay an exorbitant rate just to save myself half an hour? Also yes. Was it worth not having to hike ten blocks in killer-in-more-than-one-way heels? Abso-fucking-lutely.

Harley waits for me out front, looking like she came straight from the office. She's in a too-long black pencil skirt and matching blazer, accompanied by a white button-down and black ballet flats. She opens her arms and pulls me into a hug the moment I approach, and despite my towering over her in my heels, it's the best hug I've had in a long time.

"I need some good news; tell me you kicked some lawyerly ass today." I wriggle out of her embrace before it becomes embarrassing, blinking rapidly to dispel any tears that might've sprung into my eyes at this display of pure kindness.

"Today consisted solely of paperwork; sorry, friend." She gives me a sad smile, and I find myself blinking again.

Harley has one of those smiles that touches her big brown eyes, like it truly means something. She's stunningly gorgeous, with flawless dark brown skin and cheekbones that could cut glass, but she's also by far the most compassionate and empathetic person I've ever met, and I really have no idea why she's friends with me. Her job as a public defender—which she chose specifically to help those who can't afford legal representation, despite getting offers from all the top legal firms—actually matters in the grand scheme of life, unlike the elitist cesspool that is my job. Was my job.

She sweeps her long black box braids over her shoulder. "Want to talk about it now?"

I purse my lips and shake my head. "I think I'll only be able to say it once. Besides, we should put our name in, looks like there's going to be a wait."

She holds out her arm for me to link mine through. "I made a reservation."

I bend down so I can rest my head on her shoulder. "Of course you did."

Harley leads us into the bar, and a host takes us out to the back patio. We slide into seats across from each other, and I immediately reach for the drinks menu. The April evening air is just the right amount of chilly, but I'm going to need to either start drinking or put on my jacket, and I really don't want to detract from my cute outfit: army-green cargo pants fitted through the calf and loose around my hips, paired with a black tank top and lots of gold jewelry.

So drinks it is. I order two different cocktails while Harley requests a sparkling water.

I shoot her a death-beam glare.

"I have to work tomorrow. Justice doesn't serve itself." She gives me an apologetic shrug. "I'm sure Nick will be happy to get wasted with you."

"Speak of the devil." I raise my eyebrows suggestively at Harley while raising my hand to wave to Nick.

Nick is everything I normally like in a man: tall, muscular, floppy brown hair, family money, and a gorgeous smile. He looks like a 2005 Abercrombie ad threw up all over him, spray tan and all. Unfortunately, he's also the nicest guy I've ever met, which totally zaps all my sexual tingles. Luckily, his cinnamon-roll core wasn't immediately obvious when we shared a class together freshman year at Columbia, otherwise I never would've propositioned him. When he politely asked to get to know me better first, I knew there was no future for us, and he quickly became one of my best friends in the world, the perfect complement to the trio Harley, Gem, and I automatically formed as suitemates.

"How are two of my three best gals?" He leans over and kisses each of us on the cheek before taking the seat next to Harley.

"Thanks for trekking all the way to Brooklyn, Nicky." He hates that nickname, so of course it's the only thing I call him. "I just needed to get away from anything even remotely connected to work." Which includes my apartment smack-dab in the middle of bros-of-finance central.

"I just spent an hour on the packed-to-the-absolute-gills subway when I could've been at home relaxing with a beer and baseball, so yeah, you're welcome." He signals the waiter and politely orders a beer and three different appetizers. He doesn't ask us what we want, already knowing exactly what we would order.

"Oh my god, I swear, teenagers are the fucking worst!" Gemma makes this declaration from across the patio as she walks through a crowd toward our table, scattering people as she goes. "Seriously, how many more days left of school, because I'm about to fucking murder some of these hormonal motherfuckers." Gemma keeps her potty mouth in check all day long in her classroom and therefore tends to swear like a Real Housewife of New Jersey whenever free of impressionable preteens. She plops into the seat next to me, banging her head on the table, her thick, straight black hair falling in a shiny curtain around her face. Petite, Korean American, and sassy as hell, Gemma has never been shy about expressing her feelings. I basically want to be her when I grow up.

Harley reaches across the table and pats her head soothingly. "A few more weeks, Gem. You got this."

As Harley moves her arm back to take a sip of her water, she brushes up against Nick's hulking biceps. She bites her lip and averts her eyes while he not so subtly shifts his arm even closer to her.

Ugh. I wish those two would just bone already. But they're both too damn nice to just hit it and quit it, so the whole thing would probably end up turning into some disgusting lovefest, ultimately resulting in me in an ill-fitting pink bridesmaid's dress.

Hmm. Maybe if I start being nicer to Nick, he'll consider making me a groomswoman. I could definitely rock a suit.

"Anyway. Enough tales of woe from the classroom, Ms. Kwon. Back to me." I tug on Gemma's arm until she sits up. Then I hand her my second cocktail. Because I am a giver.

Nick takes a long swig of his beer. "Give it to us, Sade."

I can't bring myself to look any of them in the eye, so I focus on the small centerpiece—a succulent planted in a low glass jar—instead. "I didn't get the promotion. Bill gave it to his future son-in-law." Oof. It hurt earlier, but saying the words aloud is a sucker punch to the gut.

They draw in a collective breath.

Nick recovers first. "What the fuck, Sadie." He reaches across the table and squeezes my hand. "I'm so sorry. That's completely fucked up."

"Did Bill say anything?" Harley asks. "Give you any kind of explanation?"

Gemma throws her arm around my shoulder. "What explanation is there other than nepotism and the patriarchy?"

I let myself sink into her hold for a second, then pull myself upright. "That's not the end of it." I take a sip of my cocktail. "I sort of blew up in the meeting and dropped a bunch of F-bombs, and he fired me."

Their mouths drop open in perfect synchronization.

Gemma speaks first. "What a fucking dick."

"The crazy thing is, until today, he totally wasn't a dick. He gave me a job right out of college. He's always supported me. He's never once hit on me."

Nick scoffs into his beer. "He's not a dick because he's never hit on you? Is the bar really so low?"

"Yes," the three of us answer in unison.

Our server brings over an armload of plates, laden down with appetizers, saving Nick from a lecture on the evils of men. The server piles everything in the middle, and we all dive in, everyone helping themselves. I order another drink because all this food is going to dull the slight buzz I've worked up between my first cocktail and the wine I had back at home, and we absolutely can't have that.

"What are you going to do?" Harley hands me a fried chicken slider, as if she knows I'm going to need some carbs to soak up the alcohol I'm planning on imbibing.

I shove half the slider in my mouth in one bite, avoiding answering her question. A question I've been asking myself since the moment Bill made his announcement. I finally swallow and shrug, as if this whole situation isn't the most devastating thing that's happened to me since I left home for college. "I have a little bit in savings, so between that and credit cards, I'll be okay for a couple months while I look for another job." Because instead of finally getting out of debt, now I'll be falling farther down the hole.

Gemma pounds her fist on the table, making the silverware jump and the glasses rattle. "Fuck that. Seriously, Sadie. Fuck that. Think about how many hours you've given these people. *Given* them, because they sure as fuck haven't paid you for all of them. Not even close. Think about how many dates you turned down and vacations you didn't take, going into the office sick and never getting enough sleep, and this is how they treat you?"

"I know, Gem. Trust me, I know. But he fired me. What else can I do but find a new job and start at the bottom of the ladder with a whole new company?" I hold up my glass to Nick. "Where the boss will probably hit on me."

"Should I cheers to that?" Nick warily clinks his glass against mine.

"With your killer résumé, I'm sure you're going to have plenty of offers." Harley once again earns her reputation as the optimistic one.

I down the last half of my cocktail before raising my hand like one of Gemma's students so I can order another. "Yeah, maybe. I don't know. I turned off my email for the weekend. I'm going to take the next three days and digest and see how I feel."

"I imagine tomorrow you're going to feel like puking. A lot." Nick pushes a glass of water my way.

"That's the goal." Spending the day with my head in the toilet seems preferable to spending the day rehashing the ways I must've fucked up in order for this to have happened.

Harley takes the water glass and holds it up to me like I'm a toddler, not moving it until I roll my eyes and drink. "You know, taking these three days might actually be a good first step. Maybe your next job should be one that treats you fairly and actually pays you for the work you do."

"Working all that overtime was my choice." My defensive hackles rise along with my blood alcohol level, thanks to this very popular topic of conversation. My friends are always on me to work less and live more. Date more, travel more, sleep more. Blah blah blah. But I've never been the kind of employee who can say no, assuming if I did I'd be kissing my chances at a promotion goodbye. The promotion I didn't get anyway, despite never saying no.

And now that she mentions it, I can't remember the last time I took a vacation or went on an actual date. I've always been a pick-up-a hot-guy-at-a-bar-and-take-him-home-for-one-night kind of girl. Woman.

The three of them exchange a look. Harley cocks her head toward Nick.

"It was only your choice because it was made clear you'd be rewarded with a promotion, Sadie. That doesn't count as an actual choice." Nick delivers this news since he also works in finance and seemingly knows how these things go.

I open my mouth to continue the argument, but Harley holds up a hand to stop me. "We don't need to have this discussion right now. Tonight's about celebrating what a badass you are, whether your idiot boss chooses to acknowledge it or not."

Gemma holds her glass up to the center of the table. "We can say many things about you, Sadie Jane, but the one thing no one can disagree with is that you are one badass bitch."

Nick meets her glass. "I'm not going to call you a bitch, even as a term of endearment, but you know I think you're awesome."

Harley completes their triangle. "We love you."

I grudgingly hold up my glass, clinking it against theirs. "Can I please get drunk now?"

～

Two hours later, I throw my arm around Gemma's shoulders as we stroll down the streets of Brooklyn, looking for a karaoke bar. How cliché can we be? Getting drunk and going to sing karaoke.

Nevertheless, a-karaoke-ing we shall go.

Harley begged off from the extension of our "celebration," giving us hugs and jumping in a Lyft to head home. I'm 99 percent sure Nick wanted to peace out too, but he knows better than to leave drunk Gemma and Sadie to their own devices. So he follows along behind us, close enough to intervene should one of us fall into moving traffic, but walking far enough away to be able to claim he doesn't know us.

"I don't have to go to work tomorrow!" I scream at the top of my lungs, drawing amused glances from the poor souls passing us by.

"Teenagers fucking suck!" Gemma announces to the world as if we weren't already aware of this information.

At which point, Nick catches up to us, grabbing my arm and pulling the two of us into the next dive bar we see. Which is a dive, but a Park Slope dive, so, you know, still hipster AF. "Gem, might want to chill with yelling how much you hate your job in the neighborhood where you teach."

"But teenagers suck." She sticks out her lower lip for half a second before beelining straight to the bar.

Nick sighs. "I don't get paid enough for this shit."

Sticking my arm through his, I lean my head on his shoulder to comfort him. And keep myself upright. "I know I don't say this enough, Nicky, but you're the best. If you were like even a little bit mean, I might like you better. But that'd be bad actually because then I'd probably wanna bang you, and I don't think I could bang you. Not that you're not bangable, because you totes are. I just actually really like being your friend, you know?"

Nick gives me a bemused smile and a peck on the top of my head. "I like being your friend too, Sadie. Most of the time."

We make our way over to Gemma, who has ordered us a round of shots, which we pound before immediately ordering another.

I'm pretty sure I catch Nick giving the bartender some super-secret signal, requesting his shot be water and not tequila, but honestly, who has time to care about that when there's more drinking to be done?

Shots having been shot, we order some cocktails and find a high-top table tucked in a back corner.

"And another thing that really pisses me off," Gemma starts, as if we were in the middle of a conversation, which I don't think we were, "is that you could've had so many dates. Like so many dates, Sadie. And have you had so many dates?"

I hold up my hand, my fingers forming a 0, bringing it close to my eye like it's a telescope. "I've had zero dates. Lots of fucking. Zero dates."

Nick chokes a little on his beer, but like the wise man he is, he refrains from commenting.

"You should be going on dates! Have you seen you?" Gemma gestures wildly in my general direction, barely managing to not fall off her stool.

Crooking my finger in the *Come here* motion, I bring her closer to me so I can "whisper" in her ear. "You should also be going on dates because I have seen you and you're super fucking hot, my friend."

She pulls away from me, ever so slightly, tears in her eyes. "Do you really think so?"

"No. Yeah. Duh."

Nick laughs. "You get so Californian when you're drunk."

I punch him in the shoulder. Sort of. I might miss his arm altogether, but the intent is there. "Shut up, Nicky." I hop off my bar stool. "Order me another drink, bitches! I'm going to pee!"

Gemma is calling for more drinks before I even leave the table, which is why I love her. I stumble to the back of the bar, pushing into the bathroom and joining the like-minded crowd of equally intoxicated women waiting for a stall.

"I love your shoes," one says to me.

"Ohmygod, thank you so much!" I gush. "You have like the most perfect hair. Seriously, I'd kill for it."

"Please, you're like a Barbie doll come to life if she weren't all plasticky and was actually like super cool and a feminist."

I place a hand over my heart. "That's literally the nicest thing anyone has ever said to me."

A flush rings out, and one of the stalls opens up for my new friend. The woman washing her hands at the sink catches my eye in the mirror. "Girl, your man is super hot."

"He's not my man, so look all you want!"

She shakes off the excess water from her hands and grabs a paper towel. "Your girlfriend isn't so bad either."

"Also not mine, so please, have at it!" God, if only my friends knew how much I was hooking them up while I try to hold in my pee.

"Does she like girls?"

"She likes everyone." I give her what I'm sure is a very subtle wink.

She gives me a thumbs-up and heads out, and finally a stall opens up. I rush in and lock the door.

As I relieve myself, I use the precious time to think about the highlights of the night. How my job robbed me of a social life and a dating life and a romantic life and a housewife life. I might be married with kids if it weren't for that stupid job.

Ew. Definitely don't want that.

But seriously, my friends are right. I've sacrificed a lot for my career. And for what? To watch my hard-earned promotion be handed to a man named Chad? Fuck that.

With drunkenness, as usual, comes clarity.

I flush, wash my hands, pour compliments over the new girls now waiting in line, and make my way back to the table. I pause at the end of the darkened back hallway, a smile growing as I see both Nick and Gemma chatting up a pair of super-hot babes, though Nick is keeping quite a bit of space between himself and the blonde making eyes at him. The girl from the bathroom pulls her attention from flirting with Gem and gives me a salute when she catches my eye.

Skirting around the table to avoid the new happy couples, I make my way to the bar. After another shot, I slide my phone out of my pants pocket, grateful for facial recognition because I'm not sure I could handle putting in a passcode at the moment. I pull up the dating app I haven't opened in months. My last login date pops up on the screen. Yikes.

"Okay, Sadie. Let's get serious. Let's go on a motherfucking date." Pretty sure the guy sitting next to me thinks I'm either wasted or crazy, but I'm too drunk to care.

I find a button directing me to local singles. A bunch of blurry photos come up for me to look through. Honestly, not sure if the photos are blurry or my eyesight is, but it doesn't really matter. I swipe right on a couple of guys who don't look completely pathetic, pretty proud of myself for taking this bare minimum of steps.

After a few more arbitrary swipes, my phone chirps with an alert.

Someone matched with me! On like, my first try! Okay, so there were probably like twenty tries altogether, but he picked me!

The app wants me to make some sort of selection; apparently this guy already wants a date. I toss my hair over my shoulder because check me out, that wasn't even that hard. I squint my eyes until I make out the word "coffee." Yes. Coffee date. Good. I tap the box, then choose

Saturday at two o'clock. Middle of the day, no expectations. Easy peasy.

Pshaw. I don't know what everyone is complaining about. Dating in New York City is a breeze!

The word "confirmed" pops up on my screen, and I let out a little whoop. I grab another shot, head back to my table, and hold my phone victoriously over my head. "Guys! I made a date!"

Nick, Gemma, and our new friends all cheer for me like I just won an Academy Award.

I don't remember much after that.

$\backsim$

Friday rolls by in a blur of a vomit-fueled haze. Because my friends are amazing, coffee and a greasy breakfast sandwich show up at my door at one o'clock in the afternoon, right around the time I manage to scrape myself off the bathroom floor.

I take the delivered goods from a guy who looks way too smug about this whole situation, if you ask me, and make a mental note to thank Nick and Harley the next time I can make my eyes focus on a phone screen. I seriously don't deserve them.

Even though it's April and not that cold, I curl up on the couch under my favorite soft blanket, slowly taking a few bites of the sandwich, making sure it's going to stay in place before I chow down on the rest of it. "I'm too old for this shit," I tell my philodendron, which doesn't offer even one kind word of commiseration.

And with that blank stare from my plant, with a full belly and under the comfort of my blanket, I finally let the sadness wash over me.

Not just disappointment or anger but pure, unfiltered sadness. I'm certainly no stranger to feeling worthless—not meeting expectations was one of my few constants growing up—but getting fired came out of nowhere. I didn't have time to mentally prepare for the onslaught of emotions. And all those emotions wash over me now, like some kind of fucked-up tsunami.

I spend the rest of the day on the couch, chugging water and mainlining saltines, Netflix and a wad of tissues to stem my tears my only company. Around eight that night, I manage to drag myself off the couch and into a shower. I feel almost like a real live human being when I step out of the steam and into my pajamas.

I'm on my way to sleep when my phone dings with an alert.

Reminder: Coffee tomorrow at 2:00. Gran Caffè de Martini.

I don't know whether to be super impressed with myself for setting a reminder or super annoyed I made a date in the first place. I think it's a little bit of both. I consider canceling, pretty sure "I was shit-faced when I made this date" is a justifiable enough excuse. But seriously, it has been way too long and the date is already set. If nothing else, it'll prevent me from spending the whole day wallowing. "Suck it up, Sadie. One date won't kill you."

I could be officially losing it, but I'm pretty sure the dracaena in the corner of my room nods in agreement.

THREE

I'M MOST DEFINITELY running late for this date, but why the fuck
did I match myself with some guy in Brooklyn? Oh yeah, because I
happened to be drunk off my ass in Brooklyn at the time. Idiot. I finally
manage to find the café and am at least partially mollified because it's
cute as hell. The walls are a robin's-egg blue, and there's a mural of
flowers splashed on the brick.

"All right, Park Slope, you might be worth the hour travel time."
Stepping into the café, I look around for a hot, well-dressed man, because even if I can't remember what this guy looks like, I most definitely have a type. I stroll to the back of the small space, then back
outside to the patio, then back inside, checking all corners of the shop.

"Sadie?"

I hold in the groan as I turn to my left. Drunk me must have been
real drunk.

But here we are. I put on a bright smile and cross over to the literal
antithesis of every guy I've ever dated.

His eyes are hidden by black plastic glasses that probably don't even contain prescription lenses. Between those and his unruly dark curly hair, only a sliver of his so-pale-he-probably-hasn't-been-outside-in-months face is visible. He's wearing ripped jeans and old Converse and, dear god, a *Lord of the Rings* T-shirt.

And he doesn't even stand as I make my way over to the table, taking the time to swish my totally first-date-appropriate floral flowy skirt.

"Did you want to grab a drink first?" Still not bothering to stand and greet me, he gestures toward the counter.

"Oh, yeah. Sure." I spin on my heel and sashay to the register, making sure he can fully appreciate how much effort some of us actually put into our appearance for this so-called first date. And I mean, I'm certainly cool with paying for my own coffee, but we could've at least had an introductory hug first.

Whatever. I order my iced vanilla latte and take it back to the small marble table. After spending an hour trekking out here, I sure as hell am not going to head home in under five minutes. And I'm even surer as hell not leaving without coffee first.

I slip into the open chair and hold out my hand. Not going to lie, I definitely do not remember this guy's name, but I'm finding it difficult to care much at this point. "Nice to officially meet you."

His hand envelops mine, shaking firmly. "It's Jack, Jack Thomas."

"Jack." At least he's cool enough to not shame me for forgetting. "Sadie Green."

"Yes, I know." He reaches into his messenger bag and pulls out a file folder. "So why don't you tell me a little about yourself?"

My brow furrows as he flips open the folder and pulls a pen from somewhere hidden in the depths of his hair.

30

Um, what? Is this a date or a job interview?

"What exactly would you like to know, Jack?" I raise one eyebrow—a trick I spent many hours in the mirror perfecting—and take a sip of my coffee.

He doesn't even look at me. "Let's start with the usual. Job, hobbies, et cetera."

I should've chosen the cocktails option on the dating app, because despite just yesterday swearing off booze forever, I'm going to need a drink to get through this. "Well, I'm a financial analyst." The words are out before I realize they're not exactly the truth. But whatever. They'll be true again soon enough. "Went to Columbia, yada yada yada. But honestly, that's like the least interesting thing about me."

"Your job is the least interesting thing about you?" He scratches a note on whatever paper he has in his folder, finally removing his gaze from said paper to glance at me, though he still doesn't meet my eyes, focusing instead somewhere behind me.

But whoa. Even without direct eye contact, my breath still catches in my chest. Jack might have very little going for him in the presentation department, but his eyes are low-key magic, the greenest I've ever seen on a real human being. The color of moss or emeralds or some other poetic shit like that.

He clears his throat when I fail to answer his question.

"I'm sorry, what did you say?" I busy myself with another quick sip of coffee, which I just barely manage not to choke on.

"You said your job is the least interesting thing about you?" His attention returns to the file folder.

I force out a fake laugh. "I mean, isn't that true for most people?" At least those who have jobs. Unlike me.

He frowns. "I sure hope not."

Okay, Judgy McJudgerton. "Well, what do you do for a living, Jack?"

A red blush creeps over what I can see of his cheeks. "Nothing." The word comes out barely audible, and he rushes out his next words before I have a chance to respond. "Hobbies, then?"

"Working, hanging out with my friends, working more, talking to my plants, and working." I reach over to the small vase of flowers sitting on the side of the table, rearranging the buds to keep me from reaching over and grabbing that stupid file folder.

"And how would you describe your overall temperament?"

My mouth drops open. I cross my arms, leaning on the table, closing the space between us to less than a foot, ready to let this guy know what's up, because I've had *a week* and I am so not in the mood for this. "Look. I realize I haven't been on a date in like far longer than I'd really like to admit, but seriously? Is this what I've been missing? Because no thank you. I should've just stayed home with my Netflix and my plants, and yeah, I realize how pathetic that makes me sound as I hear those words coming out of my mouth, and yeah, I don't even care at this point, because that's how weird this is."

He leans back in his chair as if he can't physically stand to share my space. "Whoa. Who said anything about a date?"

"Are you kidding me right now? Am I being punk'd? This cannot be real life." I start to push my chair back and stand, but Jack places a hand on my forearm. It's warm, and soft, and his grip is surprisingly gentle.

There's a beat of silence, during which Jack seems to realize he's still holding on to my arm. As soon as he does, he drops it like I scalded him.

"Sorry. Don't leave. I didn't mean to sound like a dick, I'm just a little confused." He gestures for me to retake my seat.

I do, but I move it away from the table and cross my arms over my chest. Like the mature adult I am.

"Why'd you think this was a date?" His voice holds no judgment, only curiosity.

Pulling out my phone, I swipe over and click on the app. "I matched with you on a dating app. What else would this be?" I hold up my screen.

He purses his lips as he studies my phone. "That isn't a dating app."

"Um, hello? Yes it is. I swiped right, you swiped right, we matched, we set a date." I turn the phone back to face me, feeling like I'm in some kind of horror movie. And then true horror overtakes me.

ROOMMATEZ is splashed over the top of my screen, right there in bright orange letters.

"Oh my god. I'm a complete fucking moron." And while it's definitely not the first time I've thought those words, it might be the most mortifying. "In my defense, I was completely wasted at the time."

"I don't think that's a defense."

"I'm so sorry for wasting your time." I sling my purse over my shoulder, preparing to make a hasty retreat because oh my god, could things get any worse?

"It's not a waste of time if you're in the market for a roommate." He slides a piece of paper across the table.

I don't want to be rude—or ruder—so I take it, though I have no intention of moving in with a strange guy I've never met before, app background check be damned. I pretend to peruse the specs on his sheet before breaking the news gently. "I wish I could, but my career is based in Midtown and honestly, I couldn't afford anywhere in Park Slope." The words have barely cleared my mouth when I see his asking price. His ridiculously low, must-be-missing-a-zero asking price. "Wait, does that say . . ."

This time I let my eyes actually take in the information printed in front of me. Words leap off the page. Words like "brownstone." "Chef's kitchen." "Backyard."

Straight-up real estate porn.

"Okay, now I know I'm being punk'd." I tear my eyes away from the tantalizing details to study Jack, whom I'm suddenly seeing in a whole new light. An I-could-live-with-this-man-in-exchange-for-a-backyard light.

Jack averts his gaze from mine. "You're not being punk'd."

"So you're a serial killer, then?" I can't resist going back in for another look at the flyer. Is there anything sexier to a New Yorker than a hot real estate listing?

"Definitely not."

"But you're renting a room in a brownstone for a pittance and you just happen to want me to move in with you? Why me?" We all know it has nothing to do with my sparkling personality.

He takes a sip from his coffee, and it seems to give him the fortitude he's so far been lacking. Jack raises his eyes. "Honestly? You seem like the kind of person who likes to laugh. And I need some laughter in my life."

And something about those words, the sincerity in his gaze when it finally meets mine, well, it almost comes close to warming my cold, cold heart.

But I can't let anyone know that.

I toss my hair over my shoulder. "I'm quite witty, as you've probably already noted."

"Hmm." His answer is noncommittal, but he almost sort of smiles. He folds up his file and stashes it in his bag. "So do you want to come see the place? It's just a couple of blocks from here."

"Sure." Picking up my phone, I snap his photo before opening my group text.

"Did you just take my picture?" The little color there was drains from his face, like I just stabbed him in the chest.

"Yup, and I'm currently sending it to my three best friends. One of whom's a lawyer, one of whom's a former athlete, and one of whom teaches middle school. Honestly, I'm not sure which one of them is scarier." I tap away on the screen. "In addition to your photo, I'm sending them your address and instructing them to call the police if they haven't heard from me in a half an hour." I stand and turn for the door. "Shall we?"

Jack sits frozen in place for a minute, like he can't decide whether he should follow me or run away screaming. He should totally run away screaming. But he doesn't, rising from his seat and holding the door open for me on our way out of the café.

The air outside is absolute perfection, not too hot, not too humid, one of those rare New York days that tricks you into thinking anything is possible in life. Jack leads me down a block and over a couple more, and my eyes don't ever stop darting around. Gemma and Harley share an apartment in nearby Windsor Terrace, so I'm not totally unfamiliar with the area, but I spend most of my time on the island Manhattan, almost exclusively in charmless Midtown, and there's something endearing about the brownstones lining the street on our walk.

After just a few minutes, Jack stops in front of one such brown-stone. "Here we are."

I peer up at the towering building, the perfect slice of New York history. "Which floor is yours?"

He clears his throat. "Um, the whole thing is mine."

My mouth drops open, and I immediately turn away from the brick-building version of Chris Hemsworth to look him dead in the eye. "You rent the whole brownstone?"

"I own the whole brownstone." He shoves his hands in his pockets and shuffles his feet.

"Shit, dude, you must be a serial killer. Your mortgage must be like ten thousand a month." And even just from the outside, this place is so good I'm seriously considering moving in. I can brush up on my self-defense skills and sleep with a knife under my pillow.

He stares down at his feet. "I don't have a mortgage. I own it outright."

I may be standing in place, but I literally stumble and almost fall.

Jack reaches out a hand, grasping my elbow and keeping me steady, dropping his grip the second I've regained my balance. "Do you still want to see inside?"

"Are you kidding me? I'd walk around the block topless in order to see inside."

His cheeks flush a dark pink, and he turns away to open the iron front gate. "That won't be necessary."

"Your loss." I follow him up the short flight of steps leading to the bright red front door. I let out a longing sigh, trailing my fingers over the cherry paint. "I love a pop of color on the front door."

He turns a key in the lock and pushes the door open. "It was brown when I bought it. I decided to paint it red."

I wait for the rest of that thrilling story, but Jack just awkwardly sweeps his arm out, gesturing for me to enter. Taking a deep breath, I pray the inside isn't some kind of disgusting frat house bachelor pad. I even close my eyes as I step into the front room, crossing my fingers before opening them, scared all of my just-developed dreams might be dashed. I squint, slowly inching my lids open.

Oh god.

It's good.

Real good.

It's so so so good.

Definitely better than my last five one-night stands. Combined.

The front room is open and inviting, the walls a bright white, original molding still in fantastic shape. A comfortable-looking sofa sits across from a brick fireplace surrounded by built-in bookshelves, filled to the brim. In the back of the first floor is the biggest New York kitchen I've ever seen, with white cabinets and butcher-block counters. Bar stools line the peninsula, and a wooden farm table separates the living space from the kitchen. Behind the kitchen, a pair of French doors lead out into what I assume is the backyard.

My mouth is just permanently open from this point on.

Jack lets me look around, leaning against the arm of the couch while I explore the first level on my own.

When I reverently run my fingers along the perfectly worn wood countertops, he gestures to a staircase leading to a lower level. "The basement is kind of a hangout space. Couch, TV, pool table."

"Video game console?" I give his nerdy T-shirt a pointed look before making my way back toward the front and the stairs leading to the upper levels.

"Every single one you could ask for." He says it like that's some sort of accomplishment, gesturing for me to make my way upstairs.

The man might be awkward, but I like that he doesn't flinch under my snarky words. If we're going to be roommates—and I've already decided we're going to be roommates—he's going to have to get used to my sharp tongue.

"Your room would be the one on the left."

I push through the door, and while I wouldn't have thought it possible, my mouth drops even lower. The room is huge. And not by New Yorker standards but by actual people standards. A queen-sized bed stands center on the far wall, there's a large bay window, and there's a goddamn fireplace. In the bedroom. Everything is white, making the space look even larger, but despite the lack of color, the room feels warm and cozy. Once my plants move in, it'll be the perfect space for me.

"This would be your bathroom."

"Mine? As in all for me?" I don't actually want to leave this bedroom—I'm tempted to just curl up under the quilt and refuse to vacate—but the call of an all-to-myself bathroom is too great. And yeah, I have my own bathroom now, but it kind of sucks, and never in my apartment-sharing life have I ever had a bathroom to myself.

Peeking my head in, I have to grab on to the door to keep from fainting. "Is that a claw-foot tub?"

Jack leans against the hallway wall. "That it is."

"I think I just orgasmed."

A choke sounding suspiciously laughlike rumbles out of him, and it's in that moment I think this might actually work.

Jack pushes off the wall, gesturing to two closed doors. "My room and the other guest room." He starts to walk back downstairs.

I cross to the stairs leading to another upper level. Because of course there's another level. "What's up there?"

Jack stumbles on the steps, catching himself before he tumbles down. "Oh, nothing. Just storage space. I'd ask that you not go up there."

"Very *Beauty and the Beast*." I lower my voice into a deep rumble. "'The west wing is forbidden.'"

He doesn't even crack a smile despite my spot-on impression. Instead he continues walking, throwing over his shoulder, "Did you want to see the backyard?"

"Fuck yeah I do!" I bound down the steps, beating him to the first level and the French doors leading out back.

I don't wait for permission; I push them open, waiting to stumble into my own personal Eden, ready for this yard to be the cherry on top of this perfect New York fantasy sundae.

I stop short on the top step.

Jack joins me, his hands back in his pockets. "It needs a little work."

That's the understatement of the century.

Overgrown, dead bushes line the wooden fences. Weeds spill out of the raised garden beds. All kinds of tall green grass stalks push up between the stepping-stone path. It's an absolute crime against backyardery.

"I love it," I breathe out, already mapping what I'll plant and where.

Jack looks at me like I'm crazy, the first time he's given me such a look, which is odd, all things considered. "I was never much of a gardener."

"You're so lucky you swiped right on me, my friend. I mean, that was a given already, but especially considering all of this untapped potential."

I take out my phone, hit Harley's number, and don't wait for her to actually greet me before talking. "Hi, yes, I'm going to need you and Gem to come meet me at that address I sent you."

"Oh shit, are you getting kidnapped? Are they selling you into sex slavery?" Harley calls for Gemma in the background, and I can tell she's going into full-blown lawyer mode.

"No, but I'm about to agree to move in with a guy I just met." I throw Jack a wink as I stride past him and back into the house.

"Jesus Christ, Sadie, you'll be the death of me one day. Don't sign anything! We'll be there in twenty." Harley hangs up on me and I tuck my phone back in my purse.

Jack meets me in the kitchen, him on one side of the peninsula, me on the other. "So what do you think?"

What do I think? I think my fairy godmother just dropped the solution to all my problems in my lap. With my savings and this ridiculously low rent, I'll have plenty of time to look for a new job. Maybe even one I actually like. "I think it's fucking perfect and you're probably making a huge mistake letting me come live in your perfect house, but I don't care because I love it so much and also that's on you for matching with me." I take a deep breath, knowing I can't get into this arrangement without telling Jack the whole truth. "But I have to be honest about something. I just got laid off from my job. I do have some savings and I'm like a seriously, ridiculously hard worker. For real, my job was my life. And I promise I will find something soon and I know it's a lot to ask, but if you take this chance, I swear I'll be not the worst roommate." I clasp my hands together as if in prayer. Which they might as well be.

He slides a lease agreement across the counter. "Sounds like you could use a bit of a break."

I pull the paper to me, smiling softly. I don't bother reading it since Harley is going to examine it within an inch of its life as soon as she gets here. "Thank you, Jack." And before he can change his mind, I steer the conversation far away from my employment. Or lack thereof. "So seriously, how does someone our age end up with a free-and-clear brownstone in Park Slope? Bestselling sex tape? Lotto? Black-market drugs?"

His mouth pulls into a flat line. "Dead parents."

"Oh fuck. Oh god, Jack. Jesus Christ, I'm the worst. I'm so sorry. I want to say it gets better when you get to know me, but my friends will attest to the fact that I'll always be a huge asshole. I'll totally not be offended if you want to kick me out. I'm definitely going to cry all the way home because seriously this place is to die for, and I like really need this break so I don't go completely broke, but I'll totally understand. Fuck."

The corners of his mouth tilt up into what just might be the beginnings of a smile. "I think you're going to be good for me, Sadie Green."

"Oh, I definitely won't be. Like literally no one has ever come away from knowing me thinking that, promise," I blurt out before clamping my lips shut, not needing to dig my own grave any further.

"When can you move in?"

FOUR

AN HOUR LATER, Harley, Gemma, and I sit in a different, equally adorable café even closer to Jack's brownstone. Which is about to be my brownstone. Because holy shit, how could I even think about turning down this opportunity?

"Gotta say, Sade, definitely walked into this thinking you'd once again lost your damn mind, but now I'm just pissed you found him first." Gemma rips into her chocolate croissant, handing me a third and Harley a third before shoving her own portion into her mouth in one bite. She somehow manages to also be tapping on her phone screen at the same time. "Although, he doesn't appear to have a social media presence. Not even an old Facebook. And when I googled him, there were like eighty bazillion Jack Thomases, none of whom are your adorable hipster, which seems a teeny bit sketchy."

"Okay, one, he is not adorable. Two, at least that means he probably doesn't have a record. Surely a murderer would be among the first

Google results, right?" I check my own phone, bringing up the room-mate app. "And his profile here says he doesn't do social media be-cause it's bad for your brain."

"He's not wrong about that." Harley bites into her section of the croissant, never moving her eyes from the lease agreement. "These terms look pretty fair. Technically he can ask you to leave at pretty much any time, but you also have the right to terminate the lease and move out at any time, should things get weird. You're each just required to give two weeks' notice, so it all seems pretty standard."

Gemma sips her iced coffee. "Jesus, you're going to be able to actu-ally pay off your loans. I'd literally commit murder to pay off my stu-dent loans."

"As an English teacher, shouldn't you be more careful about using the word 'literally'?" I raise one arched eyebrow at her, then duck when she throws her straw wrapper at me. Now that they've been plied with chocolate, carbs, and caffeine, I figure I can broach the real reason I brought them here, other than abusing Harley's free legal services. "Also, I've been thinking."

"Uh-oh," Harley says.

"Fuck me," Gemma groans.

"Okay, rude." I tear my own straw wrapper in half and throw a wadded-up paper ball at each of them, trying not to be deterred by their reactions. "What if . . ." I pause for dramatic effect—and to gather my courage. "I didn't look for a new job?"

They stare at me for a solid minute without saying a word, and the silence suffocates. Not just the air around us but the tiny spark of hope fluttering in my chest.

Gemma pinches the bridge of her nose. "I realize your new rent is a pittance, but you do still have to pay it, along with all of your other bills. And you're still going to be living in New York. Shit isn't exactly free here."

I roll my eyes, sarcasm shielding my doubt. "Duh. So here's what I'm thinking. I find some kind of bartending gig, preferably at a sports-bar-type place where I can show my tits and make two hundred dollars a night. I could work Fridays and Saturdays and then during the week, I'll work on building my floral business."

Harley chokes on her coffee. Gemma's head tilts to the side like she's a confused puppy.

Their reactions completely smother what was left of the hope spark, deflating my plans entirely. Plans that, admittedly, only really took shape in the last half hour or so, but plans that have always been in the back of my mind. They just seemed so out of reach and impractical that I never spent a lot of time dwelling on them because really, what's the point of dwelling on an out-of-reach dream that can never be accomplished? And real truth be told, having faith in myself and all that self-help bullshit is just not a thing for me. Apparently with good reason, since even my best friends don't think I can do this.

"Okay, it was a stupid idea. Forget I said anything." I pull the lease agreement away from Harley and pretend to read through it. She's already given me the basic rundown so I don't have to actually read it, but it's a good reason to not look at either of them.

Harley places her hand flat over the contract. "It's not a stupid idea. Isn't that the whole reason you got a business degree? So you could eventually open your own flower shop?"

"It's not that we think it's dumb, we just haven't heard you talk about being a florist since like sophomore year. I think we all kind of figured you'd let that go by now." Gemma pats my arm somewhat awkwardly in her attempt to bestow comfort upon me.

Shrugging, I sit back in my seat, removing myself from the physical-touch range. "I kind of did. Didn't seem like it was the kind of plan that was ever going to come to fruition, so I put it aside. But now I could actually make it work, and with the whole no-job situation, it just kind of feels like a sign, you know? Like if ever there were a time, this is it." I chance a quick glance at them, and they're both smiling at me like proud parents at their toddler's first dance recital, and proud parents are such a foreign experience for me it reignites the tiniest of hopeful flames in my chest.

"This is the perfect time, and I definitely think you should go for it." Harley hands me her pen. "First things first."

I take the pen and sign the lease agreement before I can second-guess myself. "So what are the chances Jack's an actual serial killer?"

"Fifty-fifty," Gemma guesses.

"Eighty-twenty in favor of him not trying to murder you in your sleep." Harley takes her pen back and tucks it into her purse. "I think he seems like a genuinely nice guy."

"And we're totally going to be barging our way into that kitchen all the damn time, so hopefully he can hang with us." Gemma loves to cook, but the kitchen in the apartment she and Harley share is the size of a coat closet.

Harley's phone trills, and Nick's face pops up on her screen. She holds it up so he can see all of us.

"Did I read my texts right? My last Manhattan friend is abandoning me?" Nick is at his parents' house in the Hamptons for the weekend, because yes, he's exactly as stereotypical as he seems on paper. He's out in the massive backyard, the pool behind him and a glass of rosé in his hand.

"I can't even look at you right now, you're so cliché." I take Harley's phone from her. "I'm going to need you to make the trip out at least once to make sure this guy knows he can't mess with me."

"Wait, you're moving in with a guy?" Nick's definitely plucked eyebrows meet his perfect hairline.

"And she's opening her own business," Gemma chimes in, taking the phone from me.

"What the fuck? Are you finally doing the flower thing? Do I need to get on the jitney and come home?"

All three of us laugh. Nick would never take the jitney. He's as down-to-earth and humble as any upper-middle-class white man can be, but there are certain lines even he won't cross.

Harley takes the phone back, facing it out so all of us are within view. "Moving day is in two weeks, so you can meet him then. He seems really sweet. And he's kind of cute."

I barely manage to contain an eye roll. Gem and Harley might find Jack's nerdiness attractive, but I definitely don't. And thank god for that, because nothing could be more foolish than lusting after my new landlord.

"Oh?" Nick doesn't sound too thrilled about that description coming from Harley's lips.

Gemma and I share a knowing glance.

"Well, I gotta go give my new roomie this lease agreement. See you later, Nicky."

We all wave, and Harley ends the call.

"Do you want us to come back with you?" Gemma rises, already gathering her purse and coffee.

"Nah, it's fine. If he's going to kill me, it'll happen eventually anyway." I stand and grab the signed lease. "Also I'm ninety-nine percent sure I can take him."

Harley gives me a quick hug. "Text me when you get home."

"Thank you, guys." I pull Gemma in, making her join our group hug even though she hates it. "Not just for today, but for this whole weekend. You're the best."

"Yeah, yeah. Go make some kick-ass plans for your new business, you lucky bitch." Gemma pushes me away, but her smile is genuine.

I wave them off as they head back toward their place while I turn to go in the opposite direction, back to Jack's. Back to my new home.

It's been a really long time since any place has felt like home.

I knock on the door, and Jack answers within thirty seconds, like he was waiting for me to come back.

"Everything check out?"

I hand him the signed agreement. "I really hope you don't live to regret this, Jack Thomas."

He flips to the back of the form, double-checking my signature, a hint of a smile playing on his lips. "So I'll see you in two weeks?"

"Looking forward to it." I feel like we need to seal the deal with a hug or a handshake or something, so I awkwardly hold up my hand for a high five. Jack just as awkwardly tries to slap my palm. But he misses. After an uncomfortable laugh, I wave and head down the front stairs.

And just like that, I have a new roommate.

~

JACK: Hey, it's Jack. Got your number from the lease, hope it's ok to text you. I forgot to ask if you wanted me to clear the furniture out of the room or not.

ME: Texts are good. I don't answer phone calls anyway. Are you offering me the use of all that gorgeous furniture?

JACK: Please spare me the hassle of having to get it picked up before you move in.

JACK: So did you want it? 😉

JACK: Shit. Did not mean to send that emoji.

JACK: And by it, I mean the furniture. Just the furniture.

JACK: Do you want the furniture?

ME: Oh, I definitely want it. 😂

ME: Guys. I'm not sure if you know this, but there is like so much to see in NYC.

GEMMA: Yes, Sadie. We know.

HARLEY: Sounds like you're enjoying your two-week staycation?

ME: I'm soaking up as much Manhattan as I can.

HARLEY: It's only a subway ride away, you know.

GEMMA: Not that you're ever gonna wanna go back once you're out in Brooklyn living your little hipster millennial dream.

ME: Wow. I'm so not a hipster.

NICK: Sadie. Your new life plan is to open a sustainable floral design business. You might as well change your name to Juniper and start a podcast.

ME: In general, how do you feel about plants?

JACK: Fine I guess?

ME: Do you have any floral-related allergies?

JACK: Not that I'm aware of.

ME: Good.

JACK: Just how many plants are you bringing?

ME: Is it weird that I can already hear the judgment in that text?

ME: Is it weirder that I'm impressed by said judgment?

~

ME: Sup, bitches, make sure you go follow my new Insta account, @bridgeandblooms

HARLEY: Followed! Cute pics so far!

ME: Thanks! I've been doing all this exploring and I keep finding all these great floral inspiration shots.

NICK: All I can see in my head is you frolicking
through the streets of Manhattan like you're Maria
von Trapp singing "Sound of Music."

ME: Did we all just fall in love with Nicky or just me?

GEMMA: Just you. Followed your account. But if
you get a TikTok, I'm out.

~

ME: Do you have plans this weekend?

JACK: You'll find the answer to that question is
pretty much always a no from me.

ME: That might be the saddest thing
I've ever heard.

JACK: Gee, thanks.

ME: ANYWAY. Enough about you. Could I
come by and do some weeding in the backyard?
I'm already getting a late start with planting season
and I want to get to it ASAP.

JACK: Sure thing. Is there anything we'll need to
hire professionals for?

ME: Possibly shrub removal, but I'll take care of it.

JACK: Just let me know and I'll cover the cost.
Since you're doing all the work and everything.

ME: Sounds good, I'll see you Saturday.

JACK: I'll get your key printed before then.

ME: 👍

FIVE

I HOIST MY PLANT MOM tote bag higher on my shoulder as I knock on the bright red front door of the brownstone.

Jack answers almost immediately, wearing basically the exact same thing he did on our "date," only today his ripped jeans are topped with a Super Mario Bros. shirt, I'm assuming in an unironic fashion. His hair still hangs loose and wild, covering the parts of his face not already hidden by his glasses.

He flashes me something between a grimace and a smirk, gesturing for me to enter.

"Good morning." I say, once he's made it clear he won't be kicking off this conversation.

"Morning. Did you find the place okay? I mean, you've been here before obviously, but this is your first time coming here by yourself." He shuffles backward a few steps and shoves his hands in his pockets.

"Yeah, it was fine. I'm not one of those Manhattanites who never sets foot in the other boroughs; I know my way around Brooklyn. Sort of."

"Cool."

"Indeed." I wait for a second, pretty sure he has no plan to speak but not wanting to fully dominate the conversation. I'm low-key afraid he's going to tear up our lease if he realizes that I typically never shut up, especially since he seems like the quiet type. "Well, I guess I'll just head to the yard."

"Oh. Yeah. Of course." He clears his throat. "Are you going to need any help with anything?"

"Nah. It'll mostly be weeding today, so I should be able to handle it. It's basically free therapy." Emphasis on the "free" since losing my job also meant losing my health care. Yay America.

"Great. Well. I guess just let me know if you need any help." He gives me a weird little half wave.

Which I mistakenly interpret as his offering a high five. I go to slap his hand just as he pulls his back and good lord, this is painful.

I brush past him and head to the French doors leading out to the yard, desperate for a quick escape. "Okay, then."

Luckily he doesn't follow me and try to make things even more awkward than they already are. I push through the doors and can practically feel the tension draining from my body as I enter the garden. There is a lot of work to do back here, but I'm seriously stoked about it.

I set my bag down on a weather-beaten metal table and unload my supplies. Tugging on my pink gardening gloves, I dig out shovels and trowels and a knee guard and set up shop in front of the planter in the back. I figure I'll start here and work my way forward.

Once I get in the rhythm, my mind completely clears. This is my meditation, the time when I can turn off all the negative thoughts in my brain and just be. Most kids probably aren't super into gardening, but for me, the garden was always a place of quiet—both internal and external. It brought me a peace I desperately needed, and even though I haven't been able to dig my hands in the dirt in quite some time, I'm automatically transported back to my happy place. My calm place.

I work for hours, snipping and pulling, clearing and weeding, until I have huge piles of stems and branches collected and planters ready to be filled with flowers. When I finally hit the point when even I need a break, I pull off my gloves and head back to the metal bistro set. A cup of ice water sits on the table, next to a plate covered in tinfoil. I sink into one of the chairs, gratefully sipping the cool water. Peeking under the foil, I find a sandwich waiting for me. I am someone easily swayed by food, and Jack's offering completely erases any lingering doubts our awkward encounter might have stirred up. I devour the whole thing, not realizing how hungry I am until I take the first bite.

Surveying the work I've done, I decide to pack it in for the day. I shake off my gloves and bang my shoes against the concrete steps before pushing back into the house, not wanting to leave a trail of dirt as I go.

"Jack, I'm taking off," I call, striding quickly for the front door, hoping to avoid another stilted encounter.

Steps thud from the basement stairs. "Don't forget your key." Jack crosses over to the entryway table, handing me a gold key on a plastic key ring.

It's one of those old-timey-looking hotel key chains, bright pink with "Park Slope" etched in white retro letters. I don't know why, but the thoughtful gesture brings a smile to my face. A genuine one. "Thanks, Jack. And thanks for the sandwich."

"You're welcome. Thanks for doing all that work in the yard."

I tuck the key in the inner pocket of my bag. "I'll come back sometime this week to clear out all the debris. I'll text you when I know what day."

"Sounds good." This time he very deliberately holds up his hand. And I just as deliberately slap him a high five. "Bye, Jack."

"Bye, Sadie."

~

I wake easily at the chirp of my alarm on moving day, dressing in cut-off jean shorts and a worn Columbia T-shirt. Hair in messy bun, sneakers on feet, I run down to grab some coffee for the gang, which is just the first of many trips I'll be making up and down these stairs today. I'm eating only carbs for the rest of the week. Balancing our tray of coffees on top of a pink box of doughnuts, I make it back to my place with plenty of time to shove a maple bar in my face before everyone arrives.

Harley and Gemma show up together, and Nick knocks on the already open door a few minutes later.

He pokes his head through the doorway. "How much do you love me?"

"I'm not answering that after my brief foray into Nicksanity brought on by your comparing me to Maria von Trapp." I take down another doughnut because all that lies before me is stairs. So many stairs.

Nick steps into the room, then makes a sweeping gesture with his arm, signaling the entry of four college-aged guys.

"Are they strippers?" Gemma looks at each one from head to toe.

"Interns." Nick snaps his fingers, and the four man-boys each grab a box and make their way back down the stairs.

"Ninety-nine percent sure this is illegal." Harley hands Nick a cup of coffee and two sugar packets.

I give Nick a fist bump. "One hundred percent sure I don't care."

"Does this mean I can sit and watch?" Gemma hops up onto my counter, angling herself so she has a view of the door.

I yank on her arm, pulling her right back down. "I do not trust college boys with my plants. Let's do this."

We all take final swigs of our coffee and get down to business. Since I'm moving into a fully furnished home, I was able to sell my couch, bed, dresser, and coffee table, which both padded my savings and now makes for a much easier move. With the help of the strapping young interns, we've got the place loaded up in an hour, which must be some kind of New York record. We wave goodbye to the eye candy and pile into the cab of the moving van Nick rented because he's the only one with a valid driver's license.

We don't even have to double-park when we finally make our way to Brooklyn; there's a spot open on the street just in front of the brownstone. I take it as a sign from the parking gods above that this move was meant to be.

Nick whistles as he steps out of the van and crosses to the back to open the hatch. "Shit, Sadie. It all makes sense now. Even I'd move to Brooklyn for this."

"Twenty bucks says he'll move to Brooklyn within six months," Gemma mutters in my ear.

"Not dumb enough to take that bet."

Nick talks a big Manhattan game, but he loves us too much to be a whole borough away from all his best gals.

Pulling my new key from my back pocket, I bound up the front steps. I push open the front door, calling out, "Honey, I'm home!" in a way louder voice than necessary since Jack's standing right inside the entryway. "Oh, hi."

He gives me a tight-lipped smile. "I heard the van pull up."

Gemma and Harley greet Jack as they come in, each of them bearing a potted plant. They already know where my room is, so I wave them up the stairs.

Nick comes in carrying the biggest box from the van, his muscles straining against the sleeves of his definitely-too-tight T-shirt, and oh-so-casually sets it on the kitchen peninsula before crossing to Jack and sticking out his hand, keeping those muscles flexed the entire time. "You must be Jack. I'm Nick." Pretty sure his voice just dropped an octave or two.

I purse my lips as I watch this exchange. Nick squeezes Jack's hand so hard I'm surprised I don't hear bones popping, but Jack doesn't back down. And now that I see the two of them next to each other, Jack is actually taller than I would've thought him to be. Nick's definitely broader and more built while Jack is lean, but height-wise, they almost stand even.

"Nice to meet you, Nick." Jack gestures to the stairs leading to the basement. "Did you want to check out the place?"

Nick shrugs, but I can tell he's dying to explore. I nod for him to go ahead, and he practically leaps down the stairs. I'm turning to head out for another box when I hear him exclaim, "Oh shit, did you know there's a pool table down here, Sade?"

I roll my eyes, not bothering to respond. Back out at the van, I grab an armful of clothes before turning around and running straight into Jack. "Oh fuck. Sorry. I didn't know you were coming out. Is it cool to park here?"

Jack grabs a box from the truck. "Of course."

"Oh, you don't have to help unload, really, there's not much anyway, and we got it covered. Between the four of us, someone is moving every few months, so we've got our routines down." I start the short walk back to the house, Jack following behind me.

"Like I'm just going to stand around watching you all move stuff and not help?" Jack checks the label on the box and takes it over to the kitchen. "Wait, *would* a new roommate stand around and not help?"

I pause before heading up to my room, my foot on the lowest step. "Well, no, but you can certainly go about whatever your plans were for today." I climb up one step and pause again. "Have you never had a roommate before?"

"What? Sorry, didn't hear you," he calls over his shoulder, heading back to the truck.

And I thought I was the master of deflection.

But I'm not one to say no to free labor, so not only is the truck unloaded within an hour, by the time dinner rolls around, I've also managed to unpack my entire room. I wash my hands in my gorgeous new bathroom before heading downstairs to see if everyone is ready for pizza.

Harley and Gemma are sitting at the peninsula, beers already in hand.

"Where are the boys?"

They share a smirk, and Gemma nods toward the basement. "I think Nick's in love."

"With the basement or my new roommate?" Opening the fridge and pulling out a beer of my own, I lean both elbows on the counter opposite them. If I sit down, I know I won't be able to get back up.

"Both," they answer in unison.

I chug half my beer in one gulp. "You guys want your usual pizza?"

They nod, and Gemma hops up to grab them another round of beers.

I walk to the top of the basement stairs. "Boys, I'm going out for pizza. Jack, what kind of toppings do you like?"

A second later, there's a pounding on the steps. Jack runs halfway up, just enough so he can see me and not have to shout. "I already ordered. Hope that's okay. Nick told me what you guys like."

Smirking at this full-force bromance, I cross my arms over my chest. "You didn't have to do that, I was planning to treat everyone."

He shrugs and gives me a half smile. "It's no problem. I've got my favorite place on standby."

"Well, thank you. I appreciate it." I turn to head back to the girls.

"I'm really glad you're here, Sadie."

The words stop me in my tracks, because honestly, I truly can't imagine why anyone would be happy to have me here. But the look in his bright green eyes, even hidden behind those big-ass glasses, is nothing but genuine.

And so is my smile. "Me too."

~

Sunday is spent in a glorious Brooklyn hipster haze, with me strolling through the blocks surrounding Jack's brownstone, exploring farmers' markets and drinking like ten cups of coffee so I can find which place makes my favorite. Spoiler alert: they're all delicious, and the more I traverse the streets of Park Slope, the more in love I am with my new neighborhood.

I give myself the day to do whatever I want because tomorrow is Monday. Tomorrow is the first day of the rest of my life, and yeah, I'm embracing the cliché and I'm not even mad about it. Tomorrow is for bartender job hunting, and budget setting, and figuring out how the hell one starts a sustainable floral design company with no real experience.

You must be an idiot to think you can pull this off.

The words halt my steps, the negativity catching me off guard in the middle of this overwhelmingly positive day. For a second, I consider heading back to the brownstone, sprucing up my résumé, and applying for more soul-sucking finance jobs. It'd be easier to go back to the known than try for something completely new. Something risky, something that might actually make me happy.

But today is all about the good stuff. It has to be. Shoving the self-doubt into the back corner of my mind, I force a fake smile across my face, until the charm of my new neighborhood makes it real. I take about a hundred photos for my new Instagram account and buy far more bunches of flowers than I should at the farmers' market, excited to get back to the house and arrange them in whatever vessels I can manage to scrape up. I brought a few of my standbys with me, but one of my favorite things to do is create arrangements in nontraditional vases. In fact, one of the first tenets of my as-yet-to-be-written business plan will be not buying new vases but rather repurposing recycled and vintage items.

Jack is nowhere to be found when I push through the front door in the late afternoon, an iced latte in one hand and five paper-wrapped bushels of flowers tucked in the other. I drop all my goodies on the kitchen counter before running upstairs to kick off my shoes and dump my purse. I stash my receipts from my floral purchases in a folder labeled "Tax Shit" before digging out my flower-cutting shears, mentally adding a cute gardening apron to my shopping list.

Before I get to the actual flower arranging, I dig around in the kitchen to see what I might want to use for vases. I pull four beer cans from the recycling bin, along with an old coffee can, and I dig out one of my favorite ceramic vases from a still-packed kitchen box. The coffee-can lid gets tossed back in the recycling, and the vase gets unwrapped, but the beer cans require a little more work. I attack one of the tops with my shears, cutting around the edges until I can yank on the tab and rip the whole thing off, leaving me a perfect cylinder.

I'm stabbing beer can number two when Jack startles me out of my concentration. "Um, what's going on here?"

Jumping about a foot, I barely manage to avoid stabbing myself in the process. "Jesus, dude, first rule of roommating, don't sneak up on anyone holding scissors. Or a knife. Or anything sharp that could literally poke their eyes out. And by 'their eyes,' I mean my eyes, which I'd quite like to keep in my head, thank you very much."

His face scrunches up like he's making some sort of mental note. "Sorry. No sneaking. Won't happen again." He crosses over to the kitchen peninsula, which looks like a floral shop exploded all over it, which, to be fair, it basically did. "What's going on here?"

"Floral arranging." I look at him and blink a lot so he knows how I feel about questions he should already know the answer to, because hello, look at the counter.

"I thought your thing was gardening."

"It's both. And yes, you're right, the backyard is already looking a million times better than before I moved in." I meet his eyes and smile sweetly, right before piercing the top of the next beer can.

He gestures to the mounds of flowers currently covering all available space in his kitchen. "Is this going to be an everyday occurrence?"

I get to work on beer can number four. "Not right away, but hopefully once my business picks up some traction, then maybe yeah. Maybe at that point I'll have enough to rent a small studio space somewhere. Though I'd obviously have to be really raking it in for that to be a possibility. But it's totally a possibility, I mean, I definitely have 'next Martha Stewart' potential, don't you think?" I slip back into my woman-at-work mask flawlessly, charming confidence fitting over me like armor to hide all the doubts I naturally have about this business venture's succeeding.

Jack picks up a peony, examining it like it might bite him. "I thought you were looking for a job in finance."

"I was going to, but do you remember that whole thing about my job being the least interesting thing about me?"

Jack carefully puts down the bud, a look of terror growing in his eyes. "Yes?"

"Well, I've decided to open a business instead!" Taking my vessels over to the sink to fill them with water, I let the sound of the rushing liquid drown out whatever Jack's response might be.

Jack's mouth is still hanging open when I return to the peninsula. "You're opening some kind of floral business?"

"Yeah, is that okay? I mean I know I don't need permission from you to make a career change, as long as I can keep paying rent, which I promise I will. But I guess I maybe should've asked how you feel about flowers and stuff before really committing to this plan long-term since I'll need to use the kitchen from time to time and this is technically communal space." I slide my scissors through the brown paper around one of the bunches, releasing the flowers and starting to trim the stems. "I guess if you're really opposed to it I could do most of my work outside, for the spring and summer months anyway, and then we could figure out something in the fall. Assuming you haven't kicked me out by then." I flash him what I hope is an endearing grin.

He grips the edge of the counter like he physically needs the support in order to remain standing. "I'm not going to kick you out, Sadie."

"Oh, sweetie, it's day one. You're going to find so many reasons to kick me out between now and fall. It's only April." Once all the flowers are trimmed, the fun part begins. I look at the vessels, deciding which will get what flowers, and then I dive in. I attack it with gusto, willing to take risks, knowing that all floral arranging mistakes can be fixed. It's one of the things I like most about flowers—the freedom to make mistakes. Freedom not found in many other areas of life.

"I guess as long as you keep everything clean, it shouldn't be a big deal for you to use the kitchen when you need it." Jack runs a hand through his unruly long hair, pushing it back from his face.

Which is when I notice it could be quite a nice face, if it weren't so hidden by dark curls and glasses, which I'm still not sure are real.

"I promise you'll never feel inconvenienced by the dynamic and major-money-making sustainable floral design studio now taking residence in your home." I take a step back, eyeing the arrangements with a wrinkle in my nose before jumping back in and switching things up.

"Dynamic and major-money making?"

"I'm doing that whole 'manifest your destiny' bullshit."

"I don't think it counts if you call it bullshit five seconds after saying it." Jack sweeps up a small pile of loose leaves, dumping them in the trash can.

"Whatever." I take another step back, this time satisfied with what I see. I wipe down each of my "vases," clearing away any excess water or stray bits of leaves before placing them around the lower level of the house. The coffee can goes in the center of the dining room table, the beer cans are scattered around on the bookshelves, and the ceramic vase finds a home in the kitchen. I'll wait to take my pictures until tomorrow during the midday light, but overall, I'm pretty pleased with how each arrangement turned out.

Once I finish patting myself on the back for my floral brilliance, I spend a few minutes tidying up the counter, making sure I get every last scrap of waste, taking everything out back to the trash pile before wiping down the butcher block.

"See, good as new." I wave my hands around the kitchen like I'm Vanna White.

"One could even argue better than new." Jack is now perched on one of the stools at the peninsula, watching me flit about the kitchen.

"One could indeed." I head over to the fridge. "Beer?"

"Sure."

I pop the tops on two bottles, already thinking about how to cut the necks off and use them for next week's flowers. Handing one to Jack, I hold mine up. "Cheers, roomie."

He clinks his bottle against mine. "Cheers."

An incredibly awkward silence falls over us, which is something I rarely allow to happen. But this is the first time Jack and I have really been alone, with no business guiding our conversation, and I don't know what to say to him. I don't know anything about him really, other than his parents died and apparently left him a shit-ton of money. And while I'm certainly not above putting my foot in my mouth and asking the awkward questions, I also don't want to scare him too badly. It is our first full day, after all.

Jack clears his throat. "I'm just gonna go hang downstairs. Holler if you can't find something or need a towel or whatever." A red blush creeps up his cheeks, at least what I can see of them, and the overall effect borders on endearing.

"Yeah, cool. See you later." I watch his back retreat down the basement stairs, sipping my beer and starting to question just how this guy is ever going to be able to live with me.

⁓

I don't set an alarm for Monday morning, but I wake up at my usual time anyway. Thanks so much, internal clock! But I don't mind the early wake-up call as today is the first day of the rest of my life. I'm tempted to keep a count to see how many times I can say and think that phrase today but then decide it's better if I don't know.

Dressing in comfy cropped jeans, a fitted white T-shirt, and sneakers, I grab my laptop and purse and bound down the stairs, ready to meet the day.

The kitchen is empty, so Jack must not be up for work yet. I pause for a second at the front door as I realize I have no idea what Jack does for work. Mental note: stop being a selfish asshole and ask the new roommate some questions about himself.

I walk to Winner, one of the coffee shops I tested yesterday. I figure if there's any truth to the whole "If you build it, they will come" nonsense, starting off the first day of the rest of my life at a place called Winner is bound to help. Also their croissants were bomb.

Croissant and latte in hand, I nab a spot at one of the outdoor tables and set up shop. In true Sadie style, I dive into my plans for the day. First, I make a list of all the bars within walking distance of the brownstone. I plan to stop by all of them in person throughout the week, hopefully finding one desperate enough to hire me even though I haven't tended bar since college. Not that that was that long ago, mind you, but it's been a few years. Second, I submerge myself in the web presences of all of Brooklyn's top florists, taking copious notes on what to include on a website, how to market myself on Instagram, and ways to make myself stand out from the crowd. It becomes clear pretty quickly that being sustainable is going to be my niche, so I make a separate list of all the ways I want to make Bridge and Blooms the environmentally friendly florist of Mother Earth's dreams.

As I fill page after page with to-do list items—an activity that usually centers me better than any meditation app ever could—I start to freak out a little bit. This is a lot. Like a lot a lot, more than I expected. The words start to blur on the page in front of me, and I put my pen down and close my eyes, forcing myself to take some deep breaths.

You can do this. Take it one task at a time, one day at a time.

The inner-monologue cheerleading works for about a minute.

Hey, at least when you fail, you can go back to finance and be a grunt for the rest of your life.

"No." My eyes fly open and, needing something to focus on, find a glass milk bottle stuffed with a single zinnia. "I'm not going to fail," I whisper to the bright yellow bud.

Newly resolved, I pack up my stuff and head back inside to grab an iced latte for the road.

ME: I'm grabbing coffee and then heading back to the house. Want anything?

ME: If you're home, I mean. If not, kindly ignore this text.

ME: Actually don't ignore it because I'm standing here in the middle of the café waiting for your response and I look like a dweeb so let me know either way.

JACK: An iced coffee would be great. Thanks.

ME: You got it. See you in a few!

"Honey, I'm home!" I call out when I push through the front door, a coffee in each hand.

Jack is perched at the peninsula, reading a comic book and eating a piece of toast. "Do you plan to announce it like that every time you come in?"

"Um, yes." I hand him his coffee and dump my bag on the stool next to him.

He clears his throat. "How was your first morning of funemployment?"

"I'm sorry, did you mean, how was the first morning of the rest of your life?" I think that makes five times I've thought that phrase. Maybe six.

"Sure, that too." He stands and crosses to the fridge, taking out the milk and adding some to his coffee. "Why are you staring at me like that?"

"I'm making note of how you take your coffee, like a good roommate." I hoist myself onto his vacated stool. "I like vanilla lattes, by the way. Iced in summer, hot in the winter."

"Good to know."

"So, Jack—is that your full name or a nickname? If it's your full name I'm probably going to have to think of something else to call you, because while Jack is very much in line with what I know of your personality so far, it doesn't have quite enough oomph there for me. I need some more syllables." I pause for a second to sip my latte. "Anyway, it occurred to me this morning as I was putting together the plans to shape the rest of my life into something meaningful and not soul-sucking, I have no idea what you do for a living."

"Hmm." He reaches for his toast, which is now in front of me since I stole his seat.

I push the plate across the counter at the same time he grabs for it, and our hands brush up against each other. And I can't help but notice what nice hands he has. His fingers are long, his skin soft. They look like the kind of hands a doctor might have, or maybe a sculptor. Strong but gentle, purposeful but kind.

But yeah. Anyway.

"So what is it you do for a living, Jack Be Nimble?" Pulling my attention from his nice-looking hands, I focus on his equally nice-looking eyes.

He stares into his coffee like it can tell him the future.

"Oh my god, you're totally a black-market drug dealer, aren't you?"

"Technically I think all drug dealers are black-market drug dealers."

"If you think I'm going to be deterred from this conversation, then you clearly haven't been paying attention. I don't know if you remember or not, but I don't currently have a job, so I can literally sit here and badger you all day, or you can just tell me a few tiny details about yourself. Despite my assholeish nature, I'm mostly not judgmental."

He leans against the counter and crosses his arms over his chest. "I don't currently have a job."

"Dude! Are we going to be funemployed together?" I hold my hand up for a high five, but he leaves me hanging. Rude.

"I've actually never had a job. And I'm not currently looking for one. Or planning to get one."

I choke on my coffee. "You've never had a job? Like ever? Not even a babysitting gig or a bartending shift?"

He shrugs, and another one of those red flushes creeps up his cheeks. "I realize how much of a dick this makes me, but I've never needed to work a traditional job. And so I haven't."

I—the person who ran my own rip-off version of the Baby-Sitters Club until I was legally old enough to work—cannot even fathom just not working. Like just not having a job. I know that sounds like the kind of thing most people dream about, but it sounds like my worst fucking nightmare. Sitting around all day with nothing but my inner thoughts? No thank you. "So what do you do all day?" The question flies out of my mouth before I think it through.

Jack shrugs again. "I play video games and read and take lots of walks."

"And for the other twenty-two hours?" My voice screeches at a level probably only the neighborhood dogs can hear. "Sorry, I know I promised not to be judgmental and I'm not judging, really—I'm just trying to figure out how you do this, because I literally think I'd lose my mind if I didn't have some kind of structure to my life."

He purses his lips, pulling his eyes away from mine. "I probably did lose my mind there a bit. Maybe more than a bit." He pulls his arms tighter around his chest, like they're physically bracing him.

Well, shit. I want nothing more than to jump out of my seat and give him a big hug, but I don't think we're quite there yet. The man just denied my high five, for god's sake. But this is clearly a hell of a lot more than just not needing to work. If all this financial security came with the price tag of losing his parents, I can only imagine the guilt. And the grief. I don't know how far I can push him, given the whole known-him-for-two-weeks deal. Even if we are living together now, something is telling me it's time to back off.

So I do what I do best: deflect the conversation by talking about myself. "Well, I think my first few hours of the first day of the rest of my life went swimmingly. I found some bars I'm going to hit up for a potential part-time job—see, told you I'd manage to pay my rent. And I did all kinds of research about what I'll need to get Bridge and Blooms—isn't that like the most perfect name? I'm obsessed—up and running. And now I'm going to dive into one of my favorite things ever, spreadsheets. I'm not even lying about that. Finance might be boring as fuck most of the time, but I make one kick-ass spreadsheet."

A teeny-tiny hint of a smile tugs at the corner of his lips. "Something tells me you kick ass at anything you put your mind to."

My instinct is to refute the compliment, but experience has taught me that never works. So I go for casual-if-fake arrogance instead. "See how well you already know me?" I hold up my hand for another high five, and this time he slaps his palm against mine in return.

SIX

*B*Y THE END of my second week living with Jack, I've found a bartending gig, gained three hundred new followers on Instagram, and managed to completely clear out the backyard. And that's just the fun stuff. I also managed to put together a mini business plan and build a website, all by myself. Okay, Nick actually came over and helped a little with the website, but the ideas were all mine.

Jack and I have kept our conversations light and simple, and it probably comes as no surprise, but they've mostly consisted of me talking about myself and my new kick-ass life goals. I still know next to nothing about Jack, but he could probably give a TED Talk on the life of Sadie Green. The surface life anyway.

I wake up Saturday, ready to take my backyard plans to the next level. Time to germinate some seeds, mothafuckas!

After dressing in my gardening best—cut-off shorts and the standby Columbia tee—I run out for coffee, grabbing a latte for myself and an iced coffee with milk for Jack, and I'm back before the man even rolls down the stairs.

Because I'm going to need easy access to water, I set up shop in the kitchen once again, spreading out the plastic seed trays and hauling over the big-ass bag of soil I purchased at a nearby nursery earlier this week. I label the trays before scooping dirt into each of the small compartments, taking frequent coffee-sip breaks while I work.

Jack comes downstairs just as I'm filling up a pitcher of water.

"Good morning! Your coffee is in the fridge." I nod my head in the fridge's general direction; you know, just in case he forgot where it is.

"Should I even try reminding you that you don't have to get me coffee every time you go out?" Jack runs a hand through his still sleep-rumpled hair. Though to be honest, it pretty much always looks sleep rumpled.

"No. Unless you have some caffeine allergy or something, I'm never not going to bring you coffee." What kind of roommate does that? Of course, in the past, my roommates equally bestowed coffee upon me, but since I haven't seen Jack leave the house once since I moved in, I've kind of given up hope there.

"Well, thank you. I appreciate it." He grabs his coffee from the fridge and pulls up a seat at the peninsula. "Do I want to know what all this is?"

I clap my hands together. "Today is germination day!"

"Is that supposed to sound like a good thing?"

"Yes. Because it is." I hold up one of the tiny seed packets I bought earlier this week. "Today we plant the seeds, and then over the next few weeks, they germinate and grow roots. Then, when these little babies are toddler aged, we take them and move them into their new homes in the garden, where they will live long, healthy, nurtured lives."

"Should I be disturbed by the level of reverence in your voice?" Jack pokes one of the compartments and comes away with a finger covered in damp soil.

"Hobbies are healthy, I'll have you know." Opening the first seed packet, I shake four little spores into my palm.

"And how did this come to be yours?"

I'm starting to catch on to Jack's game here. Rather than leave me the opportunity to ask him deep, probing questions such as "What do you do for a living?," he's found a workaround. He asks me a million questions about myself, already knowing I physically can't keep myself from answering them.

"Do you want the actual truth or the surface answer I usually give people?" I raise my eyebrows at him in a silent challenge. An I'm-onto-you challenge. An if-you-want-to-ask-me-personal-questions-be-prepared-for-real-answers challenge.

Jack takes a long sip of his coffee before answering. "Let's go with the real truth."

"My family was pretty toxic growing up, and gardening provided me with two things: a reason to be outside the house and something I had control over." On an unrelated note, therapy is great and everyone should try it.

"Wow."

I give him a smile and make sure it's a real one. "I also really enjoy nurturing living things, ushering them from inception and into adult life."

He clears his throat, which I'm learning is his nervous tic. "That's not what I was expecting."

"What? For me to actually care about something other than

myself?" I laugh a little too loudly, pretending his words have no effect. "I know it seems out of character, but don't get me wrong, I'm still a huge asshole, and the only thing I nurture is plants. So yeah, that about covers the whole gardening obsession." Turning back to the work at hand, I continue to distribute seeds to their pods, tucking them into their little soil homes so they can bloom and grow.

"That's not at all what I meant, Sadie."

I pause my seed distribution, chancing a look at him. For once he's looking right at me, as if he needs me to see the truth in his words. I open my mouth to respond, but nothing comes out.

He clears his throat again. "Any other plans for today? Other than germinating?"

I turn back to the planters, thankful for the change in subject. "Yeah, I've got a training shift at the bar later."

"Oh, cool. Well, thanks again for the coffee. I guess I'll see you later." He gives me one of those half-hearted waves and heads down the stairs to the basement, like he's hit his conversation quota for the day and needs to escape. This is the pattern we've established. And I do my best to not take it personally. So the man doesn't want to hang out with me and plant seeds. It's not too much of an insult.

～

When I wake up on Sunday, I'm smacked in the face with the reminder of how hard it is to be a bartender. I don't know if I was just a lot younger back in college (shut up) or if bartending has gotten more physically demanding, but I hurt everywhere. After I pee, I crawl back under the covers, pulling my phone into my little cozy cave with me.

ME: What's the happs yo?

GEMMA: I refuse to respond to that text.

HARLEY: Technically, that's a response.

NICK: Why are you all waking me up so damn early
on a Sunday?

ME: It's almost noon, asshole.

ME: Dinner tonight? My place? Gem,
feel like cooking?

GEMMA: Did you just invite me over to your house
to cook for you?

ME: Yes, but only because I know you're
dying to get your hands on my
six-burner stove.

GEMMA: Sadly, you're right about that. Also sadly,
I have eight million essays to grade plus like four
million quizzes.

HARLEY: I've actually got plans for today.

NICK: Me too.

ME: WTF, traitors.

ME: Gem, come over. I can grade the quizzes at
least and we can order in.

GEMMA: Don't have to tell me twice. I'll be
there soon.

I consider getting actually dressed before going downstairs, but it's Sunday and everything hurts and I don't want to. So I stay in my flannel pajama shorts and pink tank top and figure Jack could find a million other reasons to evict me aside from my lack of proper attire.

And lo and behold, the man is actually not only awake but sitting at the dining room table when I trot down the stairs. He's dressed in his typical uniform of jeans and a nerd T-shirt, but his hair appears a little less unruly today. Almost as if he combed it.

"Morning." He takes a sip of coffee. From a mug. Like he made it himself. Which is just unfathomable to me. "How was bar training?"

"Everything hurts and I'm dying." I pick up my phone to see just how much a coffee delivery at peak time on a Sunday would absolutely drain my bank account.

"There's an iced latte for you in the fridge."

I drop my phone and practically sprint to the fridge, until I remember ow, muscles. "Did you actually go out for coffee?" I realize how bitchy that sounds the moment the words leave my mouth, but I don't bother correcting them. It's not like Jack doesn't have my number by now.

"I made it myself, actually." He nods to an espresso machine, tucked into the corner of the kitchen counter.

"You waited until *this* moment to tell me we have an espresso machine?" Rude.

"It came yesterday. I figured I should order one before you spent all of your rent money on coffee."

I take a test sip of my homemade latte, and damn if that isn't delicious. Almost delicious enough to compensate for his presumptuous acquisition of an espresso machine. "I used to work in finance, you know, I'm perfectly capable of budgeting."

"I know. But I also know you're trying to start a business, and every little bit helps, right?" A slight frown pulls down on his lips, a wrinkle creasing his forehead. "I'm sorry, I definitely didn't mean to overstep. That was kind of a dickish assumption, wasn't it?"

A little tiny piece of my frozen heart melts. "Not at all. Thank you." I hold up my cup. "And thanks for this. It's perfect." I open my mouth to finally ask the magic question, the one that will get him to reveal something of himself to me. I don't know what said question is yet, but I'm sure it's right there on the tip of my tongue.

But I don't get the chance to ask it because there's a knock on the door.

"Shit. I told Gemma she could come over so I can help her grade quizzes. Hope that's okay." I take my coffee with me over to the door, not wanting to separate myself from the much-needed caffeine.

"This is your house too, Sadie. You can have whoever you want over." He grabs his own cup of coffee and stands. "I'll get out of your way."

I turn to tell him he's not in our way, and even welcome to join, but he's already disappeared down the basement stairs.

∼

"Is it possible for the eyeballs to physically bleed? Because there must be torrents of blood streaming down my face right now." I throw down the red pen that's been gripped in my hand for the past three hours and collapse into a heap, my head resting on top of the dining room table.

"Bitch, please, this is nothing." Gemma continues to move through papers like some kind of high-speed teacher animatronic.

"How do you do this every weekend?" Sitting up, I bury the heels of my palms in my aching eyes.

"The pay is fantastic." Gemma's voice drips with sarcasm as she hands me a new stack of quizzes to grade.

"Where can I vote to give teachers all the raises? Like every raise. You guys should be paid like goddamn CEOs."

"Preaching to the super-broke choir, my friend." She shoots me an evil smile. "Aren't you glad you now live within walking distance and can help me whenever I need it?" She finishes up the essay she's grading, marks a score at the top of the paper, and moves on to the next. You'd think our piles would be smaller after all this time, but I swear, they must be self-multiplying, because the stacks just keep providing us with new torturous papers to grade.

"Damn. Are you guys still working?" Jack emerges from his basement cave for the first time since I let Gemma in. "Should I make some more coffee?"

"Yes," we both say at the same time.

My stomach rumbles so loudly both Gemma and Jack stop what they're doing and look at me. "I may have forgotten to eat today." I dig my phone out from under a teetering stack of grammar quizzes. "What shall we order?"

Jack fiddles with the espresso machine, pushing a bunch of buttons until dark liquid gold starts to pour out. "Why don't you let me go pick something up for you guys?"

Gemma pauses her intense scribbling to shoot me a look out of the corner of her eye.

"Thanks, Jack, but you don't have to do that. I can get delivery." I open up Postmates and see what's around.

He dumps the brewed espresso in a tall glass with ice, adding vanilla flavoring and milk before setting it in front of me. "I don't mind. I actually need an excuse to get out of the house for a minute. Gemma, can I make you some coffee?"

"A plain iced latte would be great, thank you." Gemma bestows a sugar-sweet smile upon Jack, while at the same time kicking me so hard under the table I'm going to have a bruise tomorrow.

"What the fuck is your problem?" I mutter under my breath.

She gives me a look. A we-are-so-going-to-be-talking-about-this-the-moment-he-walks-out-the-door look.

Jack brings over Gemma's coffee. "You guys good with sushi?"

We both nod.

"Great. Sadie, you wanna just text me what you guys like, and I'll run out and pick something up?" He shoves his hands in his pockets and it creates this low-key adorable-awkward effect.

"Sounds good."

"See you in a few." He gives us one of his signature half waves before grabbing his keys and heading out the front door.

Gemma stares at me for a solid minute, essays and quizzes totally forgotten. "He is in love with you."

I roll my eyes and take a long sip of my homemade iced vanilla latte. "Don't be ridiculous. The man isn't used to living with a woman or having friends or leaving the house, so his behaviors come across as baffling, but really, he just doesn't know any better."

"Sadie. The man just made us lattes and is now going out to pick up dinner. And he just, like, offered to go do it. We didn't even have to ask." She nudges me with her elbow. "At the very least, he wants to bang you."

"Not any more than any other person who likes women and has excellent taste." I pull a new stack of papers over to my side of the table, so desperate to end this conversation I'll happily go back to scoring seventh graders' grammar. Because there's no way Jack Thomas feels anything even close to love for me. Most of the time I'm not sure he even likes me. The man runs out of the room after a mere five minutes of conversation. It's as if he can only manage the bare minimum of politeness before needing to be free of me. He probably goes to bed every night wondering why the fuck he ever let me move in.

Gemma sips from her coffee, a knowing smirk plastered all over her face. "I like him."

"Jack's a great roommate."

"He's adorable."

"He's definitely not my type."

"As far as I'm concerned, that only speaks in his favor."

I let out a long, dramatic sigh. "Gem. I'm not hooking up with my nerdy roommate. Ever. Seriously. Let it go."

She shrugs and turns her attention back to her essays. "Okay. Then maybe I will."

My pen jerks to a stop on the paper, resulting in a long red line, straight through this kid's whole quiz. "I'd really rather you didn't." And I'd really, really rather she didn't. "But only because my roommate hooking up with one of my best friends could only lead to trouble, right? When you inevitably break up. I'd have to move again, and really, this place is just too good to give up. So I'd have to choose, you or the house, and honestly, Gem, where I'm sitting right now, it doesn't look good for you. So you might want to consider if hooking up with Jack is worth losing me as your friend before you make any rash decisions."

Gemma is fighting back a huge smile, and I know she's about to get all up in that the lady-doth-protest-too-much business, which obviously cannot happen. I can't even let myself question why the idea of her and Jack makes me want to puke up my coffee.

"But speaking of hookups, do you think Nick and Harley are hanging out without us right now?" I am nothing if not a master deflector. "Did they finally bite the bullet and go for it?"

Gemma purses her lips like she might not let me off the hook, but the chance to gossip about our two besties and their possible love story is too tempting to resist. "Do you really think they'd do that without telling us?"

"Um, yes. One hundred percent. They'd actually be idiots if they did tell us. At least at first."

Gemma frowns. "If they move in together, can I come live here?"

I drain the last of my coffee, all of a sudden ready for something a lot stronger. "You'll have to take that up with Jack."

"There's no way that man could handle both of us at once."

"Truer words have never been spoken." I take both of our empty coffee cups to the sink and rinse them before putting them in the dishwasher. Yeah. That's right. We have a dishwasher.

Gemma marks a score on a final paper, then gathers all her numerous stacks and stashes them away in her bag. "Thanks for helping, Sade. This would've been a nightmare without you."

"I hope I didn't screw it all up and you don't have angry parents calling to yell at you."

She sighs, standing and stretching. "That will happen regardless."

I open the fridge and pull out a bottle. "Wine?"

"Yes, please."

I pour each of us a glass, and by the time we've gossiped our way to glass number two, Jack's back with the sushi. The three of us sit around the dining room table, eating and drinking and chatting about nothing important. Jack seems lighter around my friends than he does when it's just the two of us. The gang has already come over a few times to hang out, and those are pretty much the only times he willingly engages. Sure, when we actually talk one-on-one there are moments when it feels easy and natural, but our conversations are always short, and we still have our fair share of awkward encounters. But that doesn't happen when my friends join the circle, and as I watch Jack and Gemma banter back and forth, it does something weird to my stomach. Like it gets all twisty and squishy.

Shit. I hope I didn't eat bad sushi.

Gemma calls for a Lyft and heads home early, since she has to actually get up and go to a grown-up job in the morning. I hug her goodbye and stand on the stoop until she's in the car. I make a mental note of the license plate number because, yeah, you never know.

Closing and locking the door, I head straight for the kitchen and another glass of wine. I've DVRed all of this week's Bravo episodes, and I'm planning on climbing into bed and imbibing three straight hours of drunkenness and debauchery.

Jack boxes up the last few remaining pieces of sushi and stashes them in the fridge. "You know, if you want to watch TV or something, you're more than welcome to use the basement whenever. I know it's kind of my territory, but it's just as much yours if you want it."

I pour the last remaining drops of the wine into my glass, saving the bottle for an experiment I have planned for this week. "It's all good. I've got a date with the Real Housewives, and I'd never subject you to that."

He grabs a beer from the fridge and shrugs. "I don't mind. Can't say I've ever watched an episode before."

"Oh, Jack of All Trades. You have no idea what you're in for." I head for the basement, testing the limits since I assume he's not actually going to join me, given how he usually cuts our interactions short as quickly as possible. I can't imagine him voluntarily sitting next to me on the sofa for three hours, especially for a Bravo marathon. But when I reach the bottom stair, I hear the thud of his steps behind me. I hide my smile.

Other than a quick peek during my initial tour, I haven't set foot in the brownstone's lower level. Probably because it looks like a frat house threw up down here. A clean frat house, but a frat house nonetheless. In addition to the pool table, there's a huge sectional sofa covered in some kind of velour fabric that belongs in a seventies porno.

The TV is bigger than some movie theater screens, and it has at least a thousand wires coming out of it like alien tentacles, each one attached to some sort of video game apparatus.

"Should I be scared about what kinds of fluids have graced this couch?" I check for suspicious stains, but it looks relatively clean.

"Other than Nick and me, no one has sat on it, so I think you're good." Jack plops down at one end of the sofa.

I curl up in the opposite corner. "Should we talk about why you haven't had anyone other than my friends over to join you in this den of all things teenage boys cream their jeans over?"

Jack looks at me, blinking slowly. "That's disgusting."

"My descriptive and spot-on language or the question?"

"Both." He picks up a remote—one of at least five—from the coffee table and turns on the TV.

I decide to leave it alone. For now. This couch is actually supremely comfy, and this sure as hell beats watching Housewives on my iPad. I take a sip of my wine. "One of these days, I will crack you, Jack Thomas."

And if I'm not mistaken, that's a smile I catch out of the corner of my eye.

⌒

JACK: Do I smell something burning up there?

ME: If you were really that concerned, you'd get
your ass up off that super-comfy couch and
check on me yourself.

JACK: Is that a yes?

> **ME:** I'm fine, thanks for your concern. Just cutting the tops off glass bottles so I can use them as vases.

JACK: You're cutting glass with fire?!?!?!?

> **ME:** Relax, I read like ten Pinterest tutorials before I started.

JACK: Fire extinguisher is under the sink.

> **ME:** Oh ye of little faith.

~

GEMMA: So I know I still have two more weeks, but what are we doing to celebrate my last day of school?

GEMMA: I need something to live for.

> **ME:** You guys could come to my bar!

NICK: Are there free drinks involved in that offer?

ME: There are heavier-than-normal pours involved
in that offer.

ME: As long as the tips are good, obvs.

GEMMA: We have to tip you?!?!?!?

ME: You do know I make less than minimum wage
now, right?

GEMMA: I also know what you pay in rent to live in
your SWEET-ASS HOUSE with your adorable
roommate.

ME: Jack is not adorable.

HARLEY: He totally is and you know it.

NICK: So drinks at Sadie's place?

ME: Hmmm. Sadie's Place. I like the sound of that.
Maybe I should open a bar . . .

~

ME: Dude, are you okay?

JACK: ?

ME: That's not an answer. Seriously, are you
all right?

JACK: I'm fine, what's the problem?

ME: I just got home and you're not here.
I thought maybe you got kidnapped
or something.

JACK: Haha.

ME: Okay, only that last part was a joke. I was
actually worried, I'll have you know.

JACK: . . .

JACK: . . .

JACK: Am I really that much of a hermit?

ME: Yes.

ME: But if you'd like to be less hermity, the gang is
all coming to my bar next Friday night to celebrate
Gemma's last day of school. We'd love for you to
come if you're free.

JACK: I'll think about it.

ME: GUYS. I just got my first official order!!!!!!!!!!!!!!

HARLEY: Woohoo! That's so exciting, Sadie!

GEMMA: Yes, girl! Get that money!!!

NICK: What did you end up setting your price point at? What are the profit margins looking like?

GEMMA: Yawn.

HARLEY: When's it for?

ME: I've got to deliver it on Friday morning 😊

GEMMA: Now we have two things to celebrate next weekend!

JACK: I was gonna order pizza tonight if you want to partake.

ME: Are you seriously texting me when I'm a floor away from you?

JACK: You're upstairs, so technically it's two floors.

ME: Wow.

ME: And yes to pizza. Obviously.

JACK: Pepperoni and black olives?

ME: You're so well trained.

JACK: Were you planning on watching Real
Housewives again tonight?

ME: Yeah, unless you have big plans for the TV.

JACK: Nope. No plans . . .

ME: Did you want to join me?

JACK: I do really need to see what happens with
Porsha.

JACK: If you don't mind.

ME: I don't mind at all, Jack in the Box ☺

SEVEN

*T*HE BAR IS packed on Friday night, as it is most Friday nights, which is good for my ever-so-slowly-dwindling bank account but not so great for my plans to low-key hang with my friends while getting paid to make drinks. Still, I manage to sneak my way over to their high-top corner table more than I probably should, stealing teeny-tiny sips from Gemma's and Harley's drinks as I do.

"I thought you said Jack was going to come by." Gemma leans in close to my ear so she doesn't have to yell over the noisy crowd.

I shrug as if I haven't been watching the door for the past hour, waiting for him to make an appearance. "Maybe he got tied up."

Doing what, I couldn't tell you, because as far as I know, even after almost two months of living together, the man still doesn't actually do anything. It's a lifestyle I find baffling, but at least he has been seen leaving the house on occasion since I moved in.

"Don't worry, he'll be here." Nick takes a swig of beer, all while managing to look super smug.

"And how do you know that?" Harley slides her drink across the table for me to take a sip.

Nick shrugs, smile growing smugger by the second. "We hung out today."

I pause midsip. "I'm sorry, did you just say you hung out today? With Jack? My roommate who never wants to hang out with anybody?"

This time Nick full-on grins. "He doesn't seem to mind hanging out with me."

"Oh, so it's just me he can't stand to be around for more than five minutes." I down the rest of Harley's drink. I'm not sure why the idea of Nick and Jack's hanging out without me bothers me so much since I love it when we all hang out together. I mean, I'm constantly baffled by Jack's isolation, so I should be happy he's making friends. It just feels a little weird that he's making friends with my friends. Especially when it sometimes still feels like he doesn't really want to be friends with me.

Nick's smile fades. "That's not how I meant that at all. And trust me, Jack's problem isn't not wanting to be around you."

"What does that mean?"

"Ho-ly fuck." Gemma's mouth drops open, her eyes locked on the door.

Her declaration is loud enough that we all swivel our heads toward the front of the bar.

And holy fuck.

It becomes immediately clear why Jack is running late. Because Jack has been to the barber. And some kind of fine establishment that sells clothes without video game logos on them.

His unruly dark brown hair has been trimmed, not enough to take away the curl, but just enough so his face is now visible. His black plastic glasses still rest on the bridge of his nose, but without the cloud of hair around him, they seem to enhance rather than detract. Because now I can see his jawline. It's chiseled and defined. As are his forearms, which are neatly framed by the rolled-up sleeves of his white button-down shirt. He's still wearing jeans, but they are darker than usual, and more fitted, and tonight's Converse look suspiciously clean.

"Did you have something to do with this?" I ask Nick, my mouth suddenly dry as the desert.

His smirk back in full force, Nick ignores my question and waves Jack over to our table.

Jack's eyes meet mine as he pushes through the crowd to make his way to us, a shy smile tugging on the corner of his lips. Lips that suddenly look fuller and just short of kissable.

When he reaches us, he gives me a rigid side hug and I get a whiff of him. At home he smells like coffee and fresh paper. But tonight he's put on some kind of cologne, and a woodsy musk fills my nose.

I completely stiffen—as do my nipples—at the weight of his arm around me. My cheeks flame, likely the color of Barbie's Dream House.

Gemma hops down off her stool and tugs Jack away, wrapping him in a hug, and I don't know if I want to punch her or kiss her. "You look amazing!"

Punch her.

She shoots me a look over Jack's shoulder, one that says, *Get your shit together, girl.* She motions for me to wipe the drool from my chin.

Kiss her. Definitely kiss her.

I beat a hasty retreat back behind the bar without speaking a word to Jack. I'm 99 percent sure I've lost the power of speech anyway.

For the next two hours, I do everything I can to avoid serving my friends, going so far as to send the other bartender over to their table when they need additional rounds. And they have quite a few additional rounds.

I've almost worked up the courage to go over and face them, under the guise of finally getting a break, when I dart a quick glance over to their table. Gemma has disappeared. A quick scan of the bar shows me she's chatting up one of our regulars. One of the regulars who's not a total tool, so I'll allow it. Nick and Harley are sitting suspiciously close together. I try to peek under the table, but I can't get a clear view. But if I were a betting woman, I'd put money on their hands being intertwined beneath the sticky marble top.

All those revelations aside, my attention snags on Jack. Still looking like the after version from some nineties teen-makeover movie. And he's sitting next to some girl, his head bent low so she can whisper in his ear.

I want to lie and say it has no effect on me, because clearly, no matter how great the glow-up, Jack and I will never be a thing. But I do feel a little burst of a stabbing pain, right in the chest, as I watch him bust up laughing at something the girl says.

And yeah. I'm definitely not here for that.

He never laughs with me like that.

So I turn away from their table once again, focusing all my energy on wiping down some already spotless glasses.

Gemma and her new friend leave first, Gem blowing me kisses and giving me the *Call me tomorrow* hand signal.

Once she's safely vacated the building, Nick and Harley head out soon after, not fooling anyone with the tiny sliver of space they keep between them as they walk out the front door.

I side-eye Jack's table and definitely do not breathe a sigh of relief when I find him sitting there alone.

I pour him a beer and finally head over. The rest of the bar is mostly empty, everything winding down for the night. My coworkers are in cleanup mode, and everyone's anxious to get out of here as soon as we can.

Setting the glass down on a fresh coaster, I stack up the empties still sitting on the table. "What happened to your friend?"

He furrows his brow. "Everyone left. Didn't they say goodbye?"

I pull a rag from my apron and wipe down the marble high-top. "Not them. Your friend." I wiggle my eyebrows a little so he gets the hint.

"Oh." He shrugs and takes a long pull from his beer. "I'm not sure actually."

"Oh." I keep wiping, even though the table is now spotless and stickiness-free. "I like your new look."

He glances down at himself, and when he raises his eyes again, his cheeks are flushed. "It's an old look, actually. Believe it or not, I haven't spent my entire adult life dressing like a hormonal teenager."

"Oh." It's the only word I can form right now because I think Jack Thomas just revealed something about himself. And it does something to soothe the leftover sting on my heart. "Well, it suits you."

"Thanks." He spins his coaster around on the table, not meeting my eyes. "Is it cool if I just hang here until you're off?"

"It's going to be a while. I've still got cleanup and stuff to do." I gesture to the tables around me, which are suddenly all empty and sparkling clean.

"I don't mind waiting." His gaze finds mine, those green eyes boring into me.

And suddenly I can't breathe. Suddenly, *I don't mind waiting* doesn't feel like a casual phrase among friends. I move a step closer to him, like there's some kind of magnetic force in his words.

"Sadie! Grab that glass and let's get the fuck out of here!" my bar partner, Sam, hollers across the room, pulling me out of my haze.

I give Jack a tentative smile. He returns it just as tentatively.

Then he chugs his beer and hands me the glass.

I take it with me back behind the bar, dunking it in soapy water before rinsing it clean and hand-drying it. Sam hands me a stack of cash I don't bother counting, shoving it in the back pocket of my tight jeans. I clock out, say my goodbyes, and gesture for Jack to meet me at the front door.

The streets are mostly empty of late-night walkers, or as empty as New York streets can ever really get. The evening air is warm, not too sticky, and there's even a slight breeze as we head the couple of blocks back to the brownstone.

Jack walks with his hands in his pockets, like he doesn't know exactly what to do with them. "How was your first delivery today?"

A smile breaks across my face. I'd meant to regale the whole crowd with the story, but since I spent most of the night avoiding them, I didn't really get the chance. "It was amazing. She loved it and told me she'd definitely order from me again and tell all her friends." Pulling my phone from my crossbody purse, I open up Instagram. "And the photo of the arrangement got a shit-ton of likes."

"Is that the official measurement these days?" He takes the phone from me, squinting a little as he studies the picture.

I placed the bouquet in one of the bottles I cut a couple of weeks ago, a gin bottle with a cool old-timey label on it. The flowers themselves are an explosion of color and texture, bright pink dahlias and orange and yellow ranunculus. I photographed it sitting on the table in front of the bay window in my room, and the colors pop against the white walls.

"Wow, Sadie, this is impressive."

"Why do you sound so surprised?" And why does said surprise sting?

"I'm definitely not, it's just, it's not just the flowers, this photo is great. The lighting, the background, the aesthetic. You nailed it." He hands me back my phone, our fingers brushing up against one another, sending a little jolt through me.

"Oh. Thanks." I put my phone away, my hands fluttering uselessly between my pockets and the strap of my purse because they suddenly yearn for nothing more than another brush of Jack's skin. Another brush of Jack's validation. Finally, I just leave them hanging awkwardly at my sides. "You sound like you know what you're talking about. Like you have an artistic eye."

He doesn't answer my non-question, letting a less-awkward-than-usual silence fall between us. As we climb the front steps of the house, he breaks it. "So I have to go out of town tomorrow. Just for one night, I'll be back Sunday early afternoon." He pushes open the door, motioning for me to walk in first.

"Oh. That's cool. Where are you headed?" It actually doesn't feel cool at all. More like the opposite, but it seems like something a nice roommate would say.

"Just a thing I have to take care of."

"I really wish you'd stop oversharing, Cracker Jack. Seriously. I can't handle any more of your secrets. They just come flowing out of you, and I'm not sure I can listen to you talk about yourself for one more second." I kick off my shoes right inside the door and leave them there, which I know bugs the shit out of him.

"Hilarious as always." He picks up my shoes and places them on the stairs, as if that will convince me to carry them to my room. "We on for pizza and Housewives Sunday night though?"

"You know it." I head into the kitchen and pour myself a glass of water before heading upstairs. "I'm taking a shower because I smell like beer and sweaty men."

"Gross."

I lean over the stairs. "Thanks for coming out tonight."

He pauses at the top of the basement steps. "Thanks for inviting me."

"Good night, Jack."

"Good night, Sadie."

⌒

I'm grateful for my scheduled bar shift on Saturday because I need a distraction. Despite the fact that Jack spends most of his time in the basement, it feels weird being in the house without him. I don't like it. And I really don't like how much I don't like it. Something shifted last night, nothing seismic or earth-shattering, but just enough to make me feel unsettled.

So I head out to a café in the late morning, catching up on some work. After my very successful Instagram post, I have three new inquiries in my email inbox, so I respond to those, chatting with potential clients about what they might be looking for. For now I'm sticking with individual arrangements, since I don't really have the space or the manpower or the confidence for any type of event just yet. But since I'm repurposing vases and sourcing all my flowers locally, I'm able to keep costs down and each arrangement is netting a solid profit. And with my bar shifts easily covering rent and my other bills, financially things aren't looking too bad these days. My student loans will still never be paid off, but that's kind of a given for us broke-ass millennials.

I don't return home until it's time to change into my tight jeans and low-cut tank top for work, the quiet house echoing around me. I haven't really had much alone time since moving in with Jack, and I'm surprised to find that I don't miss it. While I don't mind being by myself, I find comfort in knowing there's someone else there with me. Even if they aren't physically there.

Luckily nothing provides a distraction quite like thirsty-ass customers demanding all your attention. I throw myself into my shift at the bar and am heartily rewarded for my hard work at the end of the night. I make the walk home with my keys clenched tightly in my hand, phone open and ready to dial 911. Even though I make this walk alone two times a week, it feels a little more ominous knowing there's no one waiting for me at home.

But I survive, kicking my shoes off as soon as I walk in and not bothering to move them from directly in front of the door. After my shower, I climb into bed and curl up with my iPad. I'm tempted to watch a new episode of Housewives since I know I'll have trouble sleeping here all by myself, but I couldn't do that to Jack. Now that I've gotten him addicted, it just wouldn't be fair.

And speak of the devil.

JACK: How was your shift?

ME: Good. How is your super-duper mystery assignment?

ME: Oh shit! Are you in the CIA?

JACK: Can you feel me rolling my eyes, even from states away?

ME: Ha! So you've left the state of New York!

JACK: Yes.

ME: Jersey?

ME: Boston?

ME: Philly?

JACK: Anyway. Just wanted to make sure you got home safe.

ME: Regretting that now?

ME: Vermont?

JACK: I'm putting you on do not disturb.

ME: No you're not. ☺

JACK: You're right. Good night.

ME: Night.

∼

I'm somewhat disappointed when only one of my inquiries turns into an actual order. I remind myself I've only been in business six weeks and I can't expect to be a mogul overnight, but not going to lie, a small part of me expected things to take off instantly. I know that was a naïve assumption, but it still stings a little.

At least I get to spend Sunday morning the best way I know how: drinking coffee and strolling through the farmers' market. I stock up on more flowers than I need for my one order and make plans for a couple of extra arrangements for Instagram purposes, hoping to garner some more interest from my steadily growing online presence.

Once I get home, I prepare the flowers, leaving them in a giant bucket of water in the main-floor bathroom. It's small and has an air-conditioning vent, so it's the coolest place in the house aside from the fridge. Based on the florals I selected, I pick out two different vases, a vintage tiki mug I found at a sidewalk sale and another former alcohol bottle. I've been sneaking old bottles from the recycling bin at work and coming up with some pretty cool colors and shapes. And I haven't burned down the house yet with my amateur glass cutting, so bonus.

I slip into the zone of arranging, happy to lose myself while I wait for Jack to come home.

And while I lie to myself, repeating over and over how much I'm so not waiting for Jack to come home.

I stage both arrangements on the mantel, highlighting the exposed brick in the background. It's still early afternoon, so the lighting is perfect. I won't post the ordered bouquet until the flowers have been delivered to their rightful owner—I don't want to ruin the surprise—but I pop onto Insta and immediately post the other photo, spending an additional half hour engaging on the app to hopefully boost my visibility.

The front door opens just as I'm placing the extra arrangement at the center of the dining room table, the one for the order already safely stored in the fridge.

Jack tosses his keys in the bowl on the entry table and doesn't even mention my shoes, which are still right in the middle of the walkway. "Honey, I'm home."

I greet him with a grin. "How was your trip, dear?"

He throws his bag on the stairs, and I know he'll take it with him when he goes to his room, like a real grown-up. "It was fine."

"And you went where again?"

He smirks and crosses to the fridge, pulling out a beer. "Nice try."

"Sorry about the flowers in the fridge. They'll be gone tomorrow."

He hands me a beer bottle before grabbing another one for himself. "Not a problem. They look great."

"Thanks!"

"Did you photograph them already?" He pops the top on his bottle and leans up against the peninsula. He's back in his standard uniform of jeans and a nerd tee, but his shirt is fitted through the chest and arms, showing off his lean muscles, and his hair is slicked back off his face, like he's been running his hands through it and it finally just stayed that way. He's got a day or two's worth of stubble that makes him look a little gritty, a look I'm totally into. Or I would be, on anyone else.

"Yup." My phone is resting right next to him. In order to grab it, I have to cross over to him and get all up in his space, which is totally fine because Jack is my friend and my roommate and standing near him is definitely not a big deal. At all.

He smells like cologne again. And his biceps tenses when I brush up against him.

Not that I notice.

I swipe open my phone and show him the photos.

"Damn. These are even better than the first one. Gorgeous work." He taps on my screen for a few seconds.

I reach for my phone, but he holds it high above his head, still typing, out of my reach. "What are you doing?"

"Sending these to myself."

I jump up and down, not making any progress, until he finally finishes and hands me my phone back. "Why are you doing that?"

He shrugs, taking a long swig from his beer. "Because they're beautiful and I might want to look at them again."

The words zing me. Right in the heart.

It's a better compliment than if he told me I was beautiful.

That's something I kind of already know.

But his validation of my work means something else entirely. It hits me right in the center of all my feelings. Hard.

"Thanks, Jack-o'-Lantern." I make a concerted effort to remove all traces of sarcasm from my voice, because I mean it, and it's suddenly important he know that.

He clears his throat, pulling his gaze from mine. "You okay with an early dinner? I'll order the pizza if you go cue up the DVR."

"Sure thing." Grabbing my beer, I head to the basement, plopping down in my corner seat and turning on the TV.

Jack comes down a minute later, a second round of beers in his hand. He doesn't sit right next to me, but he also doesn't slide to the opposite end of the couch like he has in the past.

I bite my lip to keep from grinning and turn my attention to Bravo. Where it belongs.

$\sim$

ME: I'm going to need you to not use the main-floor bathroom, if that's okay.

JACK: And why am I not allowed to use the one bathroom on the main floor of my house?

ME: It's become my floral storage room. I know it's a pain in the ass but it's the coldest room and it's starting to get hot as balls.

> **ME:** Besides, there's a bathroom in the basement, which is where you spend 99% of your time anyway.

JACK: Fine. But I require one free beer the next time I come to the bar.

> **ME:** Fuck off.

> **ME:** ☺

~

GEMMA: Shit, Sade, your Instagram is going off the charts! Are you getting tons of orders?

> **ME:** Honestly? No. My IG is killing it but the likes aren't translating to sales unfortunately.

HARLEY: I'm sure things will pick up soon!

> **ME:** Hope so.

NICK: Hi, some of us have real jobs and would prefer to not have our phones going off every five seconds.

GEMMA: Harley has a real job.

ME: Gemma definitely has a real job.

GEMMA: Sadie is building a prosperous business.

ME: Aww, thanks, friend.

NICK: Seriously?

ME: ☺

GEMMA: ☺

ME: ☺

GEMMA: ☺

NICK: I hate you both.

~

ME: I'M SORRY!!!!!

JACK: Fuck, did you burn down my house?

ME: No.

ME: Do you seriously think I'd tell you I burned
down your house in a text?

JACK: No, you'd probably move out of state first
and then send me a telegram.

ME: We should really bring back the
telegram. Stop.

JACK: You were apologizing for something?

ME: Oh shit. Yeah. Sorry the kitchen is a mess. I had
to run out to make this delivery on time but I
promise I'll clean it all up as soon as I get back.

JACK: Business is going well then?

ME: Eh. It could be better. But I had more orders
this week than last so I'll take it.

JACK: Let me know if there's anything I can
do to help.

ME: Have I mentioned you're the best roommate in
the history of roommates?

JACK: Not nearly often enough.

ME: I'll pick up dinner on my way back to the
house. Sushi?

JACK: Sure.

ME: See you soon!

❧

NICK: So are we all good for our annual Fourth of July Hamptons beach party?

GEMMA: Fuck yes.

HARLEY: I'm in!

ME: I think so. I don't have a bar shift so as long as I don't get any orders I should be okay.

JACK: Did I just . . . am I . . . did I just get added to the group text?

GEMMA: Aw man, does this mean we have to shut down period talk? I rely on Sadie to give me a two-day warning before I'm about to start.

JACK: I don't know what that means, but please don't hold back period talk on my account.

NICK: Their cycles are all synced. Save me, Jack!

ME: You two are totes adorbs.

NICK: So can you make it to the Hamptons for the 4th, J?

JACK: I don't see why not.

GEMMA: Mmm. Jack in a bathing suit.

ME: He can see that, you know.

GEMMA: I know. 😉

EIGHT

$\int$O YEAH. JACK in a bathing suit.

By the time we arrive at Nick's parents' house in the Hamptons—beachside, obviously—we're all hot and cranky, so we change into our suits, grab a few beers, and head directly to the pool. Because why not have a pool overlooking the ocean? Rich-people logic.

But not even the intensely spectacular view can pull my attention from this other, much more interesting view. Jack may have stepped up his fashion game in recent weeks, but this is my first time getting a real peek at what's been hiding underneath those mostly baggy clothes. And it's, uh . . . not what I would've expected.

He's long and lean and cut like a swimmer. Even though I've never once seen him don workout attire, or, you know, work out, there are faint ridges of abs lining his stomach. A smattering of dark hair grazes his chest, trailing down into a thin line leading right into the edge of his waistband. His arms are sculpted without being beefy. To sum up, he's hot. Certifiably hot. And I'm definitely not the only one who notices.

"I was mostly joking in that text thread, but damn." Gemma looks him up and down from her perch on a poolside lounge chair.

"Sadie, did you know all that was under there?" Harley tilts her sunglasses down to the tip of her nose to get a better view.

I push my own sunglasses farther up on my nose, hoping to block my eyes so no one can tell how hard I'm staring. I make my shoulders move up and down in some kind of motion slightly resembling a shrug. "It's—he's—I—it's—what?"

Gemma and Harley exchange a look before bursting into laughter.

"I hate you both." Rising from my own lounger, I yank my cover-up over my head and toss it on the chair before diving into the pool.

The cool water rushes over me, and I relish the chill, though it does little to dampen the heat of my skin. Heat that is purely a result of sitting in the sun, of course.

Because Jack is nothing more than a friend. A good friend, and a supportive roommate, and really, what does it matter how good he looks in a bathing suit? It means nothing.

Even though it's really good.

I push through the turquoise surface of the pool, gliding into an easy breaststroke, hoping a couple of laps will help clear my head. By the time I've swum the length of the pool a few times and I make it back to the shallow end, the rest of the group has planted themselves in my path. Nick splashes me, which he knows I hate, so I jump on his back and attempt to force him under the water.

But the man outweighs me by a hundred pounds, so my efforts are futile. Until Harley and Gemma jump on too. The three of us manage to shove his head under for a few seconds at least, and he comes up sputtering.

Jack watches our roughhousing from his perch, leaning against the side wall of the pool, away from the fray. His lips are quirked up in his bemused smile, but when his eyes meet mine, the smile drops and his eyes darken. He swallows a couple of times.

I start to wade my way over to him, but as soon as he sees me coming, he jumps out of the pool.

"Drink time?" Jack calls over his shoulder as he heads to the cooler we brought outside with us.

Gemma catches my eyes and gives me a sympathetic smile. I shrug it off, dunking back under the water so I have an excuse to block out everyone around me. Because that rebuff actually hurt. But it shouldn't. It's not like seeing Jack in a bathing suit is so earth-shattering it changes my totally platonic feelings for him. And these feelings are only platonic. Jack is totally wrong for me. More important, I'm totally wrong for him.

After our long drive, dinner with Nick's parents, and a night swim, everyone is wiped out. We all say good night at the bottom of the stairs and head off to our respective rooms. Nick and Jack are sharing, and so are Harley and Gemma, which leaves me on my own. I should be grateful to not have to share, but I'm kind of longing for my own sleepover buddy. I need a distraction. I could crash in Harley and Gemma's room, but it's only equipped with two twin beds and I don't want to sleep on the floor.

As soon as my head hits the pillow, instead of drifting off into a peaceful and dreamless slumber, as one should, my brain decides to replay the highlights from this afternoon like a super-annoying sportsball show.

Jack rising out of the pool like some nineties perfume-ad model, tossing back his wet hair, water droplets creating a perfect trail down his cut stomach.

Jack's eyes visibly heating as he takes me in in my fabulous and definitely sexy bikini.

Jack turning and sprinting from the pool, doing anything and everything to get away from me as quickly as humanly possible.

Thirty minutes of that super-fun torture reel is enough to push me out of bed and send me tiptoeing down the stairs and into the kitchen.

Enough moonlight trickles in from the eight million windows of this fancy-ass house that I don't need to turn any lights on. I pull gently on the fridge, looking for a water pitcher.

"Sadie!"

"What the fuck?" I jump about a foot, my voice at top volume.

"Shhhh." Harley comes around the gigantic kitchen island, shushing me and closing the fridge.

"Don't shush me, you scared the shit out of me," I whisper. Fiercely.

"Sorry." She hands me a glass of water.

I gesture to the padded bar stools surrounding the marble-topped island. "What are you doing up?"

"Same thing as you I suppose. Couldn't sleep."

I take a sip of water, and my heart rate finally returns to normal. "Does your non-sleeping have anything to do with a certain man just down the hall?"

She arches one eyebrow. "Does yours?"

"I asked you first." I give her a wicked grin.

She smiles, but it doesn't reach her eyes. And she doesn't answer my question.

"It's not exactly a secret, you know. You and Nick. Gem and I have known for a while. And we'd never judge you for wanting to be together. We want you guys to be happy. Hopefully you know that."

"I know." She twists her seat, angling it away from mine.

I take a deep breath because I know there's only one thing to do in this particular situation with Harley. I need to sit in the silence and let her talk when she's ready. I literally have to bite my tongue to keep from filling the quiet with my blather, but I do it, because I know it's what she needs.

Finally, she takes a sip of her own water, shifting ever so slightly back in my direction. "Nick wants to make it official, take things public, so to speak."

Pursing my lips tightly, I just barely keep in a squeal of joy. "That's a good thing, right? I mean, you do also want to be official?"

"I do." She looks over at me and her eyes are shining. Not with tears, but with something akin to sheer joy. "I love him, Sadie. I think I've loved him for a really long time."

I reach over and grab her hand. "I think you have too. And I'm so, so happy for you. And for him. Probably more for him, since he's really scoring big-time here."

She rolls her eyes but pairs it with a smile. When her fingers grasp mine so tightly it starts to hurt, I realize there's more to it.

"I don't know what I would do if anything ever happened to our group. You and Gemma are my sisters and I'm terrified this is going to screw it up." Harley rushes out the words in one single breath.

Tugging on our joined hands, I pull her closer to me. "Hey. None of that. Nothing is going to screw it up, okay? Even if things ended badly with the two of you—which they won't, I can't even tell you how many times I've already envisioned your wedding day—nothing is going to split the four of us up." I knock my shoulder into hers. "You guys are basically the only family I have at this point—I'm not going to let anything happen to us."

She gives me a tiny smile. "Promise?"

"Promise. Is that the only thing holding you back? Wondering what might happen to the group in a worst-case scenario?" I take a sip of my water, giving her time to fill the silence if she wants to. Because I can tell she wants to.

We sit for another quiet minute.

Finally, she draws in a deep breath. "I need you to listen for a minute and not say anything. Okay?"

I mime zipping my lips shut and throwing away the key.

She takes in a long breath and lets it out slowly. "I'm worried about how Nick's parents are going to react to him dating a Black woman."

I tighten my grip on her hand but keep my promise to just listen.

"I know his parents are liberal and donated to Obama, and on paper, they do and say all the right things. But there's a big difference between being woke on paper and accepting your son is dating a Black woman. And I'm scared, Sade. Because I don't know how I'll handle it if they react badly. And I don't know how Nick will handle it either. And so in this big happy shiny relationship moment, I don't really know how to feel, you know?" Her voice cracks at the end, and I know she's holding back tears.

I pull Harley into my arms, wrapping her up tight. I'm tempted to tell her it'll be okay, that of course Nick's parents would never not accept her, but I don't, because I don't know if that's true and the last thing I want to do is lie to her.

I wait for her to disengage from the hug before picking her hand back up in mine and squeezing tightly. "I love you. And I'm here. Always."

She gives me a faint smile. "Love you back." She gulps down the rest of her water and rises to place her empty glass in the sink. "You coming up?"

"In a minute."

Harley stops at the edge of the island. "I like Jack. He's a good one."

"And here I was thinking you were a smitten kitten. You already got eyes on someone else?"

She doesn't bother to acknowledge my asinine statement because she's a smart woman and has learned well over the years. "When you're ready to talk about him, you know where to find me." She blows me a kiss and heads up the stairs.

I sit in the darkness on my own for several minutes before I can finally admit it, if only to the yellow roses on the counter. "I think I like him too."

NINE

"*SADIE JANE, IF* you don't put down that phone right now, I swear to god!" Nick throws this empty threat at me while he's waist-deep in the calm bay water.

I flip him off from my spot in a beach chair under an umbrella and return my attention to my phone. After posting another photo of a recent arrangement, I check my DMs. There are a couple of inquiries, which I answer, keeping my fingers crossed that at least a few of them turn into orders. My sales have been growing, steadily but slowly. Really slowly. And even though it's a holiday and I'm sure most people will be away from their phones, I want to make sure I address all potential customer questions as quickly as possible.

But I know Nick is probably just a few seconds from throwing me over his shoulder and carrying me into the water like the caveman he is deep down inside, so once all DMs have been answered, I click off my phone, holding it tightly in my hand like some kind of millennial rosary, praying for some good business news.

"Sadie!" This time the scream comes from my three so-called besties and my roommate—the traitor—who apparently all have little to no regard for my entrepreneur life.

"Okay, fine! You imbeciles!" I toss my phone into my straw beach bag, making a mental note to put a bouquet in it later and snap a beachside photo.

I tug off my flowy dress, revealing my very hot, hot-pink bikini underneath. Turning up my best *Baywatch* impression, I slow-motion run down the sand and into the water, diving into the cool blue and resurfacing at the little circle the gang has created. And yeah, I might throw a glance Jack's way to see if he's watching.

He's definitely watching.

Nick pulls a canned rosé from the floating cooler and cracks it open before handing it to me. "Did you really just trade one job with endless hours for a different job with endless hours?"

I take a long sip of the sparkling wine, letting it cool the heat flushing my cheeks ever since I noticed Jack noticing me. "Yes. But these are working-for-me hours, so it's different."

Harley bumps me with her hip. "I'm proud of you, girl. I know it hasn't been easy, but things are starting to pick up."

"As evidenced by the constant array of flowers all over my house." Jack gives me one of his half-cocked smiles and little bubbles float up into my chest.

But that could be the rosé.

"Maybe one day I'll actually be able to open my own shop." Assuming I don't go bankrupt first.

Nick flicks a tiny splash of water at me. "It's been two months, let's have a dose of realism here."

"It's been two *and a half* months. And I've never been a fan of realism." I argue with him not because he's wrong, but because he's Nick.

Gemma, currently perched on a giant flamingo-shaped raft, paddles back over to us after having drifted off on the current. "You're one of the realest people I know, Sadie Jane."

I push her back away from the group. "I just like talking shit, that's all."

Nick raises his beer in the air. "And we love you for it. As long as we aren't the subject of it."

"You guys are perfect, what shit could I possibly have to talk about you?" I send an air kiss to each of them.

Harley links her arm through mine. "That's the nicest thing you've ever said to any of us."

"What can I say? I'm a giver." I chug the rest of my rosé and hand Nick the empty can. "Now give me some more wine. Please."

Nick sticks a can in a pineapple-shaped floating coaster and sends it my way.

Popping the top, I hold up my can. "I can't say I've always been proud to be an American in the past few years, but one thing is for damn sure, I'm proud of all of you. Happy Fourth, bitches!"

They all echo my toast, and we clink our cans together.

"Fuck, Sade, the sentimentality is off the charts today." Gemma blows me a kiss and I flip her off.

The rest of the afternoon passes in a haze of canned cocktails and floating on the waves, until we get tired of the beach and head back to the house to kick the drinking up a notch and float in the pool. Nick's parents invited a bunch of friends over for a barbecue, so the yard fills with people and chatter and music and the occasional burst of fireworks from neighboring houses.

We stuff our faces with hot dogs and corn on the cob and fresh berries arranged in the shape of an American flag. And when the "adult" company becomes too boring for the likes of us, we grab blankets, s'mores supplies, and a few bottles of wine and head back to the beach.

Nick and Jack get a bonfire going while Harley and Gemma stab marshmallows onto the end of skewers. I open a bottle of wine and divvy it up among five paper cups. I couldn't even tell you how many drinks I've had throughout the day, but despite the constant buzz, I haven't crossed the line into drunk. At least not yet. Instead my insides feel all warm and squishy, as likely due to the company as to the booze circulating through my veins.

Nick and Harley cuddle up on a blanket, for the first time not bothering to hide their obvious affection. Gemma and I share a long look, mostly a giddy happy one, but one tinged with just the tiniest smidge of worry. Worry about what might happen to our fearsome foursome should things not go how we all want them to. Despite my declaration to Harley last night, I don't know what would happen to the group should things take a turn for the breakup, and the thought low-key terrifies me. But tonight is not the night for thoughts like that. Tonight is for realizing I've never seen two of my best friends happier, and for being happy for them.

Gemma folds herself down next to me on our blanket, linking our arms together, sharing a reassuring squeeze. Jack sits directly across from me on the other side of the fire. I meet his bright green gaze and a wide, genuine smile spreads across his face. It's been nice to see him loosen up a little bit since being here with the group. He's looking a little lighter, a little younger, and a lot more content.

It's a good look on him.

After our second bottle of wine and too many s'mores to count, Nick and Harley throw in the towel and call it a night, walking back to the house hand in hand. Judging by the lights and the noise, the party in the backyard is still going strong. I wonder whether they'll stroll in intertwined or if they'll continue to hide their relationship in front of Nick's family. I squint to try to see what they decide, but the shadows make it too dark to know for sure.

Gemma finishes up her glass of wine, then pushes up off the blanket. "I'm going to pack it in too. I'm beat."

"Do you need me to walk you back to the house?" Jack starts to rise.

Gemma shoos him off. "I'm good. Just listen for my screams."

I roll my eyes. "We'll watch you until you get to the gate."

She squats down a little so she can look me in the eye. "You good?"

There's a lot of layers to that question. Do I want to stay here alone with Jack? Am I going to do something I might regret thanks to the copious amount of imbibing throughout the day? Is there a chance I'll pass out on this blanket?

All valid questions.

But I smile and give her a reassuring hand squeeze. "I'm good."

Gemma waves good night and treks back to the house. We watch her until she reaches the back gate, as promised.

Flopping on the blanket, I lie flat on my back so I can look up and see the stars. Stars are one of the few things New York City life can't provide, but here on the beach, a ton of them are sprinkled in the midnight sky above, like a pot of glitter exploded over a swath of navy velvet.

"Get your ass over here, Jackpot." I might be tempting fate by inviting my suddenly sexy roommate to share a blanket under the stars, but I don't much care. I'd like to blame it on the rosé, but really, I just want Jack to be near me.

He chuckles, and a few seconds later lowers himself next to me, sitting with his knees pulled into his chest, a beer bottle dangling from his fingers. "You all right down there?"

"Just looking at the stars."

He tilts his head up. "It's one of the few things I miss from growing up in Connecticut."

"You grew up in Connecticut?" My attention is successfully pulled from the sky and focused on Jack. Who just revealed a truth.

He takes a long drink of his beer, like he didn't mean to actually tell me that. "Yup."

I let the quiet sit, wondering if he's kind of like Harley and needs the space to speak on his own terms. And it's a quiet I'm willing to endure because I want him to tell me more. Not just to sate my curiosity but because I want to know him.

But he doesn't say anything, just finishes his beer and lies down next to me. Only a couple of inches separate us, and heat radiates from him, warming my already flushed skin. My heart rate kicks up, and as buzzed as I still am, I'm suddenly aware of every molecule of detail blanketing us in this moment. My eyes return to the stars, the close distance/eye contact combo too overwhelming.

"Sade?" My name rolls off his tongue like a promise.

"Yeah?" My lungs are so fluttery, I barely manage to get the one word out.

He clears his throat. "Thank you."

His eyes burn into my cheek like the sunburn I know I'll have in the morning, but I avoid turning my head. "For what?"

He inches his hand a little closer to mine, leaving just the tiniest sliver of space between our pinkies. "For including me. And accepting me."

I brush my little finger against his. It's the faintest hint of contact, but it zings through every inch of me.

"It's been a long time since I've felt included." His pinky finger moves over mine, locking them together.

I turn to meet his gaze, but his eyes are back on the sky above. "It could never work between us, Jack." I mean it to come out as a joke, a pinprick in the tiny bubble of sexual tension that's been steadily growing between us. But the truth of the words makes them heavy. He's too good, too pure, a nice guy from top to bottom and back to front. And I'm none of those things. I'm the antithesis of those things. We're two vastly different people from vastly different worlds, with lifestyles that could never mesh.

"I know."

I suck in a breath, the words crumpling my heart like it's a wadded-up piece of paper. It's one thing to know I'm not good enough. It's another to hear it straight from him.

His head shifts away from the stars, finally meeting my eyes. "I'm still an absolute mess, Sadie. I would wreck you. And I could never forgive myself for that."

I tighten my hold on his pinky, mimicking the tightening in my chest. "Jack..."

He brings our joined hands up, kissing my palm before releasing my finger. "We should head back."

My lungs ache like I just got the wind knocked out of me. Which I did. I want to yank him back down to the blanket and demand we talk this out, because clearly this cannot be the end of the conversation. I can't let him walk away from this beach thinking he's the problem when I'm so clearly the destroyer between us.

But Jack is already gathering the blankets, folding them up and tucking them under his arm. He holds out a hand to help me stand, and I take it, even though the feel of his skin on mine is like ice-cold fire.

We walk back to the house in complete silence. At the bottom of the stairs, he gives me a sad smile, squeezing my hand before heading off to his room without another word.

I stand there in the dark for a few minutes before I finally force my feet to carry me up the stairs, where I fall into bed and, thankfully, into an alcohol-and-heartache-induced sleep.

$\backsim$

GEMMA: So when were you going to tell us the big news, Sade?

ME: Is the news that I'm still in bed because I was at the bar until 3 am because my business totally sucks and I'm going to be a bartender for the rest of my life?

HARLEY: Maybe you should go check your
Instagram, hon.

ME: Holy fuck, I have almost 500 new followers!

GEMMA: Yeah you do! Look who tagged you!

ME: OH MY GOD. SHE HAS 2M FOLLOWERS!!!!!!!!!

ME: Guys, I have like 100 DMs!

ME: Hopefully some of them aren't dicks!

GEMMA: If you see any good-looking dicks, feel
free to send them my way.

HARLEY: Gross.

HARLEY: Congrats, Sadie! This could be a major
turning point!

ME: I gotta go, time to sell some motherfuckin'
flowers!

∼

JACK: I don't have any plans on Saturday if you
need help making deliveries.

JACK: I know I lack the signature Sadie charm, but I'm around if you need me.

> **ME:** That's very sweet, but I can't ask you to work for me for free and I can't afford to pay you.

JACK: I really don't mind.

> **ME:** You already contribute way more to this friendship, dude. The power imbalance is wild.

JACK: What are you talking about?

> **ME:** You're the one bringing everything to the table here.

JACK: Sadie.

JACK: You don't actually think that.

> **ME:** Them's the facts, Jack.

JACK: The offer stands if you need me.

⌒〜

HARLEY: So we went out to dinner with Nick's parents last weekend . . .

ME: AND?

GEMMA: Did you double-check to make sure he's not on this thread?

HARLEY: Like ten times.

ME: OK AND???????

HARLEY: And it was great. His mom said, "We were wondering if the two of you were ever going to get your shit together."

ME: Awwwww yay!

GEMMA: I call dibs on the KitchenAid mixer!

HARLEY: Haha.

GEMMA: You think I'm joking. One of Nick's rich-ass friends can buy you a new one for your wedding 😵

ME: I'm so happy for you, Harley!

GEMMA: Me too! I promise those aren't sobs of loneliness and abandonment you're hearing coming from my room every night.

ME: Soooooooooooooooo

ME: Remember when I was all like I don't need
your help and I'm a strong independent
woman and I refuse to rely on a man?

JACK: I don't recall those exact words, but yes, I
remember the general conversation.

ME: I really need your help.

ME: Please.

ME: Pretty please.

ME: With a cherry on top.

ME: I'll buy you drinks if you come to the bar
tonight!

JACK: I'm just putting a shirt on, I'll be right there.

ME: Hmmm. Shirtless floral delivery, you might
have something there.

TEN

OKAY. SO, HARLEY, you're delivering these two to the Williamsburg addresses. Gem, you're on the Park Slope deliveries. There's four of them, but they're closer—stop whining. I've got the three in Gowanus, and, Jack, you've got the solo delivery in Windsor Terrace." I load up the final orders in their respective carriers, wagons for me and Gemma, little crates on wheels for Harley and Jack.

"Why does Jack get the solo delivery? He's the dude." Gemma accepts her wagon handle with a pout.

"That's sexist. Also, Jack allows me to live in this sweet house—which you happen to use almost as much as I do—for practically free, so shut up and get moving." I kiss her on the cheek before shooing everyone off in their respective directions. "Thank you and I love you, don't forget to spritz while you walk!"

Since one of New York's biggest influencers not only ordered an arrangement from me but shared it on Instagram, things at Bridge and Blooms have exploded. In the way I was praying for, but also so quickly that I didn't have time to prepare. All of a sudden I was inundated with orders with no way to fulfill them or deliver them, which is, you know, not great for business. Luckily, I have awesome friends and years of experience keeping spreadsheets organized and answering to demanding clients. As an added bonus, my work-centric previous life means I'm used to getting by on four hours of sleep a night. But this is our third weekend of nonstop deliveries and we've finally got our system down. Given the sticky August humidity, the flowers need to be spritzed with cool water during delivery times, otherwise they'll wilt. So each one of my friends is now outfitted with a super-cute Bridge and Blooms apron holding shears, a spray bottle, and a couple of extra flowers for last-minute replacements.

I'm only paying my wonderful and amazing and supportive friends with meals and free drinks at the bar, because despite the influx of orders and therefore cash, purchasing the blooms needed for all these arrangements, plus additional supplies, hasn't been cheap. Gemma goes back to school in a couple of weeks, which means I'll lose her mostly free labor, but I can't guarantee orders will continue at this pace once the social media buzz dies down, and I don't want to hire someone only to not have enough work to fulfill their hours.

Who knew running a business was hard? Sitcom millennials make it all look so easy, but every day there's a new decision to be made, more new factors and numbers and scenarios to consider. I just wanted to put together some pretty flowers, but this whole entrepreneur gig is a lot more work than I anticipated, even with my business and finance training. And I'm still working my two shifts a week at the bar since I'm not ready to part with my one steady income stream.

By the time I make it home from my deliveries, everyone else has already returned their supplies and pocketed their hopefully generous tips. I have just enough time to take a quick shower and change before I have to head out again to the bar.

Jack is sitting at the kitchen peninsula when I come downstairs to put on my shoes.

"You coming by the bar tonight?" I slip into my white sneakers and do one last face check in the mirror above the entryway table. I don't wear much makeup to the bar since most nights I'd sweat it off anyway, but I still dab a little gloss onto my lips.

"I think so. I was going to see if Nick was around."

"Cool. Hopefully I'll see you there." I give him a little wave and head out the front door.

On the surface, it seems like very little has changed between me and Jack, but underneath there's this simmering awkwardness that's about to boil over every time we talk. We never discussed our conversation under the stars on the beach, both of us pretending we were drunker than we actually were and feigning memory loss the next day.

But on the rare occasion he actually looks me in the eye now, all I hear is those words, on repeat in my head.

I would wreck you.

Jack and I have been living together for four months now, and I still have no idea what would make him think that. I still don't know how his parents died. Or when. Other than his slip about being raised in Connecticut, all I know about my roommate is he likes video games and has perfect eyes.

Oh, and he does a really good job of taking care of me. Making my coffee in the morning. Picking up breakfast when he knows I worked a late shift at the bar. Reheating leftovers for dinner and practically shoving them in my face when I can't force myself away from my email inbox.

I don't deserve him. Our friendship is the perfect example of how much I take without bothering to give back. And because of that, we'll never be more than friends. I can never let myself take further advantage of his supreme generosity.

And yet, when he pushes through the front door of the bar a couple of hours into my shift, my stomach does a round-off back handspring back tuck. I can't stop the smile from spreading across my face. His answering smile sends my tummy into a full-on gold-medal-winning floor routine.

He finds a vacant table tucked back in the corner, close to the bar.

"Hey." I toss a cardboard coaster on the table, leaning both elbows on the marble high-top. "Where's Nick?"

"He's with Harley." Jack leans both of his arms on the table too, leaving just a few inches of space in between us.

"Oh, cool. Is everyone coming by, then? I think I owe you all a round." I use this brief respite to stretch my aching calves. Running around all over Brooklyn and then coming straight to my bar shifts has been murder on my legs.

"I think they're all staying in. So it's just me tonight." A soft smile tugs on the corner of his lips.

I stand up straight. "Oh."

Jack hasn't ever come here by himself before. He joins the rest of the group most nights when they come out, but this is his first solo venture.

"Well, what can I get you? The usual?"

"Sure."

Heading back to the bar to pour his beer, I take longer than I really need so I can get my head together. I'm not going to pretend like the sight of Jack sitting in my bar, coming here just to see me (and also collect his free beer, but minor detail) doesn't make my heart squish. Because it does. The squishiest. Even though it shouldn't. But the whole thing seems very out of character for my boy here.

I deliver his beer but don't get the chance to chat before I'm needed back at the main bar. The place fills up, the Saturday-night crowd loud and demanding, not leaving me with even one minute to catch my breath. But I manage to keep an eye on Jack as I mix drinks and deliver sliders and wipe down spills. A couple of different people of the female persuasion approach him, and while he seems to engage in brief conversations, they never linger, heading on to greener pastures after just a few minutes.

Eventually Jack pulls out a book, somehow managing to read in the dim light of the bar, and his novel seems to act as a social interaction shield. I clock out for my break, grab another beer for Jack and a water for me, and hoist myself into the seat across from him, our knees brushing against one another under the table.

He tucks a bookmark between the pages of his novel and sets it off to the side. "Hi."

"Hi."

It stays quiet for a minute. Or at least, as quiet as it can in the middle of a crowded bar on a Saturday night.

"Thanks for the beer." He raises his glass and clinks it against my cup of water.

"Thanks for all your help with deliveries."

"My pleasure." He takes a long sip. "That's actually what I wanted to talk to you about."

A cold fist of dread punches me in the stomach. I knew something like this was going to happen eventually. Jack is tired of living in the botanical garden I've turned his house into and he wants me to leave. Of course he wants me to leave. I barged into his quiet, peaceful life and, in true Sadie fashion, made it all about me.

I rub my fingers over my forehead, trying to subtly massage away the headache that's sprung up. "I'm sorry. I can try to look for a studio space. I don't know what's out there that I'll be able to afford, but I'm sure there's something. I can get all my shit out of the kitchen, and the bathroom, and the fridge. And I'll definitely look into hiring an actual employee to make deliveries." A sudden spring of wetness blurs my vision. I stare down at the gray swirls on the white marble top, blinking rapidly to dry up any hint of tears before he can see. "Just please don't ask me to move, Jack."

One of Jack's warm hands covers mine. "Sadie."

Without thinking about it, I flip my palm over and our fingers automatically intertwine.

"Can you look at me, please?" His voice is soft, but even amid the din of the bar, each word hits my heart.

I take a long breath and slowly raise my head, eyes now calm and clear. "I'm fine."

Jack gives me his softest smile, the one that crinkles the corners of his eyes. "I don't want you to move out."

"Oh." The simple declaration brings me a small amount of relief. But instead of focusing on the positive, my brain immediately jumps to the costs of renting space and hiring employees.

"And you don't need to rent a studio, or hire anyone, if you're not ready to yet." He squeezes my hand. "I just wanted to give you a heads-up that I won't be around next weekend."

"Oh." And despite the good news, all I can focus on is Jack's not being around next weekend. The gnawing ache in my stomach at the thought of his leaving has nothing to do with being short on delivery people either. "How long are you going to be gone?"

"I'm leaving on Thursday, but I'll make sure I'm back in time on Sunday for dinner and Real Housewives."

Three nights. The gnawing morphs into a chomping, devouring, eating-a-whole-slice-of-pizza-in-one-bite kind of ache.

"Where are you going?" I don't expect him to answer, but I also can't not ask.

"Back to Connecticut. That's where I went last time too." He picks up his beer with his free hand and takes a long gulp, as if he needs liquid courage. "To my parents' house, their old house. Our old house. I still own it, and I like to go back every couple of months to check in and make sure everything's okay."

I cover our joined hands with my other one, making a hand sandwich. I'm afraid to say anything, scared that if I talk it will stop him from continuing down this path and revealing anything else. This is the first real conversation we've had since the Hamptons—not to mention the most personal info he's ever shared—and I don't want to throw up any roadblocks.

"I'm thinking about selling it." He pushes the words out in a rush, almost as one singular word, like if he doesn't get them out fast enough, he might not ever be able to say them.

"Oh, Jack." I scoot my stool closer to his, so our thighs brush and our arms press together. "How long has it been?"

"It's been seven years since the car accident. Too long, don't you think?" The corner of his lips tilts up, but it's nothing like his normal half-cocked smile.

Shrugging, I keep a tight grip on his hand. "I've never had to go through anything like that, but I think you should take as long as you need."

He takes another sip of beer and purses his lips. "I have a meeting with a Realtor scheduled on Saturday, but there's a fifty-fifty chance I'll end up canceling."

"If you get there and you feel like you need to do that, then that's okay. You don't owe anyone anything." I lean my head on his shoulder, the closest I can get to giving him a hug in these chairs.

He places a soft kiss on my forehead.

With one single brush of his lips, he destroys me. And not in the way he was so worried about. My breath catches, my heart freezing in my chest with this simple mark of affection.

"Do you want me to come with you?" I sit back up, staring head-on into those green eyes. While I can predict what he's going to tell me, his eyes will give me an honest answer.

"I can't ask you to miss a whole weekend of work. That's two bar shifts plus who knows how many orders." The expected words fly out of his mouth, but the pleading look in those eyes lets me know what to do.

"What if I came with you on Thursday and then took an early train home Saturday morning? Then I'd only miss one bar shift, and I could still get deliveries done. Gemma and Harley will cover any for Friday. Honestly, I don't even know why I'm framing all this as if it were a question. I'm coming, and I'll figure shit out on my end. So don't worry about that." I suck in a breath. "Unless you totally don't want me there and are just trying to be polite, in which case I'll obviously not intrude, because that'd be a lot even for me."

A zing of tension buzzes between us and for a second, I think he might lean over and kiss me. I'm pretty sure I stop breathing altogether.

But Jack doesn't lean in, only offers me a tiny grateful smile. "I'd really appreciate having you there with me. If you can make it work."

"Um, hello, just call me Tim Gunn. Making it work is my middle name." The alarm on my phone beeps. "Speaking of working, I've got to get back to it."

Jack releases my hand and I miss his calming touch the second it's gone. "Thanks, Sade."

"Of course. What are roommates for?" I shove my phone in the back pocket of my jeans. "You heading home or sticking around? I'm not off for a couple of hours."

He picks up his book again, flipping open the pages to his marked spot. "I'll hang out if you don't mind. I feel better when I can walk you home." He's not looking at me as he says this, eyes already scanning the words in front of him.

Which is good, because it might be the nicest thing a man has ever said to me and it takes just one breath before I realize (A) the men in my life have totally sucked, and (B) I have a super-big thing for my roommate.

Fuck.

$\sim$

"Okay, so the middle shelf of the fridge is the deliveries for Friday. Each one is labeled with a name and address. There are only four so it shouldn't be too hard." I turn the FaceTime screen away from the fridge and onto me. "You guys are the best and I love you so much."

Harley waves her hand in her *Oh, stop it, you* motion. "Happy to help."

Gemma jumps up behind her into the frame. "You can repay us with all the hot goss you're going to have about Jack when you get back." When she makes kissy faces at me, I know she has truly absorbed the full energy of her students and there's no more hope for her.

"Dude, shut the fuck up. He lives here." I search around the kitchen like Jack might spring up from behind a counter, even though I know he's safely tucked away in the basement, as always.

"While Gem's delivery might be a little off, she does have a bit of a point. This is a big deal, Sadie. The man went from telling you nothing to asking you to go to his dead parents' house with him." Damn Harley and her stupid logic and reason.

"One, he didn't ask, I offered. Two, we're just friends. Three, I hate you both." I longingly eye the wine cabinet. But it's only noon, and we're supposed to head out in an hour.

"Sorry, but Jack is too hot for all that just-friends nonsense." Gemma nudges Harley to the side so they can share the screen.

"If he's too hot for just friends, then how come you're just friends with him? How come I'm just friends with Nick?" I jog up the stairs so I can finish packing while we chat.

"Aw, you think my man is hot?"

"Nick practically has 'My Type' stamped on his forehead. If he weren't so nice." Propping my phone up on my pillows, I force them to watch me fold my clothes and stash them in my overnight bag. "Which is just another reason why this whole Jack thing is just an itch."

Gemma raises her eyebrows up and down. "So is this the weekend you scratch it?"

"You guys are terrible, and I'm hanging up now. Text me if you have any delivery problems. Love you, bye!"

I close out the call before they can protest further.

I finish packing, throwing mostly lounging clothes in my bag, but also tucking in one decent outfit in case we end up going out for dinner or something. Hmm. Jack and I going out for dinner. Just the two of us.

My mind wanders off to picture what it'd be like to go on a date with Jack but snaps back when the man himself calls my name from the bottom of the stairs.

"Coming!" I throw in my iPad and laptop and chargers and zip up my bag before bounding down the steps. In the kitchen, I hoist up the reusable tote I've stuffed full of snacks, but no sooner does it land on my shoulder than Jack takes it from me.

He peers into the bag, poking around to see what I've brought. "You do know it's a two-, three-hour drive at most, right?"

"You can never have too many snacks. Plus these have to last us the whole weekend." I refuse to be snack shamed.

"Southport does have grocery stores." Jack hefts the bag over his arm, gesturing me toward the front door.

We head out to the front stoop, Jack locking up behind us. He's parked his rented compact SUV in front of the house, and we throw our bags in the backseat. I most definitely dig through the snack bag for the gummy bears before climbing into the passenger seat and buckling up.

Jack looks over at me with a timid smile. "Ready?"

"Ready, Freddy."

I last about five minutes just sitting and listening to the weird emo music in the car before I have to pull my phone out and do something. I use the time to answer some emails and DMs, as well as comment on and like some local florists' Instagram photos. I wonder if there will come a day when I think of myself as a florist. Right now I'm a bartender who does some floral arranging on the side. And yeah, things have been picking up for Bridge and Blooms, but I still have a long way to go.

Once we get on the freeway, I have to put my phone away or risk getting carsick. I lean my head back against the headrest and close my eyes, keeping my breathing steady so my stomach stays calm.

"Sadie . . ."

A warm hand squeezes my thigh and I jump.

It takes me a minute to figure out where I am—still in the front seat of Jack's car. Though the car is no longer moving and no longer in the state of New York.

I push my sunglasses on top of my head and rub my eyes. "Shit. What happened?"

Jack smiles, unlatching his seat belt. "You fell asleep. We're here."

I subtly check my chin for any signs of drool, but luckily my skin seems to be dry. "You let me sleep the whole way?"

He pushes open his door. "You conked out pretty hard. I figured I'd let you rest."

Undoing my own seat belt and opening my door, I practically fall out of the car, my muscles are so stiff. It's afternoon, the sun still a couple of hours away from setting. The golden light reflects off the water in front of us, and my mouth drops open. The house is right on the cove, a wide expanse of blue rippling out before us.

"Holy shit." I turn around to take in the house itself. "Holy shit."

One thing's for certain: the Thomas family sure does have a knack for real estate. The house—mansion?—is massive, all gray weathered wood and white trim and exactly what I'd fantasize about if I ever wanted to live that suburban life in Connecticut.

Based on his trips since I moved in, Jack only makes it out here about every two months, but the front yard is immaculately groomed. Perfectly manicured rosebushes line the slate walkway and explosions of perennials fill the flower beds surrounding the house itself. The lawn is lush and green, and my inner Californian practically dies thinking about how much water it must take to keep it all in this pristine condition.

Jack stands a little behind me, holding all our bags. "What do you think?"

I take my bag from him, brushing off his protest. "I think it's fucking gorgeous."

He nudges me forward, and we head up the path to the turquoise front door.

I sigh longingly. "I love a bright front door."

"So you've mentioned." Jack sets down his bag so he can unlock the door and push it open.

"Is this going to be a repeat orgasmic experience?" The words come out a little breathier than I intended, but I chalk it up to the combination of just waking up and a magazine-worthy front yard.

Jack stares at me, his pupils widening, and he swallows thickly. "I'm sorry?"

"Like the first time you showed me the brownstone?" I give him a wicked little grin. "Am I in for another dash of real estate porn?"

"Oh." He clears his throat, grabs his bag, and leaves me behind on the doorstep.

Chuckling to myself, I follow him in, preparing to have my mind blown once again.

And so much of the house is mind-blowing. I mean, given its size and location, it'd be hard for it not to be. But it also looks like it hasn't been updated in at least twenty years. Which, given how long it's been since Jack's parents passed, makes sense.

But even though the furniture and fixtures are out of date, everything is clean and in impeccable condition.

Dropping my bag at the foot of the stairs, I head for the back of the house. It shouldn't even be possible, but the backyard also looks out directly on the water. I look at Jack with a question in my eyes.

He shrugs. "There are a few houses with cove views at the front and the back."

I do a little mental math as to what two waterfront views must cost, but then I stop because I don't want to pass out.

I head into the main living room, which is anchored by a ginormous gray sectional piled high with pillows in varying shades of blue. A TV the size of my bed hangs on the opposite wall, over a gray brick fireplace. To the left of the living room is an entire wall made of glass, the sunlight sparkling off the water like diamonds. The walls are all a muted cream, with nothing hanging on them, though I notice several spots of slightly discolored paint, like the photos and artwork that once hung there have all been removed. I frown a little to myself. I was hoping for some family portraits, anything to give me a glimpse into Jack's childhood.

Jack emerges from the kitchen, where's he stashed all the road trip snacks I never got a chance to even open. "Ready to see your room?"

"Fuck yeah. Lead the way."

He takes me upstairs and all the way down the hall to the last room on the back side of the house. "This is my favorite of the guest rooms."

Because there's more than one guest room. Obviously.

Pushing open the door, I immediately come to a dead stop. "Would it be rude for me to ask if I could move in here instead of living in the brownstone?"

Jack laughs softly and nudges me farther into the space.

The hardwood floors are softened with a plush white rug. The bed is bigger than any my butt's ever had the privilege of being on, dressed all in white super-soft linens and loads of pillows. French doors lead out to a balcony overlooking the water, but when I fully enter the room, my attention doesn't snag on the killer view.

Instead I cross over to the foot of the bed, dropping my bag and staring at the painting hanging over the headboard. It's so detailed it could almost pass for a photograph; in fact, I have to squint to make sure it's actually a painting. It's a beach scene, similar to the one just outside the windows. The sand looks like I could reach in and scoop it up, let it trickle through my fingers. The facets of the water catch every shade of blue. But what really captures my attention are the three figures walking down the beach, feet in the water, hands joined. In the middle is a little boy, probably about six or seven, with dark curls and bright green eyes. The woman on his left has matching curls, the man the same emerald eyes.

My breath hitches in my chest. I can feel the weight and heat of him as he moves to stand behind me. "It's beautiful."

"It was my mother's favorite."

"I can see why." Reaching back, I find his hand, tucking mine into his grasp. "Are you sure you want me to stay in here?"

"Absolutely." His fingers tighten around mine.

We stand there in silence for a few minutes. I can't move my eyes from the piece of art, but Jack's gaze flickers back and forth between me and the painting.

He breaks the spell first. "How about a swim?"

I nod, not sure I can form actual words right now. It's a lot. Being here, in this room, seeing Jack's parents, seeing the home he grew up in. This sliver of his soul. It all sits heavily on my chest, and I'm grateful when he ducks out to let me change, telling me he'll meet me downstairs.

I finally rip my eyes from the painting, quickly changing into my suit and throwing a T-shirt dress over it. Sliding my feet into flip-flops, I pull my hair into a ponytail and head down the stairs.

Jack's already waiting for me in just his suit, and I'm glad this isn't the first time I'm seeing him shirtless, because the overload of feeling might push me into some kind of spontaneous combustion. He's got two towels tucked under one arm. He reaches out the other, and I slide my hand into his.

I'm telling myself all this physical contact can be chalked up to the influx of emotions from being here, in this space, and Jack's needing my care and friendship.

In reality, I just really like the way his hand wraps around mine. It's protective and supportive, and the simple brush of his skin warms my entire body.

Jack tosses our towels on a lounge chair on the concrete patio in the back of the house. "You probably want to leave your shoes and dress here. Sometimes the tide comes up quick."

I kick off my flip-flops and tug the dress over my head.

Jack's eyes trace me from the tips of my toes up to the top of my messy ponytail, a warm smile heating his gaze.

But he doesn't say anything, just offers his hand again, leading me down a small set of stone steps to the sandy beach. The beach itself is a thin strip of sand, not enough for lying out or picnicking, and given there's only a couple of other houses nearby, it's empty.

We wade in up to our waists, the water cold and a little biting, but the afternoon sun is still warm, and the chill helps shake me back to my senses. A little bit at least.

Jack left his glasses in the house, so for once my view of his eyes is completely unobstructed. I pay attention to the way they change color based on the topic at hand, like some kind of permanent mood ring.

For a while we chitchat about nothing. Bravo gossip, how business is going, whether Jack needs to upgrade to the latest edition of some video game thing.

But then the quiet falls as the sun begins to set. A little bit of a chill cools the air, causing goose bumps to rise along my arms.

Jack trails a finger from my shoulder down to where the water meets my hands, doing nothing to help the whole goose bump situation. "Do you want to head back inside?"

Shaking my head, I cross my arms around myself to bring a little warmth. "It's too pretty to leave now."

"You should see the sunrise."

"I think I will on Saturday." I make a mental note to leave myself plenty of time in the morning to actually take it in and enjoy it before rushing to catch the train. "What was it like growing up here?"

Jack skims his hands over the water, making little ripples circle out around us. "Honestly, at the time I kind of hated it."

"Really?" I can't imagine Jack's hating anything, let alone something so beautiful.

"We're pretty isolated out here, and it was always a long drive to get to my friends' houses. I'm an only child, so a lot of the time it felt kind of lonely. I had to find ways to occupy myself, keep myself entertained." He shrugs and a small smile starts at the corner of his lips. "But now I only think about the good parts. Summers on the beach and barbecuing with my dad and baking cookies with my mom."

"Funny how memory works that way." I try not to think about how my own memories are the opposite swing of the pendulum. I'm sure there were good moments, positive experiences, somewhere in my childhood, but none of them seemed to stick. Instead my brain focuses on the singular constant refrain *You'll never be enough.* I've mostly boxed up said negative refrains, tucked them away in a back corner of my mind, but every so often they jump out at me. Like every time I even begin to think about taking things further with Jack.

You'll never be enough.

"I'm really glad you're here, Sadie." The words are spoken so softly that if we weren't standing only inches apart, I don't think I would've heard them. And they're so opposed to my internal dialogue, I almost brush them off.

But I don't, and they chase away any trace of cold, push the hurtful words to a back corner of my brain. "Me too."

ELEVEN

B Y THE TIME we get back to the patio, the sun is beginning to set, the sky turning a deep blue that blends in with the cove water. There's a real chill in the air now, one I didn't expect, and I shiver as I slip my T-shirt dress over my head. It does little to bring me warmth, so I half-run back into the house, already dreaming of a hot shower and my pajamas.

"I was going to just cook some pasta for dinner if that's okay?" Jack flips the switch on the side of the fireplace before heading toward the kitchen.

"Wait, you mean to tell me that after all this time you know how to cook?" I stop at the bottom of the stairs, just long enough to glare at him for holding out on me.

"Only pasta. That's my one dish." He's tucked his towel around his waist, and I somehow can't make myself stop staring at his chest and his smattering of hair. The smattering leading down to the waistband of his bathing suit.

"I'm always good with pasta. Is it cool if I shower?" I might actually need a cold one at this point.

"Of course. I'll get this going in the meantime." He waves me off and retreats to the kitchen.

Bounding up the stairs and into my room, I grab my toiletry bag and pj's before checking out the attached bathroom. While it's not super huge, there is a nice-sized tub I'm tempted to wallow in, but even I know pasta doesn't take that long to cook, and I don't want to keep Jack waiting. I curl my hair into a bun so it doesn't get wet and take a quick (but very hot) shower. I pull on a pair of soft cotton shorts and an old T-shirt, wishing I'd brought something a little warmer to wear for the evening, but I figure the wine-and-fireplace combo should be able to take care of it.

Jack is still in the kitchen when I come downstairs. He's changed, and from the looks of his damp hair, also taken a short shower. He's wearing a fitted white T-shirt and flannel pajama pants that are doing . . . things . . . to his rear view. Good things.

He gestures to a full glass of wine on the kitchen island. "I figured you'd want some of that."

"It's like you've known me my whole life." Sliding into the seat in front of the wine, I take a large sip.

He gestures to the chair next to me. "I also pulled that out. Wasn't sure if you remembered to bring a sweatshirt."

I turn to my right. A navy blue hoodie with the Captain America shield is draped over the back of the stool. I immediately tug it over my head, relishing its instant warmth and softness. "You know, in some cultures, giving a woman your hoodie is tantamount to a marriage proposal."

Jack stirs something in a large pot positioned on one of the eight burners on the other side of the huge island. "Would those cultures happen to consist primarily of middle schoolers?"

"Maybe." I tuck my hands into the sleeves, pulling myself farther into the cottony warmth, hopefully disguising the large inhale I take to breathe in the scent embedded in the fabric. Coffee and paper. "I do hope you know you're never getting this back."

The corner of his mouth ticks up. "You planning on walking around Brooklyn in a Captain America sweatshirt?"

"Hardly. It'll never see the light of day again." I cackle like some evil supervillain.

He turns off the burner and dumps the pasta into a strainer. "This probably won't surprise you, but I have plenty of hoodies, so you're welcome to keep it."

"Well, that takes away all the fun, then, doesn't it."

"So you'll give it back?"

"Fuck no." I already know I'll be pathetically curling up into it the next time Jack goes out of town and leaves me in the brownstone to fend for myself.

Jack dumps the pasta back into the pot, pours some sauce in, and stirs everything around a few times. He scoops two heaping portions onto separate plates, handing me one before placing the other in front of the seat next to me. After refilling both of our wineglasses, he slides onto the stool.

I hold up my glass. "Thanks for cooking."

He clinks his against mine. "I'd say anytime, but I know you'll take that literally, so I'm not going there."

"You learn fast." I shovel a forkful of pasta into my mouth, not sure what to expect from a man who has never once in the past four months been seen standing in front of our stove. "Fuck. This is actually really good."

"Did you doubt me?"

"I mean, yes?" I take another bite. "Yeah, you never should've made this for me. I'm going to require this meal at least once a week from this point on."

Jack laughs and takes a swig of wine. "And how often will you be cooking?"

I shove another huge bite in my mouth to avoid answering. "At least my friends come over and cook," I say a minute later.

"True."

We finish the meal in mostly companionable silence, aside from my outbursts of "Damn, this is good" and "You *really* need to cook more" sprinkled throughout the meal. When we're both done, I take our plates over to the sink and rinse them before stashing them in the dishwasher.

I pivot back around and meet Jack's eyes. He's watching me with an intensity I feel deep down in my core. It ignites a spark in my belly, catching fire when he gives me a slow grin. The spark travels south.

"You ready for bed, or do you wanna watch a movie?" Jack stands and stretches, his T-shirt rising and revealing just a peek of tummy.

"Are you asking me to Netflix and chill?" The question flies out before I can censor my wine-loosened tongue. And let's be real, my tongue doesn't need any help getting loose. Which is a strange visual after asking someone if they want to Netflix and chill. And thank god these thoughts are staying in my head. "A movie sounds great. Something bloody and gory." Which will lead to my turning to Jack as I shriek in fright. "Or maybe something dumb and funny. Yes. Dumb. Funny."

Like me!

Jack doesn't even try to hold in his laughter. "More wine before we get settled?"

That would probably be a bad idea.

"Yes, please." I hold out my glass for a refill.

We head into the living room, and I take my usual spot in the corner of the sectional. I've realized the corner is by far the best seat on a sectional, and it hasn't escaped my notice that Jack always lets me have it. Or that I always take it.

I set my wine on the side table and wrap a soft throw blanket around my legs. I'm not really cold, but I need an extra layer of protection between me and these feelings.

Ugh. Feelings.

It was easier when Jack was all broody and silent and I could pretend like we were just roommates and there was nothing between us.

Now he's still broody but also smiley and slightly less silent, and it's getting harder and harder to pretend like these tingles, like the steadily burning fire in my stomach, like the flutters in my chest, have nothing to do with whatever it is that's been building.

But even though I catch him watching me every so often, even though he does all these undeniably sweet things for me, there's still a constant wall up around Jack Thomas. I haven't even begun to crack all his layers.

And he's never even hinted at any sort of interest in me, because why would a man with the goodness of Jack ever be interested in me?

So I should probably lock down these tingles and flutters before I fuck things up and lose out on the best living situation I've ever had.

Jack plops down on the couch, not at the complete opposite end like he does at home, but still leaving several feet of space in between us. Notably, he drapes his arm over the back of the sofa. It still doesn't come close to touching me, but it's there.

Oh my god. I suck at this.

Okay. Locking it down. Now. Stifle that inner fire before it singes me.

I pick up the remote from the coffee table. I flip on the TV, bring up Netflix, and search for *Clueless*. "This okay?" I know he won't say no. I also know it's the kind of movie he hates.

"Sure. I haven't seen this in forever." He raises one eyebrow at me, as if he can see inside my head and knows what I'm doing.

But joke's on him, because even I don't know what I'm doing.

For the first time in a long time, I don't bother setting the alarm on my phone. Dolly Parton's "9 to 5" stays silent, and instead I wake up to sunshine streaming through the French doors, despite the thin white curtains covering the windows. All I have to do is flip over onto my side and I can see the rippling water of the cove outside. I hop out of bed for a quick second to push open the curtains before burrowing back under the soft quilt.

I didn't sleep in the hoodie, although I sure as fuck thought about it. And I may or may not have brought it to bed with me. It may or may not be tucked under my pillow.

I may or may not be losing my actual damn mind right now.

I don't know what's happened to me over the past several months, but I've never mooned around over a man before. Okay, maybe "mooning" is a strong word for it, but there's definitely something stirring around inside my brain—and my heart—that's unfamiliar and unsettling. I've never done relationships, never once felt the need for a guy for more than a night or two. I have the best friends in the entire world. I've always had a job I was good at. And I never had trouble getting off when I wanted to—with either a willing participant or a battery-operated friend. Why would I ever want that to change?

Enter Jack Thomas with his perfect house and charming smile and undeniably pure heart, and all of a sudden there are things happening inside my body I just don't know what to do with. The lust is there, which is all well and good. But I can't just ask my roommate if he wants to bone, because then what happens after?

Or, what happens if he says no?

And, like, I'm not sure I want to just bang him and be done. Which is the strangest feeling of all. Sometimes when I lie alone in bed, I think about Jack's lying next to me. Not pre- or postcoital, just lying there. With me. Sometimes my head is resting on his chest, his hands running through my hair. Sometimes my fingers trace little flower patterns on his stomach. Sometimes we talk. And sometimes we just enjoy the connection between us.

I should want to make these feelings stop, to turn them off like the tap when the bathtub is about to overflow. But I don't actually *want* to do that, I just feel like I should.

I stretch out on the bed, moving my limbs into a wide star, reaching my fingers and toes as far into the corners of the mattress as they will go.

Then I burrow my head into my pillow, sucking in one last whiff of eau de hoodie, before I pull myself out of bed and head downstairs. The house is quiet, and I don't spot Jack when I reach the kitchen, in need of coffee as always.

Jack is nowhere to be found, but there's an iced vanilla latte and a paper bag sitting on the counter with a note.

Had to run into town to talk to some people, but I won't be long. Make yourself at home, text me if you need anything. —Jack

And see? This right here? This next-level boyfriend shit?

Yeah. Not helping.

Still, I gulp down half the latte in one sip, pulling a croissant from the bag and devouring it. While I eat, I text Harley and Gemma, making sure they are on their way out to their deliveries even though I know they'd never let me down because they're kind and giving and selfless, unlike their BFF.

Harley texts me back a string of photos, one of each of her assigned arrangements, held up in front of the address it was delivered to. Gemma sends back a selfie where she's caught herself mid–eye roll.

> **ME:** I love you guys the most. Harley, a little bit more, but Gem, you're pretty up there. Drinks and dinner on me as soon as I get back!

> **HARLEY:** How's everything going?

> **ME:** Good. This house is insane. Like the brownstone but bigger and with waterfront views.

> **GEMMA:** Did you guys bang yet?

ME: Seriously? We're not banging.

GEMMA: But you want to.

GEMMA: Don't bother lying because we know. So
just admit it. You want to bang Jack.

I don't respond for a minute, taking a long sip of my coffee and then chewing on my lip before finally working up the courage to type the actual words.

ME: Okay, fine. I want to bang Jack.

The text thread explodes with GIFs. Happy dancing ones from Harley, lewd ones from Gemma.

ME: BUT.

ME: I'm not going to. I don't want to mess this up.

GEMMA: "This" being your living situation?

ME: Yeah.

HARLEY: Or "this" being your chance for an actual
relationship that includes not just hot sex but also
genuine care for another person?

ME: Yeah, maybe that too.

GEMMA: I literally just stopped in my tracks. Are
you trying to say you actually like him?

GEMMA: I don't mean that to sound like you
shouldn't because you totally should.

HARLEY: I think it's just a surprise that you're
willing to admit it.

ME: Only over text. And only to you two.

Neither of them responds, and no little typing bubbles pop up.
Which leads me to believe they've now rejoined forces in their living
room and are plotting against me. Bitches.

HARLEY: You should talk to him. I feel like there's a
pretty good chance he feels the same way.

GEMMA: Yeah. This.

ME: I don't know that he does.

ME: And that isn't a self-deprecating thing.
It's a legit I don't know if he likes
me thing.

ME: God. I made it to 28 without ever having to
have this feeling.

ME: Is this what it's like being a teenage girl? No
wonder they're awful.

GEMMA: Welcome to my world.

HARLEY: Give it time. You don't have to do
anything right now.

GEMMA: Other than live with the hot-ass man who
you are falling in luuurrrrvvvvee with.

ME: And on that note, I'm off to the
beach.

GEMMA: I can't believe we had to get our asses up
at the crack of dawn this morning so you can spend
the day on the beach.

I send them a blowing-kisses GIF and finish the last sip of my latte. Tossing my cup in the recycle bin, I venture out of the kitchen in search of a bathroom on this level to save me from having to walk back up the stairs. The hallway behind the kitchen is long and peppered with closed doors. I'm tempted to peek, but even I know that's crossing a major line. So I show a huge amount of restraint and don't open any, until I reach one whose door is already partially ajar.

Assuming it's the restroom, I push in and immediately stop in my tracks. This is definitely not a bathroom. The room is large and paneled in dark wood. There's a whole wall of built-in bookshelves, and a massive desk dominates the center of the space. It's a very manly-man study, and very not Jack. Obviously the room belonged to one of his parents, probably his dad if we're being stereotypical about it, and it feels wrong to be in here.

I'm spinning on my heel to hightail it out of there when something catches my eye. Other than the painting hanging above my bed, what I've seen of the house is completely devoid of photos or artwork. But hanging on the wall to my right is another masterpiece, and it's a familiar subject. Taking a few steps closer, I let my eyes absorb all the details, everything from the iron gate to the bright red front door. It's a perfect reflection of the brownstone. Jack's brownstone.

Our home.

I stare at it for what feels like an hour but is probably only a few minutes. When I tear myself away, I duck out of the study, leaving the door in the exact position I found it in.

⌒〜

When Jack returns a couple of hours later, he finds me on a lounge chair on the back patio, a chilled glass of sauvignon blanc in one hand and my phone in the other.

"I'm officially living my best life," I declare when he plops down on the chair next to mine.

He gives me that bemused smile of his. "Looks like it. I take it you were able to find everything you needed?"

I push my sunglasses to the top of my head so I can look at him unimpeded. "Yup. Thank you for the coffee and breakfast."

He shrugs like he didn't go totally out of his way for me. "There's no espresso machine here, and I know how touchy you are about your lattes."

"Did you get all of your errands done?" Keeping my eyes trained on him, I lean my head back against the padded chaise.

"Yeah." He shoves his hands into the pockets of his jeans. Because of course he doesn't switch up his daily uniform, despite its being a gorgeous summer day.

"Everything okay?"

I fully expect him to give me a standard Jack answer. Read: one without any sort of emotion or context behind it. But he surprises me.

"I don't know if I can do it, Sade."

I shift to my side, so my entire body is angled in his direction. "Do what?"

"Sell this house." He flops his head back against the chair but then turns to look at me. Even though his eyes are hidden behind the lenses of his glasses, I can see the sadness, the heaviness, in them.

"Okay, I'm going to ask a rude question, which obviously never stopped me in the past, but I want you to have a heads-up because I know how this is going to sound and I'd just like you to remember I'm your friend and I care about you. You as a person."

His lips quirk up just a tad. "Okay. I'm a bit terrified now, but please, go ahead."

Pulling my knees up, I tuck my feet under my butt. "Do you need the money? Is that why you feel like you should sell the house? Because you need to, financially speaking?"

He doesn't even flinch at the brazenness of it. "No. I don't need the money. That doesn't really have anything to do with it."

I want to reach out and touch him, close this physical space between us in the hopes of closing the emotional divide along with it. But short of climbing up onto his chair, there's no graceful way to do that. So I stay put, but I keep my eyes locked on his. "Then why now?"

He stays quiet for a minute, but it feels different from Jack's normal quiet. He's not avoiding the question, just thinking through what he wants to say. Finally, he takes in a long breath, letting it trickle out slowly before he begins speaking. "I was twenty-three. When they died. Even though I was already an adult and had been living in the brownstone for a few years, I relied on them for so much. Career guidance. Financial advice. Love and support. They were my best friends. We don't have any other family, so after the accident, it was just me. All on my own." He pulls his gaze from mine, like he doesn't want to see my reaction to this next part. "And I just froze. Like I was in this block of ice, captured in this moment in time. I didn't know what to do without them. Or how to be. How to grow. How to move on."

Fuck it. I push myself off my chair and sit at the foot of his. He pulls his legs up so he's sitting crisscrossed, and I do the same. Our knees press together, and I take one of his hands in mine.

"When I thawed out, I made a lot of bad decisions. I blew a lot of money, drank way too much, had a shit-ton of meaningless sex."

Oof. Not loving hearing about that part, but I try to keep my features neutral, knowing it's costing him something to reveal all of this to me.

"I'm not sure how I snapped out of it, honestly, but I think it was probably just the idea of how disappointed my parents would be if they could see what I was doing to myself. So after a couple of rough years,

I cleaned up my act and paid off the brownstone, and while I wasn't quite frozen again, I was living in this weird sort of fugue state. Like I was just numb all the time. The only people I talked to were online or random takeout people or service workers." He clears his throat. "I've been hollow for so long."

He picks up our joined hands, running his thumb over my knuckles.

My chest aches when I think of Jack alone and in pain, with no one to turn to for support. "Do you still feel hollow?"

He finally meets my gaze once again. "Not anymore, no."

"How did you come out of it?"

His face breaks into my favorite smile, the one that crinkles the corners of his eyes. "My therapist recommended I look for a room-mate."

"Oh." The admission is a direct punch to the heart, and any small slice of delusion I had left about my feelings for Jack completely explodes like a balloon full of confetti.

Jack leans back a little bit, putting some space between us, though he keeps a tight hold on my hand. "I might not be hollow anymore, but I'm also nowhere near whole, Sadie. I'm still fucked up and closed off in a lot of ways. I'm still healing."

"Oh." His declaration connects directly with my lungs, and the single word puffs out of me like a soft sigh. Talk about shattered delusions. My chin falls to my chest, and I stare at our intertwined hands. I want to tell him that it's okay and I understand, because it is okay and I do understand, but his words seem to carry a heavier purpose. Like he's letting me down easy before I even have the chance to tell him how I might feel. How I definitely am feeling.

He cups my cheek in his hand, gently pulling my eyes back to his.

"Our friendship means more to me than I could ever put into words, Sade. And I can't risk it, no matter how much I might want to. I could never be enough for you."

I swallow thickly. "Shouldn't I get the chance to decide that for myself?"

He sighs, and for half a second, I think he might lean in and kiss me. Instead he releases me, dropping his hand from my cheek, letting go of my hand in his. "Maybe. Probably. But I'm too selfish to let you."

I scoff at the irony of his words and want more than anything to move back to my own chair, but I don't trust my legs to support me at the present moment. "I think we all know I'm the selfish one in this bunch."

"You couldn't be more wrong about that." He holds up a hand to stop the protest he knows is coming. "Let me have this one."

I roll my eyes, turning and pushing myself awkwardly from his chair over to mine.

For a few minutes, we sit in silence, eyes glued on the water and the slowly setting sun.

"I think you should keep the house."

"Yeah, me too." He pulls his phone out of his pocket and taps out a quick message. "Realtor appointment canceled."

"Does that mean you can come home with me tomorrow?" I try to not let the obscene amount of hope I have color my question. "It's not a big deal if you can't, of course, and you should totally stay if you need to. Or want to."

"I can definitely come home with you tomorrow." His phone buzzes, probably the Realtor calling to beg him to change his mind. Jack stands. "I gotta take this."

I nod and wave him inside. "Of course."

He hesitates for a second, like there's something else he wants to say.

But I don't know if I can hear any more. My heart feels like a deflated bounce house. "Go, before he decides to show up at the front door."

Jack grimaces, swiping his phone to accept the call while stepping through the back door.

I turn my attention back to the ocean, losing my focus in the ebb and flow of the waves.

This heartbreak shit is overrated.

TWELVE

THE NEXT MONTH passes in a blur of avoidance. Avoiding Jack. Avoiding addressing the huge emotional elephant sitting between us on the couch every Sunday night—the only time I don't go out of my way to not see his face. And sure as fuck avoiding dealing with my feelings.

Because feelings are dumb, and surely if I just ignore them, they'll go away.

That's how these things work, right?

Luckily, business at Bridge and Blooms is, well, blooming. I was worried orders would die down after the social media hype, but they keep coming in. I still work my shifts at the bar, not ready to give up my one source of sure income just yet, but every other hour of the week is spent managing emails and social media, sourcing flowers and trying to stay local about it, and actually creating and delivering the arrangements themselves. It's beyond exhausting, and there are several days when I don't think I can take another step. But I keep pushing and pushing, determined to prove I'm capable of some sort of success. Terrified it's all going to fall away at any minute.

I still haven't bitten the bullet and hired any employees, but now that Gemma is back in full-time teaching mode, I think I'm going to have to. And even though Jack has never once complained about the literal garden his kitchen has become, it might be time to start looking for a studio. Bridge and Blooms is on the way to outgrowing its space. It also probably wouldn't be a terrible idea for me to have some space from Jack.

Because in the rare moments we cross paths during the week, just the sight of him leaves me as wilted as a hydrangea cut from its stem and left without water.

And on Sundays, when we still carve out the time we've dedicated to hanging out together, I feel his eyes on me, almost pleading with me. I want so badly to know what those eyes are trying to tell me, but I'm too chickenshit to actually look at them and see.

Jack clicks off the TV one Sunday night mid-September, shifting himself on the couch so he's looking right at me instead of at the screen.

I stay curled tightly up in my corner, a blanket wrapped around me as both a comfort and a shield.

The intensity of his gaze is burning me up, heating me from the inside out like I'm a clay pot in a kiln. Only the heat has been turned up too high and I'm about to shatter.

"Sadie."

Yeah. My name coming out of his mouth does nothing to soothe my burning core.

He sighs when I don't respond, scooting closer to my end of the couch. "Look, I get that shit's weird right now, but can you look at me, please?"

I purse my lips so tightly I'm surprised they don't glue themselves together. But I manage to look at him without screaming or bursting into tears, which I take as a win.

"I have something I want to show you. If that's okay." He stands up and holds out his hand.

I don't take it because I'm pretty sure any skin-to-skin contact would result in combustion, but I push myself off the sofa and gesture for him to lead the way.

He does, without acknowledging my hand snub, heading upstairs. Instead of stopping at the second floor, he continues to the staircase leading up to the top level of the brownstone.

"If you got me a library, you really haven't been paying much attention." The comment comes out louder and snarkier than I intended.

Jack pauses halfway up the steps and turns back toward me. "Why would I get you a library?"

"We're going to the forbidden wing." I furrow my brow at the confusion on his face. "Have you actually never seen *Beauty and the Beast*?"

"I liked superheroes." He shrugs and continues walking up the stairs.

Now I'm fully intrigued. I have no idea what to expect from this mysterious third floor, but when Jack pushes open the door and gestures for me to enter the space, I still manage to be totally and completely shocked.

The space isn't as big as the full footprint of the brownstone, but it's pretty damn close. Meaning, it's huge. And completely wide open. The floor is the washed maple you might find in a dance studio, the walls exposed brick and dotted with large, airy windows. The ceiling is broken up with two massive skylights. It's already dark outside, but the space must be absolutely flooded with sunlight during the day.

"It's incredible." My attention is focused solely on the skylights at the moment, so I don't see what Jack is pointing out at first, until he pulls my eyes from the ceiling.

"I hope this setup will work for you, but if not, we can rearrange it however you want." He leads me over to a large kitchen island, simple white cabinets, and a butcher-block top, just like we have downstairs.

There's also a sink in the corner with more counter space, and off to the side, two big cooling fridges, the kind you might find in an actual florist's shop.

It finally starts to sink in what is happening here. This is for me. He arranged this space for me and Bridge and Blooms. I run my hands along the worn wood countertop, taking a minute to collect myself. Pesky emotions swirl around in my mind like a damn whirlpool and I'm caught in their pull.

"You did all of this for me?" My words are thick with unshed tears, and fuck, I'd give anything to not actually cry right now, as if letting out my tears is tantamount to cutting myself open and baring my soul. Which it kind of is.

"I didn't really have to do much. The space was just sitting up here unused." He steps closer to me, closing the distance between us to just a couple of feet. "I'm tempted to pretend I wanted my kitchen back, but we both know how I feel about cooking."

I appreciate his attempt at humor, but I can't make myself laugh. Or even smile. It's too much. It's all too much.

Wetness streams down my cheeks, and I don't even try to stop it. I'm not sure I could.

"Shit, Sadie. Why are you crying? Did I fuck it all up?" He reaches out a hand and covers one of mine.

I pull away, under the guise of needing to wipe at my eyes, but mostly I'm just afraid of what his gentle touch will do to me.

He crosses to the sink in the corner and comes back with a wad of paper towels. "Will you talk to me, please? Whatever it is I screwed up, I promise I'll do what I can to fix it."

Rubbing at my eyes with the scratchy paper leaves them more raw than they already were. "You didn't do anything wrong." I gesture helplessly to the space around us. "This is the nicest, most perfect, most thoughtful thing anyone has ever done for me."

He steps back into my space, and this time I let him. Removing the paper towels from my hand, he gently wipes away my last stray tears with the pads of his thumbs.

I force myself to look in his eyes, grateful when my own tear up again, blurring this perfect vision in front of me. "I don't deserve you, Jack. Not as a roommate, or a friend, or . . ." I don't finish the thought, but it ends with *I sure as fuck don't deserve you as any kind of romantic partner.*

"Why would you say that?" He continues to catch my falling tears, his thumbs gentle on my rubbed-raw skin.

"Because I'm a selfish asshole, and you're the kind of person who does this"—I throw my arms out wide to encompass the entire space—"for someone you've known for five months." I know what those fridges cost, not to mention the logistics of purchasing them and getting them set up on the top level of the house without my realizing what was going on.

Jack drops his hands from my face and takes a step back. "Why do you continue to think the worst of yourself, Sadie?"

"It's not thinking the worst if it's true." I know I sound like a petulant teenager, but I don't care. My reaction to his generosity only serves as further proof of how terrible I am.

"No." He crosses his arms over his chest and glares at me. "I'm not letting you do this. Tell me why you think you're a selfish asshole."

"You've lived with me for months; I would've thought you'd seen enough of it for yourself by now." The overwhelming emotions—many of them of the happy and positive variety but also guilt and confusion and embarrassment—are starting to coalesce into one big emotion: anger. Anger is so much easier to deal with than all those other feelings tap-dancing around inside my heart. Rejection and self-doubt and inferiority and self-loathing.

Jack refuses to be cowed by the venom I'm dripping into my voice. "Give me one example."

I mimic his pose, arms crossed defiantly over my chest. "I forced my friends to work for me for free for half the summer."

"Your friends are grown adults who were happy to help you because they love you. Myself included." A dart of something flashes through those green eyes on that last sentence. "Next."

My breath hitches in my chest. I know he didn't mean it like that, and I'm not backing down. "I moved into your house and took the whole place over without ever even asking you if it was okay."

"Have you ever once heard me complain about that?"

"No, but that's only because you're a good person."

"And you're not?" He looks like he wants to throttle me, and honestly I don't blame him.

"Obviously."

Jack pushes his glasses up on his forehead, pinching the bridge of his nose between his thumb and index finger. "I have a real question for you, and I'd like a genuine answer."

Shrugging, I hop onto the counter. This conversation is wearing me out and I'm about to fold. Also, it gives me a good excuse to not have to look at him.

"Why can't you see the good in yourself, the good that we all see in you?"

"I know my positive traits, Jack. I'm a hard worker. I'm smart. I'm pretty hot and good in bed." I lean back on my hands, kicking my feet like I'm a kid on a swing. "I'm also a selfish asshole."

His eyes burn into the side of my face. "Who told you that?"

I study the plaid of my flannel pajama pants with great interest. "What do you mean?"

"Exactly what I said. Who told you you're selfish?" He moves so he's standing directly in front of me. "You didn't come to that conclusion on your own, so who told you that?"

"You gonna go beat him up or something?" I attempt to infuse the words with sarcasm and good old-fashioned deflection because the tears are coming again. The pressure continues to build in my chest, and I'm one more thoughtful comment away from breaking.

"Maybe."

I chance a glance up, expecting to see one of his quirky smirks. But he's serious. And pissed. Brows furrowed and eyes dark.

"Do we really have to do this, Jack? I don't want to talk about my fucked-up childhood, okay? I don't need to cry to you about my parents."

He sucks in a sharp breath. "Are you kidding me right now?" He shakes his head slightly, and his anger morphs to disappointment and hurt.

And my heart falls. "I didn't mean it like that." I reach for him, but he steps away from me. "Fuck. I'm sorry, Jack."

And I'm a sorry excuse for a human being, because a little part of me feels vindicated. See, I told you so, I am a total asshole. I wait in silence for Jack to leave, because that's what people tend to do when you hurt them over and over again.

But even though he maintains the space between us, he doesn't leave. "Sadie, I could give you a hundred examples of the things you do on a daily basis that are the antithesis of selfish. You're one of the most giving people I've ever met." His lips tilt up in a bemused smile. "And yeah, sometimes that generosity comes with a dose of snarky honesty, but it doesn't negate the kindness. Not even a little bit." He places his hands on the counter, one on either side of me. "So should I start listing all the nice things you do, prove to you that you are one big marshmallow of feelings, or do you want to tell me how we ended up here?" He leans in, letting his warmth wrap around me.

I inhale deeply. Coffee and paper and what I've come to think of as home. We're the same height in this position and he completely fills my line of vision. And I don't want him to move. It's suddenly imperative he remain right where he is, as if he's the only thing holding me together. So I start talking.

"My dad is a narcissist. And not the kind who thinks he's a hotshot or whatever. Like the actual clinical, sociopathic definition of the word." For a second, I focus on Jack's eyes, watching as they darken to a deep emerald, but then the emotion in them overwhelms me and I let my gaze drift down to his chest, to the dragon crest printed on his soft cotton T-shirt. "He was pretty abusive, emotionally and verbally. Liked to call me stupid if I brought home an A minus, tell me how dumb and petty my feelings were when I would tell a story, that kind of thing." I give him the least of it, because I can't bring myself to say the rest out loud. "I actually stopped talking at home for a while, believe it or not. I couldn't ever seem to find the right words, the magic words that would make him happy, so I stopped trying." Huh. I never really made the connection until now. I went from being afraid to open my mouth to never shutting up, a trait that really only kicked in once I became friends with Harley, Nick, and Gemma in college.

"And your mom?" Jack's voice is low, rumbly with suppressed anger.

"She got it just as badly as I did." I shrug it off. "I don't blame her. Not anymore."

"You should. She should've protected you." Jack's grip on the counter tightens, those beautiful fingers turning white with tension.

"She did her best. She's as much a victim as I was." It took me a long time to get to that place with my mom. In my head, I mean, since I haven't ever shared this with her, since it would involve talking to her, and that's not a thing I do. But holding on to all that anger wasn't good for me (yay for college mental health services!), and I had to let some of it go before it ate me up inside. "Besides, it's all in the past now. I left California right after high school graduation. Moved to New York, and I haven't been back since. No lasting harm done."

"Except for the lasting harm that prevents you from seeing how amazing you are."

I open my mouth to argue with him, but he places a single finger there, and the brush of his skin on my lips is enough to stop the words in their tracks.

"I didn't do all of this as some sort of gesture out of the goodness of my heart, Sade. I did this to put a tiny dent into the debt I owe you. Because you've done more for me in the past five months than I'll ever be able to repay you for." He traces his thumb over my bottom lip.

And oh god, I'm pretty sure my insides just melted into a pile of actual goo. And please, god, let this be the moment he kisses me. Because there's a good chance I might die if he doesn't kiss me. I don't think I've ever wanted anything as much as I want, right now in this moment, for Jack Thomas to kiss me.

He removes his finger and takes a blasted step away from me. "I'm the one who doesn't deserve you. And I'm trying, I promise I'm trying to get there. I just need a little more time."

It's the closest he's ever come to acknowledging this zing between us, and I don't know where exactly *there* is, but I know I'll give him all the time he needs. I still can't wrap my head around Jack's thinking he's the one who needs to come up to my standards; the idea is too ridiculous to make any sort of sense in my brain.

He shoves his hands in the pockets of his jeans. "I don't expect you to wait for me or anything."

"I haven't even looked at another guy since I moved in here." I blurt out the words before fully thinking them through.

And I don't even realize the truth of the statement until I say it out loud. It's been five months, and I can't remember the last time I went that long without so much as a flirtation over a drink. But no one has piqued even a hint of my interest since I met Jack, even when I still thought of him solely as my nerdy, sweet roommate.

"So does that mean you think you could give me a little more time?" There's such hope in his voice, my already melty insides turn completely liquid.

I can't do anything other than nod and agree. Because he means too much for me to do anything else, and I want him to have that time, to feel ready for whatever the next step might be. I hold open my arms and he steps into my embrace. And we've hugged before, mostly awkwardly, but this is something different. His arms wrap around me, his strong hands flat on my back, pulling me close. I bury my face in the crook of his neck, letting my fingers tangle in the curls at the nape. I breathe in every inch of him, holding on for as long as I can.

When he finally separates himself from me, I give him a cheeky smile. "We're doing it on this counter one day."

His cheeks flame a bright red, his pupils exploding, darkening his eyes. "Jesus, Sadie." Finally, he bursts out laughing. "I'm holding you to that."

⌒

GEMMA: Um, excuse me, Miss Sadie. WTF am I seeing on your IG right now?

HARLEY: What's on her Insta?

HARLEY: Wait, why am I asking that when I can open it up and check for myself?

NICK: Oh shit. Where is that?

GEMMA: WHY ARE YOU IGNORING US RIGHT NOW.

GEMMA: Sadie.

GEMMA: Sadie.

GEMMA: Sadie, I have literally 20 minutes between classes to pee, shove food in my face, and regroup and I'm using those 20 minutes to text you, so you better fucking answer!

        ME: Jesus. I was on the phone with a customer.
                         Good lord.

        ME: Hi, all! What's everyone up to?

GEMMA: I'm going to kill you.

HARLEY: My caseload is full, so you might want to rethink murder at this point.

NICK: Good god, Sadie. Tell her so my phone stops blowing up please.

ME: It's not really a big thing, it's just the top level of the brownstone.

GEMMA: The top level of the brownstone has coolers, a sink, and an island perfect for flower arranging? Convenient.

ME: Jack provided some of those things. Obvs. I think he was sick of me taking over the kitchen every day.

HARLEY: I'm sure that's it ☺

NICK: Yeah, that shit looks expensive. He wants to bang.

GEMMA: He wants to do more than bang.

NICK: True. He's probably in love with you.

HARLEY: Probably?

NICK: I mean, I wanna say definitely, but I also don't want to jinx it.

ME: He's not in love with me. I straight-up propositioned him and he still hasn't touched me.

NICK: Oh shit, yeah, then he definitely loves you.

ME: That doesn't make any sense. If he loved me, he'd want to sleep with me.

GEMMA: Oh you sweet sweet summer child.

GEMMA: I have to go, but we'll be continuing this conversation.

ME: Is this like one of those telemarketing texts I can opt out of?

GEMMA: No.

HARLEY: Definitely not.

NICK: I've been trying to opt out of this group text for YEARS.

⁓

JACK: Is it weird that I miss seeing the kitchen full of flowers all day every day?

ME: Um, no. My creations are stunning and you were lucky to be able to behold them.

ME: Also, this space is perfect for me and have I said thank you yet?

JACK: About a million times.

ME: Let's go for a million and one.

ME: THANK YOU!!!!!!!!!!!

JACK: You're welcome.

ME: If you miss the flowers that badly, you're welcome up here anytime. Obviously. Since this is your house and all.

JACK: I may take you up on that.

JACK: Did you have a plan for lunch?

ME: Not at the moment.

JACK: Want to go grab something? Or I could pick something up and bring it back, if you're busy.

ME: I could come with you to grab something quick.

JACK: Cool. Text me whenever you're ready.

⁓

ME: So you know that feeling when you're secretly crushing hard-core on your roommate and he like kind of knows it but you haven't explicitly discussed it but when you subtly discussed it he asked you to give him some time and wait for him to be ready and you agreed because you like him too much to say no but you're also super impatient and so now every time you've looked at him since then—FOR TWO WHOLE WEEKS—your stomach has gone all flippy and you think you might be losing it if he doesn't kiss you soon but he shows no sign of kissing you?

GEMMA: . . .

HARLEY: . . .

GEMMA: What the fuck did I just read.

ME: I think I might be losing my mind.

GEMMA: Ya think?

ME: So, real question: can I just jump his bones?

HARLEY: Verbal consent, Sade. Before and during.

ME: Why you gotta be all legal about it?

HARLEY: Just trying to keep you out of jail.

GEMMA: Practically a full-time job on its own.

ME: Wow. Rude.

HARLEY: Seems like you might be in need of a girls' night.

ME: Yes please.

ME: God I'm so horny.

GEMMA: Not that kind of girls' night.

⁓

ME: Okay, I can't take this anymore.

ME: What is hiding underneath that giant tarp in
the corner of the studio space?

JACK: First of all, way to give a guy a heart
attack.

JACK: Second, it's just some stuff from the old
setup in the studio. I can get rid of it if you need
the space.

ME: I have plenty of space, I was just curious.

ME: Is it stuff you're going to get rid of? Can I
rummage through and see if there's anything
I can repurpose?

JACK: I'll go through it. I'd really rather you not, if
that's okay.

ME: You do know telling me you don't want me to
see what's under there only makes me want to
look all the more, right?

JACK: I can see how that might be a problem for
you, but I also know how much you respect your
very kind and giving roommate and therefore will
not violate his privacy like that.

ME: Ugh. Respect is the worst.

JACK: If I make you pasta tonight will that make you feel better?

ME: It's a start.

THIRTEEN

*T*O GIRLS' NIGHT!" I raise my margarita to the center of the table, waiting for Harley and Gemma to clink glasses before taking a large sip of my frozen beverage.

"I can't believe you convinced us to come out for drinks on a Tuesday night." Gemma pouts, but it doesn't stop her from sucking down half of her margarita in one gulp.

"I'm sorry, guys, the weekends have been crazy for me. Besides, you have a half day tomorrow." I dip a chip in salsa and shovel it in my mouth. I didn't have time to eat lunch today and I'm starving.

"You do know that means I still have to see teenagers in the early hours of the morning, right? And then I have to sit through staff development, which, nine times out of ten, is worse than teenagers." She raises her hand to signal for our server, ordering another drink before Harley and I are even halfway through our first round.

"Well, if you'd like to make a career change, I may have a spot as a floral assistant opening up soon." My offer is mostly a joke, since I know Gemma doesn't actually want a new job. Though I am basically working from sunup to sundown, and it might be starting to take a toll on me both mentally and physically.

Harley takes a dainty sip of her drink, which will probably last her the entire meal. She's such a grown-up. "That's awesome, Sade! I can't believe how things exploded overnight." She pops a chip in her mouth. "Actually, that's not true. I can totally believe it, because you kick ass at everything you attempt."

"Aw, thanks, friend." I take a swig of margarita. "That's so not true, but I appreciate your confidence in me."

"So should I be interested in a career change, what are we looking at? Pay? Benefits? Hit me." Gemma folds her arms and leans across the polished wooden table.

"Um, minimum wage and my undying love?" I lick some salt from the rim of my glass before taking another long drink. Damn, that's good. It's been a while since I took some time to meet up with just the girls. And it's been a while since I actually sat down to eat. Usually I'm shoving food in my mouth whenever I can find a second to spare.

Gemma starts in on drink number two. "Sadie. You're a millennial businesswoman. You're supposed to care more about your employees than minimum wage and no health care. Should we even touch maternity leave yet?"

"Dude. It's been six months, you gotta give me a little time." I poke her in the arm with my unused straw. "Also, I can't tell if you're joking right now."

"Yeah, are you actually thinking about looking for another job?" Harley shoots me a look like this is the first she's hearing of it too.

Gemma shrugs. "I don't know, honestly. I love teaching, I adore my students. Even when they're hormonal assholes. But everything that happens outside of the classroom is just exhausting, you know?"

Harley pats her arm. "We know, Gem. Did something specific happen?"

"No. Just more of the same. I just keep waiting for things to get better, get easier, but it seems like every year is worse. Higher, more unrealistic expectations. Less support. Always less money." She bites her lip. "It's just a lot."

"You're doing the lord's work, Gem. I would've killed twenty teenagers on the first day." Signaling to the waiter, I order us all another round. At least one of us is going to really need it. And what kind of friend would I be if I left Gemma to drink alone in her time of need?

She gives me a sad smile. "They're far and away the best part of my job."

"Well, should Bridge and Blooms explode into celebrity florist status, I'll happily offer you a job with double minimum wage." I drain the dregs of margarita number one and move on to number two.

"And benefits."

"Sheesh, you drive a hard bargain for someone who doesn't even know if she wants the job or not." I throw a chip at her. "But I suppose I can give you benefits too. Because I'm a giver."

"Speaking of givers . . ." Harley raises one eyebrow at me, and I'm regretting ever teaching her how to perfect that move.

I raise one eyebrow right back. I'm not giving them an inch in this conversation. If they want the deets, they're going to have to come right out and ask.

"You and Jack fucked yet?" Leave it to Gemma.

Pursing my lips, I hold back the sigh threatening to spill from deep within. "No, we have not fucked yet. As I've said many times, it's not like that. Also, since when do we come right out and ask about fucking?"

"Um, when have we not done that?" Harley asks.

"Okay, you and Nick fucked yet?"

Harley swirls her straw around in her still-on-round-one margarita. "Obviously."

Gemma covers her ears with her hands. "I don't want to hear this." A second later she drops them and leans closer to Harley. "Just kidding, I totally want to hear this."

"How'd we go from Sadie and Jack to me and Nick?"

"There's nothing happening between me and Jack, so it's your turn." I don't mention how badly I *want* there to be something to report between me and Jack. Since the night he gifted me with the studio, nothing much has changed. There have been a few more long looks and hand brushes and he sits closer to me on the couch now, but it's still super G-rated all up in the brownstone.

Harley takes a long sip of her drink. "It's good."

"The margarita or the sex?" Gemma asks.

"Both." Harley can't hold back her grin, the cheeky minx.

I hold my glass in the air once again. "To Harley, out here proving you can have a good man and a good job, all at the same time."

"Don't forget good sex, lucky bitch." Gemma bashes her glass against mine a little too hard.

I shoot her a look, but she's gone back to drinking margarita number three. Harley nudges me under the table, and we exchange a glance. Gemma has had plenty of moments of career dissatisfaction since she started teaching, but never to the point where she might want to quit. Gemma is brilliant, and I have no doubt she could find success at any career she tried. But hopefully this is just a phase and she'll find the joy in teaching once again.

"Now that I've passed my interrogation, I do actually want to know what's going on with you and Jack." Harley diverts attention away from Gemma's career angst like the best best friend she is. She can always tell when we've hit our limit with sharing and need to move on to a new topic.

And, only because I love Gemma and want to help take her mind off her shitty job sitch, I give in. "Ugh. Fine. Still no fucking. What else do you want to know?"

"Any kissing at least?" Gemma perks up now that the conversation is back to titillating territory.

I attempt to shake my head while also going for my margarita straw, which doesn't work out how I want it to. "No kissing. Some subtle touches, and some even subtler eye fucking, but that's all she wrote."

"What is he waiting for?" Gemma raises her hand like one of her students, ready to order another drink.

Instead Harley hands off her as-yet-untouched second round. "More importantly, how are you feeling about everything?"

Bleh. It'd probably do me some good to talk about all this. In fact, I know it'd do me some good to talk about all this. But I also have no idea how to approach this conversation, even with my best friends. Alas, not knowing exactly what to say sure as hell never stopped me before. "I think I really like him. Like, not just in an I-want-to-bang-you way, but in an oh-shit-there's-actually-some-feelings-in-there kind of way. He makes my stomach flip. And he gives me these little chest aches. And every time he does something nice for me—which is, like, all the fucking time—I just want to squeeze him." I stab the ice in my drink with my straw. "Guys, I haven't flirted with another guy since I moved into the brownstone. I didn't even realize that until recently. And like, I don't feel like I'm missing out on anything, you know?"

"You're not, trust me on that." Gemma holds out her fist and I give her a half-hearted bump. "So what's his problem?"

I purse my lips, not wanting to divulge too many of Jack's secrets without his permission. "I think he still hasn't fully dealt with his parents' deaths. And he's been alone for a long time. Not just single alone. Like actually alone. I can't imagine going through what he did without you guys there to support me."

"You'll never have to find out." Harley pats my hand. "I imagine a lot of his hesitation comes from not wanting to end up alone again. You blew into his life, brought all of us with you, and he wants to make sure he's ready so he doesn't mess it up. I know it's frustrating for you, but I think it's actually a really smart way to go about things."

"Yeah, I get it." I break a chip into tiny pieces. "Not going to lie though, I definitely feel like the longer we wait, the more likely it is he'll never want to take things to the next level."

"Why would you say that?" Gemma has slowed down on her alcohol consumption and is now shoveling chips in her mouth, probably with the hope of soaking up some of the booze.

"I mean, you can only live with me for so long before growing to hate me."

Harley and Gemma exchange a look, and Harley opens her mouth, I'm sure with the intention of saying something calm and measured.

"Why the fuck would you say that?" Gemma blurts out before Harley can even start her sentence.

I ignore the looks of horror on their faces, knowing they're my friends and will try to placate me no matter how much they agree with the sentiment. "Come on, guys, you know me better than anyone, you know what an asshole I can be."

"We do know you better than anyone, Sadie. You and I lived together for years and I've never come anywhere near hating you." Harley crosses her arms over her chest, leaning back in her chair and studying me like she's my therapist.

Whom I should probably make an appointment with. Since I started Bridge and Blooms and moved in with Jack, the feelings of inadequacy that always live in the back of my mind have been much more vocal.

"You're my friends, so you have to say that." I cross my own arms over my chest, giving her a pointed look.

"No, we don't. And just for the record, I fully agree with the asshole part. In the most loving of ways, of course." Gemma opens a new straw with the sole intention of shooting the wrapper at me. Which she does, the thin paper landing in my untouched glass of water.

"How did you get back here, Sadie? I thought you dealt with all of this dad stuff in college." Harley was the one who originally encouraged me to visit the mental health clinic on campus, and I'll forever be in her debt for that.

"Daddy issues never truly go away, do they?" It's a bratty answer, but I'm in a bratty mood. This is the second time I've had this conversation lately, and that's two times too many if you ask me, which no one has bothered to do.

"Ah, so now that you have the prospect of a new man, a good man, and a real relationship on the horizon, all the self-doubt is coming back?"

"I don't need you to psychoanalyze me, Harley."

"I think you kind of do, Sade. Because she's totally right. Selfish people don't offer to help their friends grade grammar quizzes." Gemma reaches over and fishes the soggy paper out of my water glass.

"And selfish people don't stay up late listening to their friends freak out about their new relationships." Harley nudges my elbow with hers.

Damn them both for zeroing in on my trigger word without my even mentioning it. "Okay, so I've done two nice things recently. Big whoop." Seriously, why can't anyone just leave this alone? Why do I have to continue to have this discussion with people?

Gemma sways a little in her seat and I'm thinking she might be calling in sick tomorrow. "You do nice things for people all the time. Just shut up and accept it. Fuck, your whole career is doing nice things for people. Either bringing them flowers or serving them drinks. Nice things."

"I don't think it counts if I get paid for doing the nice things. But anyway, can we get back to the real topic at hand?" That's how desperate I am to never have to hear about how nice I am again; I'll willingly change the subject back to me and Jack. "I thought you both cared so much about how much I like Jack and how much he doesn't want to kiss me."

Gemma rolls her eyes. "He so wants to kiss you."

"I think that has been well established at this point, Sadie. I think the real question is, will just a kiss be enough, for either of you?"

I know it won't be for me. I don't even have to think about it or consider Harley's question. I want more than just a kiss from Jack. More than just a one- or two-night bang sesh. But saying it out loud is a totally different animal.

Gemma hands me her remaining margarita. "Drink this and then answer."

I chug the remainder of her cocktail, even though it's mostly melted ice at this point. Whatever. Liquid courage is liquid courage. "I don't want to just kiss him. I want him to be my— Fuck, I've literally never even had a real one. Not once."

"You want him to be your boyfriend!" Gemma squeals, punching both arms in the air triumphantly.

I bury my hands in my hair. "I want him to be my boyfriend."

Harley claps her hands, and I'm pretty sure the entire restaurant is staring at us. "This is so exciting!"

"It's not exciting at all. It's nauseating. And terrifying. Why do you people put yourselves through this?" My head falls onto my arms, crossed on top of the sticky table.

Harley runs a soothing hand through my hair. "It's worth it."

"What if he thinks I'm not worth it?" I mutter into the crook of my arms, mostly hoping they don't hear my question.

"Then he's an idiot and we'll kick his ass." Gemma could do it too.

I sit up and look at each of them. "I don't deserve you guys. And I'm scared I don't deserve him either." That's the sentiment I was trying to convey to Jack the night of the studio surprise. I don't feel like I deserve him, and I don't know what I could possibly bring to the table, to a man like him.

Harley grabs my right hand, holding it tight in hers. "You absolutely deserve him. He'd be lucky to have you, Sadie."

Gemma takes my other hand. "And you deserve us. And we know how fucking lucky we are to have you."

"You guys are the best, and I love you." That blasted wetness springs up in my eyes again, but at least this time I can blame it on the margaritas.

I wake up the next morning, not *not* with a hangover. It's a weird haze of too much emotional conversation combined with too much tequila and not enough water. My head aches, but not so much as to be debilitating. I'll be able to function, but movements will be slow today.

The weather is starting to cool down as we head further into October, so I pull on my favorite jeans and a light sweater before heading out the door and straight to Bagel World for the biggest breakfast sandwich they make and coffee for me and Jack. The air is crisp and cool on the walk back home, and the long cleansing breaths I take help further clear the alcohol-and-emotion fug from my brain.

Even after talking things out with Harley and Gemma, I still can't piece together the puzzle that is me and Jack. I know I like him. I'm pretty sure he likes me. I know we both have some serious mental blockages due to our unfortunate parental situations. I think these are things we could work out, and work on, together.

I've never wanted to work on anything with anyone, together or not, so this thought alone should be a good indicator of just how deep I'm in. But knowing this frisson with Jack isn't just some lust-fueled fling doesn't do much for me in terms of filling in the blanks. I'm still left wondering if he feels the same way. If he'll ever be able to get past his hang-ups.

The not knowing, and the living in a constant state of *What the fuck is happening here*, is a lot. It'd probably be a hell of a lot easier to just cut my losses and bail now, but the whole living-together situation kind of makes that impossible. Unless I want to move out. Which I definitely don't.

So I guess I just have to hang in there and wait, see whether he returns my feelings and whether he eventually wants to be with me too. And I just have to hope he's worth the wait.

Actually, that's the one thing I don't need to bother to hope for. I know he is.

I leave Jack's coffee on the kitchen counter, sending him a quick text to let him know it's there. Climbing an additional flight of stairs multiple times a day to get to the studio is hopefully doing wonders for my butt, because damn, it's tough sometimes. I stop in my room to change into an old T-shirt I don't mind getting dirty, kicking off my shoes in the process. One of the best parts about working from home is never having to wear uncomfortable shoes ever again.

I grab my laptop and head up to the studio space, which I have lovingly dubbed BaBs (for Bridge and Blooms). I dump all my stuff on the counter and climb onto the bar stool I found at one of the local flea markets. Going through my calendar, and emails, and DMs, I put together a to-do list for the day. Since I don't have any deliveries scheduled, today is mostly about catching up on admin stuff, which, not going to lie, has been kicking my butt. I love spreadsheets, but I've fallen so far behind on inputting info, I'm going to need the whole day to catch up.

When my eyes feel like they might actually fall out of my head, I push the stool back and go for a walk around BaBs. The space is big enough for me to do a couple of laps when I need a break. Normally it's just a quick jaunt to give my eyes a rest and get the blood flowing, but today's jaunt brings a small surprise.

Jack's forbidden tarp still lives in the corner of the studio, and typically I breeze on by it, continually impressed with my no-peeking restraint. But today, said tarp has been haphazardly replaced, leaving a whole corner of the hidden contents exposed.

I check over my shoulder, even though Jack rarely comes up here when I'm working and usually sends me a text beforehand to give me a heads-up. Creeping on tippy-toes, I inch my way farther into the corner, low-key expecting some serial killer–esque corkboard with red string and pictures of his victims.

But that's not at all what I find.

My brow furrows as I take in the smallest sliver of what's revealed. And then I throw caution to the wind and push the tarp to the floor to get the full picture.

The full picture is three paintings, of three very familiar images. Images I'd know anywhere, because I created them. I take a step closer to the one on the far left, examining every inch. It's almost an exact replica of one of my floral arrangements, the colors and shadows and details of the flowers captured as brilliantly as my camera caught them. I move along to the middle painting, another one of my arrangement photos. Jack has transformed the image I posted to Instagram, of the arrangement posed in front of the brick wall in the living room, so painstakingly perfectly someone might mistake it for a photograph. The third painting isn't finished yet, but I can tell by the background and the rough sketch marks it's going to be another one of my Bridge and Blooms pics, completely brought to life by this new medium.

"What the fuck?" I mutter.

"My thoughts exactly."

I freeze, like Jack is a T. rex and he won't be able to see me if I don't move. "Shit."

"What are you doing?" He stalks across the room, covering the distance from the door to the corner in just a few steps. The anger in his voice is foreign and startling.

"Look, I didn't purposefully go snooping, but the corner of the tarp was sliding down and I saw a sliver of the painting and I'm really sorry for peeking, but holy shit, Jack. These are incredible."

Jack pushes past me, grabbing the tarp and throwing it over the paintings. As if covering them up will make me forget them. "They weren't meant to be seen."

"Why not? I've never seen anything like them before." It dawns on me that that's not entirely true. "Wait. The painting in the guest room?" And the one of the brownstone, though he doesn't know I saw it.

He nods, yanking down the corner of the tarp, making sure everything is sufficiently hidden.

"Jack, these are really remarkable. Why didn't you tell me you were an artist?"

"I'm not." He crosses away from me to the window, shoving his hands in his pockets.

"Clearly, you are. Why would you want to keep this talent hidden?" I take a few tentative steps toward him, but he halts me with a glare.

"It's nothing. Forget you even saw those." He rakes his hand through his hair.

I shut up for a minute, using the quiet to inch closer to him. When I get close enough, I reach out my hand, placing it gently on his forearm. "I'm sorry for snooping, but I'm also really not because I'm glad I saw the paintings. I wish you would've told me about them."

He steps back, moving out of my reach. "Yeah, well, not everyone likes to talk about themselves twenty-four/seven."

I freeze once again, the chill of his words an ice pick piercing my heart. My head falls, and I blink rapidly, sucking in short, rasping breaths. I force my feet to move, stumbling over to the counter to grab my laptop, abandoning my coffee and my phone, anything to get to the door as fast as possible.

"Sadie," Jack calls, but I ignore him, bolting down the stairs and into my room, shutting and locking the door behind me.

He knocks on my door five minutes later, but I continue to ignore him, pretending to work, though how I'd be able to input numbers onto a spreadsheet when tears are blurring my vision is beyond me. His words weren't a surprise. Anything but. I guess I'd just deluded myself into believing Jack actually liked me, maybe even cared about me as more than a friend. But of course, all along he's been thinking I'm insufferable. Because I am.

I wait an hour before I open the door, and I only venture out because I have to pee. My phone and my coffee are waiting for me right outside the door. I scoop them up and scamper to the bathroom.

I don't check my phone until I'm safely locked back in my room, buried under my covers for good measure.

> **JACK:** I'm sorry. I didn't mean that, and it was a
> horrible thing to say, and I'd like to apologize when
> you're ready to hear it.

Ugh. Even his apologies are mature.

An hour later my phone chirps again.

> **JACK:** If you let me talk to you, I'll answer all your
> questions . . .

He already knows what to say to make me give in.

I wait another half an hour before I respond.

> **ME:** Fine. I'm coming downstairs. Have wine ready.

I let another twenty minutes pass, taking the time to wipe under my eyes and fix my hair.

When I head downstairs, Jack is already waiting at the sofa, two glasses of wine sitting on the coffee table. I sit as far away from him as I can and drink half of the glass before turning my attention to him.

"I'm sorry, Sadie. That was a shitty thing to say. The shittiest. I never should've said it, and I sure as fuck didn't mean it." He clasps his hands together, knuckles turning white. "This is probably going to sound terrible, but I love listening to you talk about yourself and your life and your friends and your work."

I purse my lips. "Is that all?"

His brow furrows. "Yes. I mean, I'm sorry. Again."

"Why didn't you tell me you could paint?"

He releases his clenched hands, wiping his palms on his jeans. "I couldn't. Not for a long time, anyway."

"How long?"

He meets my gaze head-on. "Seven years."

I suck in a breath, the full impact of his words washing over me. He hadn't painted since his parents died. "Are those the first ones you've done? Since?"

He nods, letting me put together the unspoken sentiment on my own.

The first thing Jack painted since the death of his parents was my flowers.

"If I hadn't snooped, would you ever have shown them to me?" The words come out in a squeak of a whisper, my lungs barely functioning enough for me to breathe, let alone speak.

He clears his throat. "I don't know, Sade. I wish I could give you a different answer, but I'm not going to lie to you."

"How does it feel? To be painting again after such a long time?" There's clearly still so much I don't know about Jack, and his history, but this obviously isn't just a hobby. Or wasn't just a hobby.

"After what I said to you, you're concerned about *my* feelings?" He shoves his hand through his hair, and this time the curls stay pulled back from his face.

"You were justifiably upset and said something dickish out of anger. It's not the end of the world." I fail to mention just how badly a comment like his actually hurts since I can see he genuinely feels bad. And it's not his fault I'm programmed to run all insults on a loop inside my brain forever until the end of time.

He scoots closer to me on the couch, close enough to reach over and pick up my hand. "That's not an excuse. You didn't deserve that, even if I was upset. You shouldn't have to suffer because I'm still an emotional disaster."

I squeeze his hand. "You're not an emotional disaster."

"I am. But maybe slightly less of one since you came around." He rubs his thumb over my knuckles. "And it feels really good to be painting again."

"You painted my flowers."

"I did."

"They're beautiful." I meet his gaze, my breath fluttering in my chest once again.

"You inspired me." He leans in and brushes the softest kiss on my cheek.

But before I can fully register the sensation of his lips on my skin, he's pulling away, rising from the couch.

"I'll let you get back to work." He crosses over to the basement stairs, pausing at the top. "When we do this, Sade—and for me, it's a when, not an if—I want to be all in. I want to give you everything. I'm just not there yet. But I'm trying." He flashes me a half smile before heading down the stairs.

Like I'm going to be able to work after that.

GEMMA: Halloween is happening at your place, yes, Sadie?

GEMMA: And Jack. Since you also live there.

JACK: And just what do we mean by "Halloween is happening"?

JACK: On a scale from kindergarten costume parade to frat party?

HARLEY: Somewhere around "drink a lot of wine and order takeout while also passing out candy to cute kids who come knocking on the door."

NICK: You know, a guy from my office is throwing an actual Halloween party we could all go to.

                                            ME: No.

GEMMA: Fuck no.

HARLEY: Love you, babe, but no.

ME: OMG DID YOU JUST SAY I LOVE YOU IN THE
GROUP TEXT?!?!?!

HARLEY: Just an expression.

GEMMA: I can practically see your blushing cheeks
from across the apartment, Harley.

JACK: Wine and takeout and passing out candy
works for me, guys!

HARLEY: Now I love you too, Jack.

NICK: Whoa. Let's take that one back several
notches.

ME: Yeah, what Nicky said.

ME: Also, eff you guys for making me agree with
what Nick said.

HARLEY: Oh my god, I love all of you equally,
okay?

NICK: But me just a little bit more, right?

HARLEY: Obviously. 😊

GEMMA: Me on the other hand, I hate all of you. I'm dressing as an old maid for Halloween.

ME: Gem, be serious. There might be hot single dads out there.

GEMMA: Sexy librarian it is.

⁓

"Is this going to be enough candy?" Jack holds up three bags, each the size of my upper body.

I purse my lips to keep back the smile, and yeah, I notice how his arms bulge a little, laden down with pounds and pounds of sugar. "How many did you go through last year?"

He tosses them on the kitchen peninsula. "I don't know. I usually turn the lights off and hide in the basement."

"Oh my god, you're the cranky-old-man house!" Taking a few bottles of wine out of the cabinet, I also pull down five glasses and arrange them all on the counter.

"I don't know if I'd go that far." He frowns, his brow wrinkling in a way that's adorable and also makes him look kind of like a little old man.

"Every neighborhood has one, buddy, and looks like you're it for Park Slope." I rummage around in the cabinets until I find a huge bowl. "If your old-man muscles can handle it, can you rip one of those bad boys open?"

Jack glares at me for a solid thirty seconds before grudgingly tearing open one of the bags.

I transfer the candy from the bag to the bowl, only pausing twice to take a bite of chocolate for myself. "You changing or is that your entire costume?" I wave my hand, currently holding a Twix, in his general vicinity.

He captures my wrist in his hand, biting off half of the candy bar.

And I have to grip the counter to keep myself from face-planting on the hardwood floor. Was that—is this—does that count as foreplay?

Jack releases my wrist, a smug smile tugging on his lips. He pulls a red cape from one of the bar stools, tying it around his neck. He points to his blue shirt, a big red S on the center of his chest. "Shirt, cape, Clark Kent glasses, I think I'm good to go."

"Well, which are you, Superman or Clark Kent?" I'm arguing for argument's sake. And because he caught me off guard with that wrist grab/bite and I don't like it.

Things have been . . . playful . . . around the brownstone since the whole I-hadn't-painted-for-seven-years-until-you-came-along-to-be-my-muse fiasco. We seem to have moved from easy friendship to mostly innocent flirting, though the sexual tension is still most definitely present and accounted for. Even if it never goes beyond tension. Jack's grabbing my arm and chomping half of my chocolate bar is the most action I've seen in months.

Which reminds me, I need to charge my vibrator.

"As with most things in my life, Sadie"—the rumble of Jack's voice distracts me from the needs of my sex toys—"I find myself caught somewhere in the middle."

"How poetic." I reach for a bottle of wine, popping it open and pouring myself a glass. A big one.

"What about you?" He takes the bottle from my hand and pours himself a glass.

"What about me?"

"Is this your costume?" He looks me up and down, even though there isn't much to take in.

That doesn't stop me from feeling every inch of his gaze as it rakes over my jeans and tight white tank top, Bridge and Blooms emblazoned across my chest in glitter letters. I open the fridge and take out the pink and lavender floral crown I crafted earlier today, settling it on top of my loose curls. My once-highlighted-into-blond-oblivion hair has faded and grown out, slowly returning to its natural brown, but I've been so busy I haven't even had time to think about it. Things like regular hair appointments just don't feel like priorities anymore.

"Wanna hand me my wings?" I gesture to the back of the bar stool where Jack is standing.

He hands over a pair of iridescent, sparkling fairy wings, which I slip over my shoulders.

"Voilà. Flower fairy." Spinning around, I kick up my heel in a princess pose.

"Cute and promotional." Jack holds up his wineglass.

I clink mine against his. "Happy Halloween, Jack-o'-Lantern."

He takes a long sip of wine. "I'm pretty sure you've used that one before."

"Doesn't matter, it's fitting for the occasion." I pick up the bowl of candy and take it over to the entryway table, swishing my hips a little more than necessary when I feel Jack's eyes on my ass. I'm checking my flower crown in the mirror above the table when he comes up behind me, his hand resting on my hip, the heat of his fingers burning through the denim of my jeans.

"I'm kind of hoping none of those hot single dads come by." His breath tickles my neck, sending a shiver through me.

I meet his gaze in the mirror. "You really want to jinx Gemma like that?"

He grins at me, his fingers tightening on my waist. "No, I guess not."

The sound of the doorbell trills through the house, and Jack leans forward to open the door, the weight of him pressing into me and stealing my breath.

"Better not be any hot single moms either," I mutter.

His hand trails up my back, gently squeezing the nape of my neck. "It wouldn't matter if there were."

I lean into his touch. "You do realize when you say shit like that it makes me want to throw you up against this wall and kiss you senseless, right?"

Another knock pounds on the door and Gemma's voice bleeds through the wood. "I'm carrying a fuck-ton of wine here, open the door, assholes!"

"She really leans into being off duty, doesn't she?" Jack grins, reaching around me to open the door for my boisterous, chockful-of-bad-timing friends, who push right past us into the house. "I'll take a rain check on that offer, though." His lips brush the shell of my ear before he leaves me standing in the doorway to pass out candy to our first trick-or-treaters, while the rest of the gang heads to the kitchen to start drinking.

I drop candy bars into the bags of a princess, a pirate, and a fire-fighter, all while trying to stem the ache in my chest and between my legs, before closing the door and joining my friends.

We spend the evening doling out full-sized chocolate bars (because of course Jack got the good candy) and drinking wine, our sugar highs and wine buzzes keeping us laughing long after the trick-or-treaters have stopped knocking. Gemma ends up spending the night at the brownstone after Nick and Harley leave together to stumble their way back to the girls' shared apartment.

"They'll be banging for hours," she confides to me and Jack, the three of us draped over the couch in the basement, *Hocus Pocus* playing on the TV in the background. "Seriously, I don't know how they manage to keep their energy up."

Jack shoots me a look, his eyes hooded, the wine-fueled lust obvious even from the opposite side of the couch. I squirm a little in my seat, my clothes suddenly feeling too tight, my skin buzzing with tension and anticipation. I bite my lip, feeling pretty sure I shouldn't bound right over Gemma and jump on top of him, but also not totally ruling out the possibility.

Jack clears his throat and stands, adjusting his jeans before begging off for the night. He gives me a parting look that lets me know I could definitely sneak into his room later and put an end to this months-long standoff.

Apparently all I needed to do this whole time was get the man drunk on wine and chocolate.

"Oh god, not you two, too. Where the fuck am I going to sleep?" Gemma elbows me in the ribs.

I elbow her right back. "Nothing is happening tonight, calm down."

"I mean, don't get me wrong, I'm pushing hard for this hookup, but not while I'm in the next room, yeah?"

I turn up the TV, shifting my focus to the Sanderson sisters and away from the hot piece of ass who just vacated the room. "I'm beginning to think you're right."

"Obviously." She sits up straight on the couch. "About what?"

"Maybe I'm not completely selfish, because did you see what just walked out of here?"

She smacks me in the head with a pillow. "I saw a man who'd wait for you until the end of time, so take it easy over there." Her arm drapes across my shoulders and I expect her to pull me into a headlock, but instead, she tucks us both underneath the soft blanket she's cuddled under. "And I'm happy for you. Because you, my beautiful, giving, totally-not-selfish-but-still-kind-of-an-asshole friend, deserve nothing less."

~

ME: So how do you feel about Thanksgiving?

JACK: What, like in general? As a holiday?

JACK: It's probably a pretty shitty thing to celebrate, you know, given the mass genocide and total destruction of an entire people's way of life.

ME: Wow. Okay. So yes, recognize all of that.

ME: Also, how do you feel about having everyone over for Thanksgiving! Yay!

JACK: Oh.

JACK: Who's everyone?

ME: Us, obvs. Gem, Nick, Harley. Usually we have Harley's parents too. And I guess this year possibly Nick's parents if they're going to do the whole one-big-happy-family bullshit.

JACK: Are they not one big happy family?

ME: Sigh. They are. Disgustingly so.

JACK: I'm not opposed to the idea, but I definitely haven't ever hosted anything like this before.

ME: Gem and I will take care of everything.

ME: You just have to show up and look cute 😉

JACK: That's a lot to ask.

ME: Please. You could do that in your sleep.

ME: Oh man, I bet you're fucking adorable when
you sleep.

JACK: I definitely don't snore as loudly as someone
else who lives in this house . . .

ME: Fuck off, I hate you.

JACK: Yay Thanksgiving!

~

ME: OKAY SO DOES EVERYONE KNOW WHAT
THEY'RE BRINGING?!?!?

GEMMA: WHY ARE YOU SHOUTING.

ME: I'm sorry, I just really want everything to go
smoothly.

ME: Jack hasn't explicitly said anything, but I'm
pretty sure this is the first time he's celebrating
Thanksgiving since, you know, losing his entire
family in one terrible accident, and now we're all
barging in and taking over his house and I want
everything to be perfect.

NICK: Way to bring down the mood, Sade.

HARLEY: We understand, and we promise to make the day as perfect as possible.

GEMMA: I mean, I'm cooking, it's gonna be fine.

NICK: I'm bringing a shit-ton of booze, so it's gonna be better than fine.

HARLEY: My mom's making mac and cheese and pie, so pretty sure all our bases are covered.

ME: And I've got the flowers and decor covered, obvs.

ME: So I guess we're in good shape.

ME: If you can all promise not to be totally embarrassing.

GEMMA: I promise nothing.

NICK: Jack loves me no matter how embarrassing I am.

HARLEY: Sadie. It's going to be fine. Now go get your orders done so you can relax.

ME: Lol. Relax.

ME: I DO NOT KNOW THE MEANING OF THE
WORD.

GEMMA: Oh god, we're back to shouting.

∾

ME: Okay. So plan for this week: Monday I'm out
picking up flowers, Tuesday I'm arranging,
Wednesday morning I'm delivering, Wednesday
afternoon I'm cleaning the house from top to
bottom so please don't leave anything gross lying
around. Wednesday night I'm baking and arranging
flowers for us. Gem will be over early Thursday
morning to start cooking.

ME: I don't know why you'd suddenly need to know
my detailed schedule for the week, but some of it
involves you, so there you go.

JACK: I'm around if you need help with deliveries or
lugging stuff up the stairs.

JACK: I also scheduled a house cleaning
for Wednesday, so you can cross that off
your list.

ME: You scheduled a house cleaning?

ME: Like with people who know how to clean houses?

JACK: That's usually who I hire to come clean the house, yes.

ME: I COULD KISS YOU RIGHT NOW.

ME: I won't, because you haven't given me explicit verbal consent and Harley doesn't have time to represent me, BUT WHAT I'M TRYING TO SAY IS THANK YOU!!

JACK: Nick was right, you're very shouty lately.

ME: Omg, you and Nick have your own text chain? Adorbs.

JACK: Will you please actually ask me for help if you need it this week?

ME: I'll think about it 😉

~

GEMMA: Kiss update?

ME: Do we seriously have to do this every day?

GEMMA: Yes.

HARLEY: Yes.

> ME: There hasn't been any kissing today or any other day, thanks so much for the reminder.

HARLEY: Hang in there, friend, it's going to happen soon!

GEMMA: In the meantime, let me know if you need me to bring over some batteries 😂

> ME: I hate you.

FOURTEEN

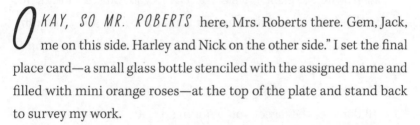

O KAY, SO MR. ROBERTS here, Mrs. Roberts there. Gem, Jack, me on this side. Harley and Nick on the other side." I set the final place card—a small glass bottle stenciled with the assigned name and filled with mini orange roses—at the top of the plate and stand back to survey my work.

The Thanksgiving table is set, even though it's only Wednesday night. I wanted everything done ahead of time so I can devote my morning hours to helping Gemma cook and taking care of last-minute emergencies. The centerpiece is still upstairs in my floral cooler, but everything else is ready to go. The table looks like it was set by a hipster Martha Stewart, which means my job here is done.

Jack climbs up the basement stairs just as I'm heading to the fridge to pour myself a big-ass glass of wine. "Wow, this looks great, Sade."

"Thanks." I hold up a wineglass as a silent offering, and he nods. "I know technically you should be sitting at the head of the table since it's your house, but I figured since Harley's parents are the only adults willing to put up with us, we'd let them have that honor. If it's all right with you."

Jack takes the glass of wine I hold out to him and shrugs. "Whatever you think is best. I'm definitely not up-to-date on holiday protocol."

"Lucky for you, we don't have protocol. We eat a lot and drink a lot and play some games and call it a day." I clink my glass against his before taking a long sip. Mentally, I run through everything I was supposed to accomplish today, checking off boxes as I move down the list.

"What time is Gemma coming by tomorrow?" Jack leans his hip against the kitchen counter, perching himself just a few feet away from me.

"She'll be here at eight, but sleep as late as you want." I subtly shift, closing the distance between us just a smidge. "Also just a warning that we will be watching the parade and I will dance and sing along at opportune moments."

"I'd expect nothing less." He pairs his words with a teasing smile. "You all done for the day or you planning on tackling any more projects tonight?"

So yeah, I might've gone a little project crazy this week, but I really want everything to go smoothly tomorrow. I want this to be the perfect Thanksgiving for everyone. I want it to be the first of many this group spends together. Well, this complete group, the group that now includes Jack. I've been invited to Thanksgiving with the Roberts crew ever since freshman year, when Harley found out I was planning on spending the weekend alone in the dorms. It was the first time I'd ever seen her put her foot down, insisting I come home with her and spend the holiday weekend with her parents. Since then, Gemma has also joined us almost every year. Nick's attendance is more sporadic, somewhat based on his parents' random travel urges, but I'm guessing now that he and Harley are bumping things up a notch, he'll be a more permanent fixture at the holiday table, even if his parents are spending this year in Italy.

I swallow the last of my wine. "I think I'm packing it in for tonight. Going to take a quick shower and head to bed. You?"

"I think I'm going to go paint for a bit." He finishes his wine and takes both of our glasses over to the sink.

He's painting a lot more these days, though never at any time when I'm also working in BaBs. I can see how my frenzied work pace and penchant for loud off-key singing could be distracting, but at the same time, I'm dying for the chance to watch Jack work. Though something tells me we might end up rolling around on the floor naked, our bodies covered in a layer of paint.

Which I wouldn't be mad about.

"Cool. See you tomorrow, then." I brush past him on my way out of the kitchen, relishing the zing the slightest hint of skin-to-skin contact brings.

Somewhere in the space of the past couple of weeks, I've stopped looking at this building tension as a thing to defeat. A thing that makes me uptight and impatient. Instead I'm savoring it. Allowing the anticipation to mount, reveling in each near miss, knowing the buildup is going to make the payoff that much sweeter. Which, honestly, feels mature as fuck.

∽

When I bound down the stairs on Thanksgiving morning, just a few minutes before Gemma is set to arrive and take over the kitchen, a pajama-clad Jack and a vanilla latte are already waiting for me at the kitchen peninsula.

"I was going to start something for Gemma, but I couldn't remember what she likes," Jack says by way of greeting.

I pick up the Wonder Woman mug filled with my coffee and breathe in the heavenly scent. "No worries. I'll make it for her. Thank you for this." I lean over and plant a soft kiss on his cheek. His skin is smooth and smells of some kind of woodsy aftershave, the scent of which will soon disappear beneath his normal coffee-and-paper fragrance.

Jack's cheeks flush a bright pink, but he pins me down with a stare that's neither embarrassed nor tentative. It's searing. "You're welcome. Happy Thanksgiving."

"Happy Thanksgiving."

To distract myself from the urge to climb into his lap and shove my tongue down his throat, I find the remote for the living room TV and flip to the parade. We rarely watch TV on this level since the basement is bigger and the couch more comfortable, but the parade is a nonnegotiable for me. And Nick and Mr. Roberts will want to watch some kind of sportsball later on, I'm sure.

Gemma knocks on the door a minute later, and after I make her a latte, she puts me to work as her sous chef. She immediately slips into her zone, controlling the kitchen with the practice of an Iron Chef and the grace of a ballerina. I chop and dice and check on things in the oven, following the orders of my commander as best I can, so as not to get chewed out. Jack, in the meantime, keeps our cups filled, first with coffee and then, at a more appropriate hour, with white wine.

A half hour before the rest of the crew is set to arrive, I dash upstairs to grab the centerpiece from the cooler. I pulled together a collection of brown glass vessels—beer bottles and growlers, and even an antique bleach bottle—and filled each one with handfuls of orange and red and cream blooms. I arrange them all in the center of the table in a clump, taking just a second to check everything over before I snap some quick photos and run upstairs to change.

We're a casual bunch, so I stick to my jeans, but I pull on a cute sweater and suede ankle booties, before tousling my hair and slicking on some lip gloss. I've gone pretty minimal with the makeup since leaving my "real" job, but I always feel better with a little lip gloss.

When I make it back to the kitchen, I do a final check-in with Gemma, who's all set until everything is finished cooking/heating/baking. We've got a silver tub stocked with ice, beer, and white wine. Nick is bringing the red and the hard stuff.

I turn to Gemma and hold my hand up for a high five. "We fucking adulted the shit out of this Thanksgiving."

She slaps my hand. "That almost doesn't even make sense. But yes, we nailed it."

Jack joins us in the kitchen, grabbing a beer from the fridge so as not to mess up our perfect display. "Everything looks amazing. And smells amazing."

"Thanks, Jackalope." I give him an aw-shucks punch on the arm. Gemma rolls her eyes.

"That's not an actual thing, you know." He pops the top on his beer, and I'm so far gone at this point, I watch the bulge of his lean biceps even during this most minuscule of flexing.

"Literally couldn't care less." Reaching over him to the appetizer tray, I grab a cracker and pop it in my mouth.

The doorbell rings a second later, and we usher in the Roberts family plus Nick, taking coats and pouring drinks and getting everyone situated. The men naturally gravitate toward the TV, where Jack hands off the remote to Nick. They all settle into the couch and armchairs around the coffee table, where an additional appetizer plate sits ready with snacks.

Gemma and Mrs. Roberts huddle in the kitchen, going over timing and temperatures and probably solving world hunger between the two of them while they're at it. Harley and I hop onto the bar stools at the kitchen peninsula, the perfect place to observe both groups and have easy access to the charcuterie.

"Sooooooo." I nudge her with my elbow. "First major holiday as a couple. How's it going?"

Harley rolls her eyes, but a slow smile also spreads across her face. "It's not like this is the first time Nick and I have spent Thanksgiving together."

"No, but it's the first time since you fell in loooooooovvvvee." Seriously, it's a wonder I have any friends at all.

"God, I can't wait for you and Jack to finally get it together. You're so going to get what's coming to you." Harley grabs a bottle of wine from the bucket, pouring herself a glass before topping mine off.

I sigh. "I should probably get some kind of reward for how patient and noble I've been."

Harley snorts into her wineglass. "One, you and patient are not a thing together. Two, you *will* get a reward."

I look at her questioningly, my eyebrows raised.

"Jack's the reward." She flicks me on the forehead, and I forgot how much that hurts.

"You're such a sap now that you're in loooooovvvvve."

She laughs and pushes me, almost knocking me off the stool. "Talk to me in another month. You'll see."

My gaze wanders over to the menfolk, lounging around in the living room. Jack meets my eyes, giving me a cute little wink and an adorable grin. Which causes me to also grin, probably adorably.

Harley catches me and chuckles. "Scratch that, talk to me tomorrow and you'll see."

An hour later, everyone files into their assigned seats and the bonanza begins. Platters are passed, wineglasses filled, meat carved. Once our plates are loaded to the brim, the four of us regulars turn our attention to Mrs. Roberts, who leads us in a quick prayer. Most of us don't really go for the whole religion thing, but we also know it's important to the Robertses, so we go with it.

And then for a couple of minutes, there's nothing but the clatter of utensils on plates, peppered with an occasional "Mmmmm." Because damn, Gem can cook.

Mr. Roberts finally breaks the silence. "Gemma, you've outdone yourself. Everything is delicious."

We all murmur our agreements around mouths full of food, not willing to stop eating in order to compliment the chef. Which in itself is a compliment to the chef. The frenzied eating starts to slow down not long after, as we all shift to savoring the tempting morsels left on our plates rather than tasting each new bite of deliciousness as quickly as humanly possible.

"I think it's time," Mrs. Roberts says a few minutes later.

We all groan, knowing what's coming and pretending to hate it even though it's my favorite part of Thanksgiving. Aside from the mac and cheese.

Harley sits up a little straighter in her seat. "I'll start. Mine's easy this year." She turns to Nick, and the smile they share almost makes me want to puke up everything I just ate. "I'm so thankful for you, Nick. Thank you for loving me, and for letting me love you."

We shower them in a chorus of "Awwwwww," and Nick actually blushes.

"Can I just say ditto?" Nick asks after leaning over and planting a kiss on Harley that has her dad squirming in his seat.

"Yes, because I might throw up if I have to hear any more from the two of you." Gemma rips off a chunk of her roll and throws it at Nick, who happily picks it up and eats it.

"My turn," Mrs. Roberts volunteers. "I'm so thankful for my lovely daughter, and I'm so thankful she ended up stuck with all of you. And I'm thankful you continue to let the old folks hang out with you all, year after year."

Mr. Roberts clears his throat.

"Oh, and I'm thankful for my husband. Of course." She flashes him a blinding smile.

"And I'm thankful for you, my darling." He pats Harley on the hand. "And you, my darling."

Gemma takes a long swig of her wine. "Not going to lie, guys, there's been some times lately when I haven't felt all that grateful."

Harley and I exchange a heavy look across the table.

"But even though shit sucks sometimes, I know I can always count on everyone in this room to support me, and I'm very thankful for that."

I reach in front of Jack and squeeze her hand. When I pull my hand back, my arm brushes up against Jack's chest and his breath hitches at the contact.

Technically it should be Jack's turn since he's next to Gemma, but I decide to jump in and go first. "I have a lot to be thankful for this year, namely everyone sitting at this table. Thank you all for supporting me when I decided to pull the ultimate millennial move and open my own florist business. Thank you for listening to me plan and whine and complain, and thank you for making deliveries and pitching in any time I needed help." I angle myself slightly toward Jack. "And thank you, Jack, for being literally the world's best landlord and letting me live in your beautiful home for such a pittance it should be an actual crime. None of this would've ever happened without you and your generosity, so thank you."

The corners of his lips turn up in the sweetest smile and he gives me a look filled with such powerful emotion, if I didn't know any better, I might call it love.

Jack clears his throat, turning his attention to the table at large. "This might sound like a cop-out, but honestly, the thing I'm most thankful for in this moment is Thanksgiving." He pauses, clearing his throat again. "It's been a long time since I celebrated any sort of holiday, and for many years now, I assumed a scene like this, being surrounded by family, just wasn't in the cards for me."

I attempt to blink a lot, and surreptitiously, but I don't think it works. My heart is pounding out an accelerated rhythm in my chest, so hard it almost hurts.

Jack cocks his head in my direction. "And then this one blew into a café, late and loud, never stopped talking the whole time." He pauses while everyone at the table chuckles. "And she changed my life." He shifts in his seat, turning to face me. "You changed my life, Sadie. You brought family and friends and laughter and happiness and a whole damn floral shop into my home. Our home. And with all of that, you brought me back to life." He reaches over and takes my hand in his. "And for that, I will be eternally thankful."

I want to open my mouth and say a million things, but I know if I do, I'll completely lose my shit. So instead, I dab my eyes with my napkin, somewhat comforted to notice Harley and Mrs. Roberts doing the same, and I squeeze his hand like I don't ever want to let go. Because I don't.

"Fuck, man, how is anyone ever supposed to top that?" Nick wisecracks the emotion in the air like it's an egg.

Jack smiles and shrugs. "At least I went last, and you have a whole year to think about it."

We all laugh and dry our tears and drink more wine and eat another round of mac and cheese. And all the while, Jack keeps hold of my hand.

~

Everyone says goodbye a few hours later, buzzed on laughter and wine, sleepy from turkey and a long day. I close the door behind Gemma, who promises to come over tomorrow to help do dishes, even though she definitely won't. Not that I care—I'd do a million dishes if it meant getting to repeat this night.

Jack is in the kitchen, surveying the mountain of china and platters.

I lean my butt against the peninsula. "Don't even bother starting now, we can deal with it tomorrow."

He throws down the dish towel he was holding. "Don't have to tell me twice." He crosses over to me, landing just a few inches outside of my personal bubble.

When I definitely want him all up in my bubble. I reach out a hand, hooking my finger through the belt loop on his jeans. "Thank you for what you said tonight."

He runs his fingers along my forearm, cupping my elbow in the palm of his hand. "I meant all of it."

I give a little tug and he comes a few inches closer. "You've given me more than I could ever repay you for, Jack."

His hand travels up my arm and he takes another step in, our chests now pressed together. His other hand reaches up, his thumb tracing along my jaw. "You have given me everything."

We both inhale a deep breath, the movement bringing our bodies even closer.

He gently tilts my head up, his mouth hovering an inch away from mine. "I want to go all in, Sadie."

"Fuck yes," I breathe.

He grins and closes the space between us, with a brush of his lips so gentle I don't know if I'll even feel it.

Except I feel it.

Electricity shoots through my veins, and for a moment I'm breathless.

Jack puts the tiniest sliver of space back between us, for the tiniest sliver of a second, before his lips come crashing down on mine, and what was a bolt of electricity turns into a lightning storm. He cups the nape of my neck with those strong, perfect fingers, clutching me to him like he doesn't ever want to let me go. And I so hope he never lets me go.

My hands roam, up his back and over his chest, until they slip under his shirt and he groans into my mouth. My fingers latch on to those lean muscles, tracing each ridge and cut, skirting up over his chest, finally reaching up to the curls at the nape of his neck, twisting into them. I rise up on my toes, needing every inch of me to be pressed into every inch of him.

All the while he kisses me, his lips soft and sweet before they turn hard and demanding. I open up to him, drinking in his every breath.

When we finally part it's out of sheer necessity, both of us panting, hearts pounding, synchronized thuds beating between our pressed-together chests. Jack hoists me up on the counter, stepping between my legs, his forehead coming to rest against mine.

I place a soft, closed-mouthed kiss on his lips. "That was definitely worth the wait."

He grins, lowering his mouth and nibbling at my jaw. "Most definitely." He brings his lips back to mine, wrapping my legs around his waist and pressing into me.

His kiss is consuming, burning from my lips down to the tips of my toes, which are currently curling inside my boots.

And I want him. I want him in a way that's different from how I've ever wanted anyone before. I want him around me and over me and inside me. But I also want him next to me, and beside me, and with me.

I cup his cheeks in my hands and drag my lips from his. "Would it be totally hypocritical for me to ask if we can take this slowly?"

Jack's eyes search mine. Somewhere along the way his glasses disappeared and the green has darkened, a shady forest. "'All in' means 'all in,' Sade. However you want it. However you need it."

I wiggle my eyebrows. "Don't get me wrong, I both want and need it." I press my hips to his, feeling the evidence of his own want and need. "But I also don't want to fuck this up."

He laces our fingers together. "We're not going to fuck this up."

"I might."

He plants a soft kiss on my cheek. "I won't let you."

I loop my arms around his shoulders. "I hope you know what you're getting yourself into, Jack Thomas."

"You're not nearly as scary as you think you are, Sadie Green." He cups my ass in those big hands, pulling me from the counter. "Want to go downstairs and watch a movie?"

"Is that code for 'wanna go downstairs and make out'?"

"I mean, yes? If that's okay?" He finds his glasses and slides them back on, giving me a sheepish grin in the process. The result is so cute I want to bite him.

"Yes, that's okay. If I can put my pj's on first." I'm already heading for the stairs, running up to change. And when I meet him down in the basement, I'm dressed in my flannel pajama pants and an oversized T-shirt. And he looks at me like I'm the most beautiful thing he's ever seen.

I don't remember what movie we put on in the background because it doesn't matter. The night is for kisses and cuddles and falling asleep in Jack's embrace.

$\sim$

"Sadie." Jack's soft whisper tickles my ear.

I groan and try to roll over, but I'm trapped in the cage of Jack's arms. Which is actually a good thing because I almost rolled right off the couch. "What time is it?"

"Either super late or super early. I think it's time to head up to bed."

I nuzzle into his neck, planting sleepy kisses on his throat. "I think that depends on whose bed."

He turns his head, his lips capturing mine. "Do you have a preference?"

Never having actually seen Jack's bed, I opt for the known. "Mine, please."

We head upstairs, hand in hand. I peel off to my bathroom so I can brush my teeth. Jack heads to his own room to change.

Once in my room, I pull down the covers and shimmy out of my pajama pants. I tuck myself under the covers, pulling the duvet up to my chin. Jack comes in a minute later, having shucked his sweater and jeans for just a pair of flannel pants. He slips into bed, pulling me into his embrace. I hitch a leg over his, tangling us up completely, tucking my head underneath his chin.

He runs a hand over the bare skin of my calf. "You really had to come in here with no pants, huh?"

I splay my hand over his bare chest. "I'll have you know I hate sleeping in pants. Much as you seem to hate sleeping in a shirt."

His fingers dance up my thigh. "You probably wouldn't believe how many times I've dreamed of having these legs wrapped around me." His strong fingers grasp behind my knee, pulling me closer to him.

"I'm guessing about as many times as I've dreamed of those fingers doing... things... to me." I tilt my head up, placing a soft line of kisses along his jaw. Where it was smooth this morning, it's now stubbled and rough.

He brings his mouth down to mine. This kiss is long and slow, Jack deliberately exploring the dips and curves of my lips. He kisses me

with the attention to detail I would expect of an artist, taking everything in, noticing when his movements make me gasp, make me
moan. His mouth eventually trails down the curve of my neck. He
nibbles along my collarbone, slipping the wide neck of my T-shirt off
my shoulder.

I want to rip my shirt off and beg him to move his ministrations
lower, but I said slowly and I meant it. Even if my hips seem to invol-
untarily be rolling against Jack's thigh, firmly planted in between my
legs. My core is aching for touch, for pressure. I've never been so turned
on by a kiss before, and I want more. I need more.

"Jack," I gasp when his mouth moves back to my neck, biting me
softly before licking the light imprint of his teeth on my skin.

He pulls away, and I get my first good look at his eyes, his pupils
black and wide, the green almost as dark. "Do you want me to stop?"

I shake my head, any and all words merely an incoherent jumble in
my brain.

He puts even more space between us. "I'm sorry, Sade. You asked
for slowly, and this is clearly not slowly."

I grab his hip, pulling him back into my space, intertwining our
limbs as close as they can be. "I still want to go slowly, but I also want
you to touch me."

His already stiff cock, pressed up against my belly, hardens notice-
ably. Jack reaches down to adjust his pants.

I place my hand lightly over his. "Is this okay?"

He nods, removing his hand and setting it on top of mine, guiding
my pressure as I stroke his thick length, just a layer of flannel separat-
ing us from skin-to-skin contact. But after a second, he picks up my
hand, kissing my palm and placing it back on his hip. He brings his

mouth back to mine, his lips searing and demanding. "You first," he mutters into my neck.

"You'll find I'm never one to argue with that command." I roll my hips, producing a spine-tingling growl from Jack.

He puts a sliver of space between us. "If it goes too far, just tell me to stop. I don't want to do anything you're not ready for."

I twist my fingers into the curls at the nape of his neck, bringing his lips to mine. "I know. I trust you, Jack."

A flash of something, bright like lightning, darts through his eyes. "Sadie." My name is a breath, a whisper.

I don't let him continue, pressing my mouth to his almost desperately. His strong arms wrap completely around me, his hands flat on my back, melding us together. He holds me for a minute, tightly, as if he's worried I'll push him away. But all I want is him closer. I want him everywhere.

His hands slip under the edge of my shirt, his fingers darting across the expanse of my stomach before they circle around to my back.

Finally, I figure, fuck it. I sit up and tug my stupid shirt over my head, tossing it off to the side of the bed before flopping dramatically back on the pillows.

Jack perches above me, his eyes silently sliding over my bared skin. "You're beautiful." He reaches out a single finger, tracing over the curve of my breasts, before placing his palm flat against my stomach. "I know you've heard that before, how beautiful you are. Because it's true." He lowers his head, placing a single kiss on the flat divot at the center of my chest. "But your heart is the most beautiful thing about you, Sade."

I swallow back the lump that seems to have jumped right up in my throat. It's by far the nicest thing anyone has ever said to me while naked, and I don't know if I can handle any more of his perfection. "I'm already half-naked, Jack and the Beanstalk, you don't have to flatter me."

He trails his mouth to the right, placing kisses over the swell of my breast. "One of these days, I'll get you to admit you're a good person." His tongue flicks out, teasing my nipple, before he takes it fully in his mouth.

My hips buck and I gasp when his teeth graze my sensitive flesh. "Keep doing that and I'll nominate myself for sainthood."

He chuckles, the vibrations making me moan. His attentions turn to my other breast while I tangle my fingers in his hair, my other hand clutching his shoulder. My skin burns all over, every inch of my body lit from within. I'm a dam about to burst, so I yank Jack back up, my tongue sweeping into his mouth. The smattering of hair on his chest rubs against my tight nipples, and my hips continue to roll of their own volition.

Jack slides a hand down my belly, his fingers dancing along the edge of my panties. "This still okay?"

"Fuck yes." I hook my thumbs in the waistband and shimmy out of them, kicking them far and away.

He runs a hand down my thigh. When he lands on my knee, he presses me open, baring me to him. He nips at my jawline. "I'm tempted to tease you, make you beg for me to touch you."

"There's plenty of time for that on literally any other night." I glare at him until he moves his hand, hovering over me until I can feel the heat of his palm.

"I should've known you'd be demanding in bed." He doesn't let me respond, his lips devouring mine at the same time he paints a single finger over me.

I moan into his mouth and he grunts, his hips thrusting, his hardness caught between us. He strokes me, never moving his lips from mine, until my entire body is tight with tension. When I'm teetering on the edge, he pulls his hand back and I whimper. He swallows the sound, a devilish grin on his unrelenting lips.

When I think I might actually combust, he slides a single finger into me. I have to pull away from his mouth so I can cry out because the torture of it is exquisite. His movements are slow, deliberate, and he hits every single nerve ending in my body, teasing my clit before plunging back inside me, this time with two fingers. And when his mouth lands back on my breast, tonguing and biting my nipple, I explode, tightening around his fingers, my hips thrusting until I come down.

I take his face in my hands, dragging his lips to mine. His fingers continue to tease me, stroking lightly as our mouths melt together. My hand travels down his flat stomach, over the ridges of his lean muscles. I push his pants down just enough so I can wrap my hand around him unimpeded. He's hot and hard in my palm, and the groan he releases into my mouth almost makes me come again.

"Is this okay?" I stroke him once, over the long length of him.

"Fuck yes."

I grasp him tighter in my hand and he does the work for me, thrusting into my fist, even as he continues to stroke me, bringing me to the brink before backing off again and again until I want to scream.

"Please," I finally whimper. "Don't stop, Jack."

And he doesn't. I tighten around his fingers for the second time, crying out in release. Jack pumps into my hand harder, shuddering out his own release a second later.

We collapse back onto the pillows, Jack taking my hand in his, locking our fingers together as we catch our breath. Once his breathing has steadied, Jack climbs out of bed, disappearing into the bathroom and returning a second later with a damp washcloth. We clean ourselves up and he slides back under the covers, tucking me into his embrace.

We don't say another word. We don't need to. We just wrap ourselves around each other and fall into a blissful sleep.

I wake up first, stretching slowly and carefully, making sure I don't stir Jack out of sleep. Moving an inch at a time, I slip out from under the covers, grabbing my shirt and panties before heading into the bathroom. I spend more time in there than I really need, low-key freaking out about walking back into my room and finding it empty.

Though even if I did, the farthest Jack could go is down the hall to his own room.

Because we live together. Fuck.

I spent the previous night with my lips seemingly permanently attached to my roommate's. Not just my roommate, my landlord. The man who could decide to kick me out of his house at any time. If and when I mess this up, he can send my entire carefully constructed financial-spreadsheet life plan into total upheaval.

And yeah, I realize Jack knows me fairly well by now—I'm not exactly shy—but what are the chances his perfect self can actually handle my asshole self for the long term?

My heartbeat picks up speed and my chest tightens.

I flick down the lid of the toilet and collapse onto the seat, tucking my head between my knees.

I really fucked it up this time.

I'm 1,000 percent sure Jack is currently scrambling back to his room and will spend the rest of his day—the rest of his life—trying to avoid me, forever regretting his one-time lapse in judgment that ended with his hands down my pants.

I squeeze my thighs together, the memory alone enough to make me ache for him.

Once I've given Jack plenty of time to get the hell out of dodge, I creep back into my room. He's still there, still asleep, still burrowed under my covers. He's on his stomach, his hands tucked under the pillow. If I didn't know better, I might think he's smiling in his sleep. But that can't possibly be. There's no way he could truly be happy after what happened between us.

Climbing back onto the bed, I gingerly balance my weight so as not to shift the mattress. I shimmy over to the farthest edge, putting the absolute maximum space between us, bringing the covers up to my chin and watching him sleep like the total fucking creeper I am. This might be the last time I see his face at peace. Surely once he opens his eyes and sees us in the same bed, said beautiful face will be overcome with horror.

While Jack enjoys his peaceful slumber, I mentally start making a checklist of all the things I'll need to do when he asks me to move out.

Find a place to live, obviously, and it'll have to be cheap. Ask the bar about taking on some extra shifts since I'll never again in my life have the good fortune to pay so little in rent. Possibly see about renting a studio space as well since any apartment I can afford on my bartender salary is going to be tiny and definitely won't have room for things like floral coolers.

I'm so lost in thought, I don't even notice Jack's eyes flutter open.

"Why are you so far away?" His voice is groggy with sleep, all low and rumbly and sexy as fuck.

Which is just rude, since I know he's about to tell me to leave his perfect house and never come back.

"Sadie?" He flips over onto his back and holds out his arm. "What are you doing over there?"

"Giving you space." I curl myself up into a little ball, wanting to be as small as possible.

"I don't want space. Get your sexy ass over here." He grins, but it fades quickly. "Shit. Unless you don't want that. I can go." He tosses the covers off, revealing his still-very-much-bare chest.

"Jack, it's your house. I can go." I unfurl my limbs and slip out from under the covers. "I can stay with Harley and Gem until I find a new place. Or maybe Harley will just move in with Nick and I can take her room. That'd actually be best-case scenario, even though I don't want to push them into something they're not ready for, obviously. But I'm that desperate for a place to live, so knowing me, I'll push away."

Jack stands at the foot of the bed as I start riffling through the drawers of my dresser, not even sure what I'm looking for.

"You want to move out?"

I stop riffling, but I don't turn to look at him. "Of course I don't want to move out. But I also don't want you to have to feel like you have to let me stay here."

"Why would I feel like that?"

"Look, last night, yesterday, emotions were running high, okay?" I spin around to face him and the look in his eyes—pure unfiltered sadness—almost breaks me in two. "So I get that you said some things and did some things that you wouldn't have normally said and done and I get it. I'm not going to go all stage-five clinger and hold you to promises made in the heat of the moment."

He stares at me in silence for a minute. "Do you really think so little of me?"

My voice drops. "I think the world of you, Jack. You're the best man I've ever known. Which is how I know you'd never actually want to be with someone like me." I bite my lip, doing my best to choke back the flood of words threatening to burst out of my mouth. I won't resort to begging.

He crosses over to me, reaching out for my hand and lacing our fingers together. "Do I get any say in this, or do you just make all the decisions here?"

My lips purse, and I shake my head, unable to open my mouth without breaking down.

He tugs on my hand, pulling me into his embrace, tucking my head under his chin. "I'm not sure what you think 'all in' means, Sade, but for me it sure as fuck doesn't mean waking up the next morning and walking away from the woman I'm falling for."

I turn my head into his chest, not wanting him to see my face. "How could you ever possibly fall for an asshole like me, Jack?"

He separates us, cupping my chin in his hand, forcing me to look at him. "Stop calling my girlfriend an asshole." He tries to keep a serious face, but it doesn't work, a grin tugging at the corners of his lips. "Can I call you that?"

Has anything on this earth ever sounded so sweet as Jack Thomas's referring to me as his girlfriend? I honestly don't know what to do with his declaration, or the affection it implies, but it does something to soothe my worries. Somehow Jack's calling me "girlfriend" feels more intimate than his hand down my pants. But because I can't just accept the actual sentiment behind his words, I do what I always do and deflect. "Are you asking if you can call me 'asshole'?"

He moves his hand to the nape of my neck. "No. 'Girlfriend.'"

I don't resist when he pulls me closer. "It does make me feel like we're in seventh grade. Which I think is the last time I had a boyfriend."

"Do you want me to be your boyfriend, Sadie?" There's a wicked glint sparking in his eyes.

My lips pull down, doing their best to fight off the growing urge to smile. "Are you always going to be this cheesy?"

"Are you always going to be this stubborn?"

"Fuck yes. I can't believe you even have to ask me that."

He chuckles, leaning down to dot a line of kisses along my jaw. "Please say you'll be my girlfriend, Sadie."

"Well, since you asked so nicely." I turn my head, capturing his mouth with mine, very glad I took the time to brush my teeth during my low-key anxiety attack in the bathroom.

Jack pulls away long before I want him to. "I could do this all day, but if I don't stop kissing you now, we're going to end up back in that bed, and I don't think we'll be coming out for the rest of the day."

I rise up on my toes so I can nibble his neck. "Is that a problem for you?"

He wraps his arms around my waist, lifting me off the ground and carrying me over to the door. "No. But we've got a sink full of dishes, and I'm mostly sure you have orders you need to fulfill."

I wiggle out of his arms on the landing, not trusting anyone to carry me down a flight of stairs, no matter how perfect he seems. "Why do you have to be all practical and logical about things?"

"I don't want to distract you from your blossoming business, rosebud."

"Did you just call me rosebud?" Coffee is calling, so I head immediately for the espresso machine as soon as I reach the kitchen. "I think I'm going to have to veto that nickname."

Jack bumps his hip into mine, nudging me out of the way of the caffeine, prepping the ingredients way faster than I would've been able to. "This from the woman who calls me everything from Jack Be Nimble to Jack-o'-Lantern."

I hop up onto the counter next to him, reaching into the cabinet for two mugs, relishing this easy morning choreography between us. "Yes, but it's funny when I do it."

Jack rolls his eyes, turning a knob on the machine and watching the espresso drip into my mug. "Whatever you say, snapdragon."

"Oh god. I've created a monster." I lean over and plant a soft kiss on his lips. "Good thing you know your way around an espresso machine, Jack of Hearts."

He carefully pours steamed milk over my espresso, handing me a perfect latte and pairing it with another kiss. "I know my way around a lot of things, dandelion."

"Technically that's an herb, not a flower."

"Yeah, yeah." He turns his attention back to the coffee, making a latte for himself too.

We take our mugs over to the living room sofa, sitting and chatting about nothing of importance. Eventually we make our way back to the kitchen, tackling the mountain of dirty dishes before I head up to BaBs to work on arrangements that need to be delivered the following day. I go back downstairs to join Jack for a dinner of leftovers, followed by a "movie" on the basement couch. When bedtime rolls around, we automatically head to my room, as if we've been dancing the same routine for years. It's easy, and perfect, and I still can't fully accept Jack wants to be in this, with me, for anything remotely termed "the long haul." But my heart is full and happy, so I decide to ride the wave for as long as I can.

⌒

ME: Soooooooooooooooooo

GEMMA: Oh my god. Finally.

ME: You don't even know what I'm going to say.

GEMMA: We totally know what you're going to say.

GEMMA: Harley, do we not know what she's going to say?

HARLEY: How about we just let her say?

ME: Thank you, Harley.

ME: . . .

ME: I kissed Jack.

GEMMA: Okay, I'll admit, that was slightly less graphic than I was expecting.

GEMMA: Did said kissing lead to the horizontal tango?

ME: Who says that?

ME: And no. It did not. We're taking things slowly.

HARLEY: I think Gem just fell off her bed.

GEMMA: Yeah. I absolutely did. Did you just say you're taking things slowly?

ME: Yup. And I'm dying, I want him so bad.

ME: But I think this is the right decision.

HARLEY: Wow. I'm proud of you, Sade. And happy for you, obvs. Jack is amazing!

                    ME: He is, isn't he. *sigh*

GEMMA: Oh god. She's been replaced by one of those relationship pod people. It's all over now.

~

JACK: You working tonight?

           ME: Yup. I got the early shift so hopefully I can manage to get some sleep before deliveries tomorrow.

JACK: What time do you think you'll be home?

                    ME: Hopefully by ten.

JACK: Want me to grab dinner?

          ME: Nah, I can just get something there when I take my break.

                    ME: Thanks though 😊

JACK: In that case, how about dessert? 😉

ME: How about you have a bath ready for me when I get home and we'll talk.

JACK: You got it, sweet pea.

ME: Fuck.

JACK: What?

ME: I kinda like that one.

FIFTEEN

HE BAR IS crazy busy, and though I'm happy for the fat stack of tips currently building up in my apron, I was mostly hoping for a calm night. The holiday season is in full swing, at both the bar and Bridge and Blooms. I've had multiple deliveries to make every day this week, and I've got a full morning of running around Brooklyn ahead of me tomorrow. My feet are already aching. Jack better have been serious about that bath, because I'm going to need it.

I've got an hour left on the shift countdown clock when I see a short head of straight dark hair pushing its way through the crowd.

Gem elbows her way onto the one open bar stool, giving me a tight smile that doesn't come close to touching her eyes.

I pour her a glass of wine and head down to her end of the bar. Setting down the glass, I lean over and give her a quick hug. "I didn't know you were coming in tonight."

She takes a long sip of her wine. "I didn't either. But Harley and Nick are at the apartment and I just needed a break, you know?"

Nodding, I rest both elbows on the bar in front of her, taking some of the weight off my feet in the process.

She eyes me warily. "Jack isn't showing up here anytime soon, is he?"

"Not that I know of."

"Good. I can only handle so much adorableness in one night." After another swig, her glass is almost empty.

I reach for an empty glass and fill it with water, pushing it over to her. "What's going on, Gem?"

"Uh-oh, have you turned into one of those bartender-slash-therapists?" Her words are cutting, but I've known her long enough to know I shouldn't take it personally.

"Nope. I don't give a shit about other people's problems unless those other people happen to be my best friends. Then I want to know why she looks like I just told her *Top Chef* was canceled." I nudge the water glass closer to her, and once she takes a begrudging sip, I refill her wine.

"Don't even speak those words into the universe," she mutters. "I don't really want to sit here and complain about how my job sucks and I hate it and how I'm super miserable while all of my best friends are pairing up with their perfect partners and living happily ever after." She runs both hands through her hair, letting it fall in front of her face like a curtain.

I don't bother telling her that Jack and I have been together for maybe five minutes and are nowhere near happily ever after yet. Or that Harley and Nick fretted about their feelings for each other for months before finally having the guts to give it a shot. I let her sit for a minute, tending to other customers until I see her emerge from her shell.

"So," I say, as if our conversation never halted. "You wouldn't have come here if you didn't want to talk. There are at least twenty bars between your place and here. Clearly you wanted to vent, and clearly, I'm going to listen. So have at it."

"I hate my job." She drinks some more wine, but this time, in a reasonable measure. "I don't know why I keep hanging in there, thinking things will get better. They're not going to get better." As she says the words out loud, it's like they finally sink in, and her face comes close to crumpling. But she pulls it together before completely breaking down.

Seeing how on the verge of losing it she is, I skip the pity and go straight to problem-solving. "Okay. If you could be doing anything in the world right now, if money and bills and all that shit weren't an issue, what would you want to do?"

"I'm not sure. But possibly something in the restaurant industry." She doesn't look at me when she says this, as if she's admitting some kind of dirty secret.

"I think that'd be awesome for you." Because duh, the girl can cook her ass off.

"But it'd be super irresponsible of me to leave a steady job, with benefits and retirement, and attempt to break into a field I have zero experience in. Especially one that's as unstable as the restaurant business." This time she does look at me, her big brown eyes almost pleading. "Right? That'd be super irresponsible?"

I gesture to our surroundings. "You're not exactly asking the right person if you want to hear that it would be stupid to quit your job, Gem."

She takes another large gulp from her wineglass. "Yeah, well, my quitting definitely wouldn't come along with a brownstone room at a shoebox price."

"Well, how about this? You start looking for a restaurant job in late May, see what's out there. Get hired because you're a badass. Work through the summer and see how it goes. If you love it, quit teaching. If it's not for you, go back to school at the end of summer." I stop polishing glasses so I can lean back on the bar, putting us face-to-face. "I'm not going to lie to you and tell you a career change is easy, because it's not. I've been super lucky to have you guys and stupid-cheap rent, and I've still had plenty of moments of wanting to throw in the towel and go back to the stability of finance. But I guess the good news about teaching is you have the summer off to give things a trial run."

She considers my words for several quiet moments. "That's actually not a terrible idea."

"Duh. Since when do I have terrible ideas?" I hold up my hand the second she opens her mouth to respond. "Don't answer that. Think you could survive the rest of the school year if you knew it might be the last few months you have to endure?"

"It might actually be the only thing making them bearable."

The wheels inside Gemma's mind are turning; I can tell by the dreamy look in her eyes and the frown lines furrowing her forehead. I flick the creases with my finger. "You're gonna get wrinkles."

"Yeah yeah." She rolls her eyes, but there's a tug of a real smile for the first time since she walked in. "Thank you for listening to me complain."

Twirling my hand, I give her a courtly bow. "'Twas an honor and a privilege."

She finishes the last of her wine. "You off soon?"

"Yup. You want to stick around?"

"Sure." She holds up her glass for another refill. "And then bring me my check so I don't drink any more."

I wave her off. "On the house. As is the therapy." She starts to push a twenty across the counter anyway, but I reach over and stick it down her shirt. "Seriously, Gem. Put it in your I-wanna-quit-my-life-suck-of-a-job fund."

I rush through the rest of my closing-out duties, stocking and cleaning and tallying up receipts. Gemma and I walk out of the bar a half hour later, arms linked and huddled together for warmth. The December temperatures dropped seemingly overnight, and the air is chilly around us.

About a block from the brownstone, Gemma stops in her tracks. She tugs on my arm, pulling me over to a brick building, pressing her face way too close to a window with a For Lease sign hanging in it. "Look at this space, Sade."

I give it an obligatory peek. "I'm all for quitting teaching and pursuing what you love, but even I know restaurants are a terrible investment. You might want to work in one first before you think about opening one."

She elbows me in the gut. "Not for me, asshole. For you." She yanks me closer, practically pushing my face up to the smudged glass. "This would be a great spot for the first Bridge and Blooms shop."

I pull her away from the window. "Yeah, I definitely am not big enough to be able to afford whatever astronomical rent they're asking."

Tucking my arm back into hers, I drag her away from the building and toward home.

Home. It still tickles me, bringing an automatic smile to my face when I think of the brownstone as home. When I think of Jack as home.

But Gemma doesn't let the subject drop. "You at least have to check it out. It could be way more affordable than you think. And who knows, maybe you could get investors. Look how much business has grown in just a few months."

I brush off her suggestion because on the surface it sounds crazy. I can't afford Brooklyn rent. And to turn an empty space into a shop takes money and employees and licenses and permits and all kinds of things I don't want to think about. "I just want to arrange flowers, Gem. And I've got the perfect setup in my very own home. Why would I want to spend all that money opening up a shop when I have this gorgeous studio space right upstairs?"

We reach my front stoop, and Gemma stops at the bottom stair. "This would be all yours, Sade."

She doesn't say it, but the implication is there. What I have now isn't all mine. My studio is Jack's. And so much of my success is due to the incredible rent deal, also provided to me by Jack. And while I certainly don't plan on driving a wedge between us anytime soon, the facts support its happening at some point. Almost undoubtedly because of me. And where will my business be then?

"Fine. I'll think about it." I gesture to the front door. "You wanna come in?"

"Go from one happy couple to the other? No thanks." She slips her phone from her purse, calling for a Lyft.

"I'll wait with you." I toss my arm around her shoulders, pulling her close to me for warmth. And because I know she needs a hug but would never dream of asking for one. "Whatever you decide to do, you know we'll all be here for you. And Jack or no Jack, you're my number one. I've always got your back."

"So much same." Her car pulls up, and we wrap each other in a final hug. "Love you."

"Love you too. Text me when you get home." I make a mental note of the car's license plate number. Just in case.

I pull out my own phone while I wait for her to get in the car and take off.

> **ME:** I'm out front. Bath ready?

> **JACK:** You know it, pink peony.

> **ME:** What happened to sweet pea?

> **JACK:** Gotta keep you on your toes.

My phone beeps with an incoming photo.

The bath is drawn. And Jack's already in it.

I race up the stairs of the stoop and push through the front door. "Honey, I'm home!"

～

After deliveries the next day, I plop down on the couch in the living room. Everything aches. Even after a very hot, very "relaxing" bath the night before, my muscles are protesting the constant motion of the past few days. Between deliveries and bar shifts, I feel like I've been on my feet for a week straight.

Jack bounds down the stairs a minute later. "I thought I heard you come in."

"I'm dead." I fling one arm over my face, the other dangling off the side of the couch. If the floristry business doesn't work out, I might have a future in acting.

He sits on the end of the couch, taking my feet in his lap. Making good use of those strong fingers, he presses into the balls of my feet until I'm literally moaning out loud. He gives me a bemused smile. "Would another bath help?"

"Probably. But only if you're not in it, and even then I don't know if I can ever fully relax in a bath again after last night." The water wasn't the only thing that was hot, if you know what I mean. "I'm like one of Pavlov's dogs. See bath, get turned on."

"What if I promise to stay out of the bath, and also promise to take care of resulting turned on–ness whenever you're ready for me?" He moves his hands up to my calves, those fingers kneading my aching muscles.

"That offer sounds like it's too good to be true." I prop myself up on my elbows so I can look at his adorable face properly. "What's the catch?"

"You let me take you out to dinner tonight."

"So you're actually offering me a massage, then a bath, then an orgasm, then dinner?" I flop back on the couch. "Now I know I must be dreaming."

He stands, gently replacing my feet back on the sofa, before heading up the stairs to my bathroom. "I usually like to go for two."

"Two what?"

He winks at me. "Orgasms."

⌇

Two hours later, dressed in comfy jeans and bundled up in our cozy coats, we head out of the brownstone and over to PDA Pizza, all the while indulging in a little PDA ourselves. Jack takes my hand the moment we reach street level, lacing our fingers together, his thumb rubbing my knuckles as we walk.

It's weird.

Nice, of course. But weird. I wasn't actually exaggerating when I told him my last boyfriend was in junior high. I don't do relationships, I certainly don't do living with boyfriends, and I sure as hell don't do PDA. But the warmth of Jack's palm pressed against mine, and the steady feel of his walking beside me—well. It does things. To my insides. They're considerably warmer and squishier than ever before. And I like it. I like him.

Not even Jack's hands are enough to distract me as we walk by the space for lease, still just a block away from the brownstone, still empty and waiting. I subconsciously drift closer to the brick building, my eyes roaming the window as if there might've been some change in the less than twenty-four hours since I last saw it.

Jack notices my distracted gaze and pulls us out of the way of foot traffic. "What's this?"

I tug on his hand, not wanting to get into all of that while we're on our way to dinner, but he doesn't budge. "Nothing. Just a space for lease Gem noticed last night when we were walking home."

He cups his hand against the smudged glass, leaning in to get a better look. "You didn't mention it last night."

"I was distracted for some reason." I bump his hip with mine. "And it's no big deal. Really, nothing to mention."

"Have you been thinking about opening a storefront?" He pulls away from the glass, eyes searching mine.

"No." I pretend to be casually looking through the window, but really I'm just avoiding his gaze. "I mean, it'd be a big step, and not one I can afford at the present moment. I don't know if I'm ready for such a huge leap."

"Did you look to see what they're asking for rent?"

"Nah. No need." I tug on his hand again. "Let's go. All those orgasms made me hungry."

But the man will not be deterred. He doesn't even blush at my mention of multiple orgasms. Instead he takes out his phone, punching in the number listed on the sign.

"Jack, what are you doing?" Shifting my weight between my feet, I'm tempted to reach up and try to grab his phone from him. "I said I wasn't interested."

"No, you didn't. You said you didn't know if you're ready." He holds up a hand to stop me from responding, turning his attention to whoever is on the other end of his phone call. "Hi, yes, my name's Jack Thomas, and I'm interested in your space for lease on Sixth in Park Slope." He's quiet for a minute, nodding and driving me crazy, giving me no indication of what's being said. "Oh, great. Yeah, we're right out front. See you soon."

"See you soon? See who soon?"

He tucks his phone back in the pocket of his jeans. "The Realtor's finishing up a meeting a block away, she said she'll be here in five."

"Jack, we shouldn't be wasting this poor woman's time when I have no intention of leasing this space." I shove my hands into the pockets of my coat, under the guise of needing the warmth but really needing a little bit of space.

"What's the harm in looking, sweet pea?" He shrugs, slipping his own hands into the pockets of his jacket. "If you don't like it, no damage done."

"I'm not worried about not liking it," I mutter. I've given the space enough of my thoughts over the past day to know I'll probably like it. Scratch that. I'm definitely going to like it.

"So then what's the problem?" He pushes his glasses up, as if he can't fathom what the problem might be.

And he can't.

Sometimes I forget, but moments like this are a stark reminder of one of the biggest differences between us. Jack doesn't have to worry about money. From what I can tell, he's never had to worry about money. He's so low-key about it, it can be easy to brush aside the knowledge that the man outright owns a brownstone. In New York. And a two-million-dollar home in Connecticut. Whether he abuses the privilege or not, the simple fact is if Jack wants something, he has the means to acquire it.

I collect my thoughts before stepping into him, tilting my chin up so I can look in his eyes. "Jack. I can't afford this. And the harm with looking is it can make me want things I know I can't have. Which can cause me to make bad decisions. And I don't like making bad decisions. It's why I haven't gone shopping since I got fired. I know my limits. When I see something, I go for it, even if it ends up costing me in the end."

Jack considers my words thoughtfully. "If it's purely about money, there are things you can do, Sade. You could look for investors."

"I don't even have a real business plan." I tuck my hands under his arms, trying not to fixate on how both he and Gemma suggested investors like they're an actual possibility.

"You have a business degree, right?"

I nod.

"So write a business plan. Think about how far Bridge and Blooms has come in the past few months. How much you've been able to grow your business even just working out of the kitchen. I'm sure there are tons of investors who'd be interested." He leans down and plants a soft kiss on my upturned lips. "And if there aren't—which there will be— then you happen to have one right here."

I take a step back. "No." I shake my head, as if the very clear declaration isn't enough. "Nope. No way. I don't want your money, Jack. I don't want you giving me this space."

He holds up his hands in mock surrender. "First off, I wouldn't be giving it to you. It'd be an investment. Second, I believe in your business and would be happy to support you. And third, I . . ." He trails off, running a hand through his curls, making them stand straight up in a really stupid-cute way.

"Third?" Stepping back into his bubble, I grab the front of his coat.

"I want you to be happy."

"I don't need you to buy me a business in order to make me happy, Jack of Diamonds."

"I feel like that one is a little on the nose for this particular moment." He wraps his arms around my waist, pulling me into his chest. "Let's just look at the space and go from there, yeah? You might not even like it."

"Jack Thomas?" A chipper voice, accompanied by the click-clack of high heels on concrete, interrupts us. A woman in her midthirties, dressed in fantastic skinny jeans, an emerald-green silk blouse, and a black blazer under her wool coat sticks out her hand for Jack to shake. "Kristen Sullivan. Pleasure to meet you." She holds out her hand to me next.

"Sadie Green."

Her shake is firm and quick. She gestures to the front door of the storefront. "Shall we?"

Jack and I follow her into the building, and I realize I've been holding my breath. When we cross the threshold, it slowly trickles out of me. Kristen flicks on the overhead lights and gestures widely to the open space.

Jack stays by Kristen as she starts rattling off facts about the property. Size, square footage, blah blah blah.

I wander around the room, trying and failing not to let my imagination run away with me. The coolers could go in the back corner, out of the way enough to not draw attention. The front windows could be filled with seasonal blooms, and the area in front of the exposed brick wall would make a great display backdrop. There's room for a large counter in the middle where I could work. I like the idea of customers' being able to see arrangements being put together while they shop. The vision pops into my head a little too clearly, already formed and morphing to fit the space.

Jack continues to ask likely pertinent and important questions as I make my way to the back hallway. There's a small bathroom and a tiny office, and a door leading outside. I unlock it and push it open, barely registering the blast of cold air as I reenter the December evening.

"What the fuck," I mutter to myself, coming to a halt in the middle of an outdoor space.

I was expecting an alley filled with trash. Instead, I'm standing in the center of a large (by Brooklyn standards) plot of dirt. It's fenced in and completely bare and basically begging me to plant it full of gorgeous flowers. With a space this big, I'd be able to source my own blooms. Or a lot of them anyway.

But I shake my head at the thought. I didn't pay attention when Kristen dropped the price, knowing no matter what number she revealed it'd be too much for me.

"Sade?" Jack peeks his head out the back door before joining me in the expansive outdoor area. "Whoa."

"Yeah." My mind is racing, darting off in a million different directions. But I keep my face totally neutral, not wanting to reveal how much I like the space. How much I could actually envision this as some kind of real possibility.

How absolutely perfect it would be.

Jack studies me for a second. "What do you think?"

I shrug, shoving my hands in the back pockets of my jeans, turning to head inside. "It's all right."

He purses his lips, following me without a word.

"What did you think of the outdoor space?" Kristen looks up from typing on her phone when we come back into the main room.

"It's big."

She nods, her eyes scanning me from head to toe as she sizes me up. "Jack mentioned you're a florist. There's a lot of ways you could utilize the room."

"Yeah. I'm just not sure I'm ready to make that kind of commitment." Ignoring the steady burn of Jack's eyes on me, I reach out my hand to shake Kristen's even as I head for the door. "Thank you so much for your time."

"Please let me know if anyone else expresses interest," Jack mutters to her as I push my way outside.

He doesn't take my hand as we resume our walk to dinner. I expect a barrage of questions, a litany of reasons why I should lease the space, why I should push myself and go for it. But he stays quiet, letting me burrow deep into my own thoughts.

It's exactly what I need.

We grab a table at the small pizza restaurant, ordering wine and a pie to share and not saying anything to each other until we each have a full glass of red sitting in front of us.

"How much?" I finally relent, letting the question burst from me, knowing I won't be able to focus on anything else until I can fully write off even the remote possibility of this happening.

Jack sits back in his chair. "It's not cheap, but it could be worse."

"How much?" I hold up my hand and gulp down half of my wine. "Okay, now tell me."

"You'd need at least a hundred to secure the lease for a year. Plus whatever else you'd need to spend to get the space set up how you want it." He watches me over the rim of his glass as he takes a much smaller sip of his own wine.

A genuine smile spreads across my face. "I'm actually kind of relieved."

His brow furrows. "You are?"

"Yeah. I mean, it's not an unexpected number, but it's definitely high enough that I don't even need to think about it any further. I can't afford anything close to that, so we can just put the whole thing to bed." If I let myself think on it, I could start to get really pissed that he made me see the space even though I told him it was too much. Because now I know how awesome it could be. Now I'll spend the next few weeks thinking about what kind of shelves I'd buy and how I'd create the window display.

I'll be thinking about how gorgeous Jack's paintings would look hanging on that stupid brick wall.

I never should've gone in there. But at the same time, it somehow feels like I was meant to see it.

Jack crosses his arms, leaning on the tiny table, putting his face a foot away from mine. "You do realize that number is a pittance to many investors, right? You could get that in a heartbeat, Sade."

I purse my lips so I don't take him to task for referring to over a hundred thousand dollars as a pittance. "I don't want an investor, Jack. I don't want to be beholden to anyone but myself."

"If you won't take my money, what about asking Nick?" He leans back as the server arrives with our pizza, setting it in the middle of the table and handing each of us a plate.

Pulling a slice from the pie, I slide it onto my plate quickly before the crust has a chance to burn my fingers. "Mixing friendship and business is almost as bad as mixing sex and business."

Jack pauses in the middle of freeing his own slice. "I really hope you aren't suggesting this is just sex, sweet pea."

Rolling my eyes and huffing out a breath at the same time doesn't hide the small smile tugging on my lips at his declaration. "It's obviously more than sex, Jack of Hearts."

"You've really run out of new nickname options, huh?"

"I happen to like Jack of Hearts, and it fits in the moment, thank you very much." Blowing on the still-hot pizza, I take a large bite.

We both sit in silence for a minute. My mind keeps wandering back to the storefront, and I keep swigging my wine, trying to erase all images of it from my brain.

"Look." Jack finally breaks the silence after the waiter comes around to refill our wineglasses. "I don't want to push you into something you're truly not ready for. But I've seen you attack this business with a ferocity that leaves me with no doubt you'd make a storefront a success. You're unstoppable, Sadie, and it doesn't seem like you to hold back when you really want something." He reaches across the table and takes my hand in his. "If you really don't want it, then this is the last time I'll mention it. But if you do think there's even a chance you want to go for it, I can put out some feelers, talk to my financial guy and see if he knows anyone who might be interested in becoming a silent partner."

I'm tempted to just shoot him down right now and put us all out of our misery. But he's trying, and he's just so damn nice, I don't want to put a damper on the evening. "I'll think about it."

"And if you need to skip rent for a few months, or more than a few months—"

"Jack. Stop." I set down my slice of pizza. "We've been together five minutes. You're my first boyfriend in fifteen years. You're going to need to slow shit down, like several notches."

He grins, his green eyes sparkling even behind the lenses of his glasses. "At the risk of sounding like a total sap, I really like it when you call me your boyfriend."

I wad up my napkin and throw it at him. "You are a total sap." But I rise up in my seat and lean over the table to plant a kiss on his waiting lips. "It's a good thing you're cute."

"Cute enough for you to just take my money?"

"So cute I refuse to take your money." I turn my attention back to my pizza. "But you can totally pay for dinner."

After another bottle of wine, Jack pays the tab and grabs our leftover pizza. We walk back to the brownstone, and I tense up when we pass the space. The possible brick-and-mortar location of Bridge and Blooms. And I definitely feel a little tug of possibility, but I'm grateful when we pass by it without Jack's mentioning a word.

Back at home, we change into our pajamas and climb under the sheets of my bed, immediately wrapping ourselves up in each other. Jack falls asleep almost instantly, the bastard.

I spend the next few sleepless hours mapping every possibility in my brain. What I'd need for the shop. The associates I'd need to hire. The business plan I'd need to create.

When I break it up into small, doable-sounding tasks, the whole idea becomes a hell of a lot less overwhelming. At the very least, it might be worth sketching out a budget. Seeing how much I'd really need to spend up front. Calculating how much I'd need to bring in each month in order to break even, how much I'd need to turn a profit. These are all things I'm capable of doing. Shit, numbers and spreadsheets were my life up until a few months ago.

I finally disengage from Jack's embrace, scooting over to the side of the bed so I can lie flat on my back, staring up at the ceiling. I know when the numbers shake out it won't be impossible. The upfront cost will sound daunting, and it will definitely be risky, but when I truly break it down, and compare it to what I've been bringing in over the past few months, it won't be totally out of the question. I'd be putting everything on the line, but if it worked, it could turn a big profit. The real question would be whether I can handle someone else's owning a stake in a business that's taken root—pun intended—inside my very heart.

"You okay?" Jack's raspy mumble pulls me out of my thoughts.

I turn on my side to face him, unable to hold back a smile when I see his adorable sleepy face. "Just thinking."

He reaches out an arm, draping it over my waist and pulling me back into him. "You know whatever you decide, I'll support you. Whatever you need."

I lean over and kiss his cheek. "I know." I hesitate before speaking again but bank on his being only half awake for this conversation and therefore not super likely to remember the details. "I think I'm just scared of the idea of other people relying on me. Employees and investors. If I screw up, then other people lose out. If I keep things small, the only person who loses out is me. And maybe you if I can't pay rent."

"I promise not to evict you." He tucks me into his embrace, planting a soft kiss on my shoulder. "I want to see you live your dreams,

Sade. I gave mine up a long time ago; you shouldn't have to give up on yours."

I pull away from him, brow furrowing at that cryptic comment. "What dreams did you have to give up?"

But he's already fallen back asleep. Leaving me with even more endless questions to keep me awake.

SIXTEEN

*J*ACK IS STILL asleep—seriously, bastard—when I slide out of bed the following morning. I dress in jeans, my stolen Captain America hoodie, and Uggs; grab my laptop; leave a note for Jack on the kitchen counter; and head out.

I need to see all of this—numbers and commitments and a real business plan—in black and white. It's the only way I'll truly be able to make an informed decision, the only way I can finally put the whole thing to rest. Or dive in headfirst.

Walking over to Café Regular, I purposefully pass by the storefront one more time. Not much has changed since the night before, obviously. The windows are still smudged, a For Lease sign still propped inside. The brick is still hipster and cool. And even though I can't see it, the outdoor space is still practically begging for a garden.

I let the sight of it fuel me, ordering a large vanilla latte and holing up at a table in the corner, ready to hunker down for the day.

The morning is filled with numbers and research and figuring out how much it costs to have employees. Once I have an estimate for monthly expenses, I break it down by week, and then by day. I use that number to figure out how many arrangements I'd need to sell each day and how much they'd need to be priced at. I price out utilities, and taxes, and health care, and décor. And as much as I've never regretted leaving my career in finance, I've never been more grateful for it.

After googling a hundred examples of successful business plans, I make edits and adjustments to the original one I wrote for Bridge and Blooms to include the storefront and all the new numbers. It's probably a little sassier than needed, but I figure anyone who's going to write me a check for a couple hundred grand should know what they're getting themselves into.

Around noon and latte number three, my phone buzzes.

> **JACK:** I don't want to interrupt you while you're in
> the zone, just wanted you to know I'm around if
> you need anything.

His words make me smile. It's still kind of mind-blowing how he's able to tell exactly what I need in any particular moment. Whether it's space or silence or a hug, it's like he can see inside my brain and determine how best to soothe me. If this is what having a boyfriend is all about, I've been missing out.

But something tells me Jack is not your average boyfriend.

> **ME:** Thanks, babe. I'm probably going to be out for
> a couple more hours, but I'll let you know when
> I'm heading home.

JACK: Sounds good. You're killing it, sweet pea.

                                                 ME: Thanks, Jackpot.

                ME: And yes I know, I've used that one before. Can I
                  help it if I feel like I won the boyfriend lotto,
                                aka the Jackpot?

JACK: Shit. That was sappy as hell.

                      ME: This is what you've done to me.

JACK: I like it.

                                    ME: 😌

I tuck my phone back in my purse so I'm not tempted to spend the rest of the day exchanging flirtatious texts with Jack. Instead, I read over all my documents and spreadsheets again, before compiling them in a file and emailing them over to Nick. I find him on G-chat so I won't be tempted by my phone.

                ME: Hey. I just sent you a whole file of shit.
                    Can you look at it and tell me what
                            you think?

NICK: Is this about the storefront?

ME: Good god, are there no secrets among us anymore?

NICK: Gem told us the other night and Jack mentioned it this morning.

ME: Jack mentioned it? How so? What did he say? Is he trying to finagle something?

NICK: Oh my god, chill. He just said you guys found a cool space last night but that you seemed really against him giving you the money.

ME: I'm not taking his money.

NICK: If you wanna throw away $200k from a man who is clearly beyond when it comes to you, not my place to try and change your mind.

ME: See, the way you phrased that makes it seem like you want to change my mind.

NICK: I'd take his money.

ME: That's because you've always had money and you don't know what a serious power imbalance it'd create in our relationship.

NICK: Yeah yeah. It's free money.

                                          ME: It's not free.

             ME: I really like him, Nicky. I don't want to fuck
                                           this up.

NICK: I don't want you to fuck this up either.

             ME: Thanks for the vote of confidence. Can you
                    look everything over please?

NICK: Yeah, give me an hour.

I spend the hour doing more research. All right, much of said research happens on Pinterest, but it still counts. Trying to find the cutest DIY ways to spruce up the shop is a 100 percent productive use of my time.

My phone chirps almost exactly sixty minutes after our conversation.

NICK: Is there any way you can set up an
appointment with the Realtor for this afternoon?
I'd like to meet you both there, take some pics, add
them to your business plan so I can pass it along to
some people.

                                            ME: Um, yes?

ME: You think it's ready for that? You think I'm
ready for that?

NICK: I'm not gonna lie, it's a risk, but I think you've
got a solid presentation and an opportunity for
decent profit. Let me know when to meet you.

Two hours later, after running home to change into something less college finals week, I meet Nick and Kristen back in front of the store. Before she even opens the door, Nick peppers her with questions, and this time, I actually listen, making note of utilities and décor restrictions and permit requirements.

Nick snaps photos as we walk and talk, jotting down notes, and once even pulling out a measuring tape to check the numbers. After a quick but thorough inspection of the outdoor garden, Nick asks Kristen to give us a minute. She's already got her phone pressed to her ear as she makes her way back out front.

He doesn't say anything for a minute, flipping through the pages of my business plan on his iPad screen.

I shift my weight from one foot to another about a hundred times before I finally can't take it anymore. "So? What do you think?"

He looks up from his screen, giving me a soft smile. "I think you should go for it."

"Really?" Based on my morning of numbers and calculations and projections, I know a profit is a ways off, and certainly not guaranteed. But it definitely boosts my confidence to hear it's possible from someone who knows what he's talking about. "And you think you might have some people who could be interested? I think we're going to have to move fast or this place is going to get snatched up."

"I'm sure I could find someone."

"Okay. Can we get that ball rolling, like today preferably?" Now that I've made the decision, I need this place to be mine. My brain has latched on to all the possibilities and I want contracts signed and keys in hand.

"I could. But I'm not going to." He crosses his arms over his chest, like he's preparing for a standoff. "Let me do this with you, Sade."

I open my mouth to list all the reasons why it's a terrible idea.

"Stop. Just listen for one minute, okay?"

I glare at him, but I purse my lips and tap the nonexistent watch on my wrist.

"This is a good investment. I spent the afternoon double-checking your numbers, and everything checks out. You know I've always had plans to invest in some small businesses, and if I'm going to invest this money in someone's risky idea, why shouldn't it be yours?" He drops his hands, placing one on my shoulder. "I know you want to say no, but—"

"Of course I want to say no, Nicky. Not because I'm not grateful or because I don't trust you, I just worry about what this could do to our friendship if things don't work out." Losing Nick might actually be worse than losing Jack at this point, he's been a staple in my life for so long. And even if I trust Nick implicitly, which I do, there are no guarantees in business. My old job burned that lesson in my brain. Would he hold it against me if I ended up losing his money?

"Nothing could ever change our friendship. You mean way more to me than money, Sadie." He gives me a little shake. "I have the means, you have the idea. You're family. Let's do this together."

Ugh. He had to go and pull the family card. He knows how I feel about that. Nonetheless, it works. Because the pro side of going into business with one of my best friends might be even stronger than the con side. Why shouldn't I take this opportunity to put the fate of my business in the hands of someone I trust? Someone I know will always have my back and my best interests in mind. Someone I know will never screw me over or betray me.

But I can't let him win this too easily. "If—and that's a big if—I were to agree, you'd be acting as a silent partner. Emphasis on the silent."

"Not like you'd let me get a word in anyway."

"And friendship comes first. Always. If shit starts to get weird, either I'm buying you out or I'm finding someone else to buy you out." Because the thought of anything coming along and busting up our fearsome foursome is unacceptable.

"I can live with that." He starts tapping away on the iPad, like he's drawing up the contract as we speak.

"What's your number?" I hold my breath, even though I know he's going to be more than fair.

"Two hundred for twenty percent."

"Fifteen." I hold out my hand.

"Done." Nick clasps my hand in his, giving me a firm shake before pulling me in for a hug. He then gives me an actual noogie. "I would've taken ten."

I push him away from me. "I would've given you twenty."

For a minute we just look at each other, grins of disbelief wide on our faces. Then Nick heads out front to talk to Kristen, and I stand in the center of the empty space that's now mine. My store. My business.

I can't believe this is my life.

Until the closet in the back of my brain cracks open and that mostly-shoved-away negative talk starts to creep out.

You think you can do this?

There's no way you can do this.

You could never accomplish something like this.

"Sade, let's go." Nick waves me out the front door, closing up the shop and my inner voice behind him.

Kristen promises to have contracts in our email by the end of the day, and as long as nothing weird comes up, keys should be in my hands in two weeks.

We wave goodbye, and I practically skip along the sidewalk. "Nicky, you just signed up to be tied to me for life. How does it feel?"

"I'm sure you want me to make some kind of sarcastic retort about how I'm already in a deep state of regret, but I'm not doing that. I'm pumped. You're going to rock the shit out of this, and I'm happy to be along for the ride."

"Silently, of course." I combat my bitchiness by looping my arm through his.

"Of course."

We reach the brownstone a minute later—hello, best commute ever—and jog up the front steps.

I'm all set and ready to bellow my usual greeting, but as soon as I open the door, I hear a cork popping. One of my all-time favorite sounds.

Gemma, Harley, and Jack are waiting for us in the kitchen with champagne and cheers. We all pile in for a big group hug, and after a toast and the clinking of glasses, I pull Jack off to the side.

He runs his thumb over my cheek. "I'm so proud of you, sweet pea. You're going to kill it."

I lean up for a quick kiss, head and heart equally bolstered by his continued faith in me. "You're not mad?"

"Why would I be mad?" His brow furrows.

I smooth out the wrinkles with my finger. "Because I wouldn't take your investment, but I took Nick's."

He loops his arms around my waist. "Are you happy, Sadie?"

I bite my lip to control the insane grin threatening to take over my face. "I literally have never been happier."

"That's all that matters to me, sweet pea."

The keys to the storefront are placed in my grabby hands five days before Christmas. The whole group is there with me to celebrate, Gemma streaming the whole exchange on my Instagram. My followers are already asking for renovation updates, and the store transformation is going to be social media gold.

The following couple of days consist of cleaning and painting, two of my least favorite things, but necessary steps in order to be ready for the good stuff that's to come after the holiday. I do a fair amount of online shopping, trying to find repurposed and upcycled pieces for the store. And I draw up a preliminary plan for the back garden, mapping out what blooms I want to go where. I'm going to turn part of BaBs into a mini greenhouse so I can start germinating seeds in January, and I need to figure out which kinds of flowers will be the best bang for my buck.

It's a whirlwind couple of days, and I'm happy to take a break with the rest of the crew on Christmas Eve. Christmas itself is one of the few holidays we don't usually spend together. Gemma heads home to Virginia for the Kwon family celebration. Harley and her parents usually travel out of town the week between Christmas and New Year's. And Nick's presence is required at his grandmother's under threat of losing his trust fund.

For me, Christmas means Chinese food and vintage Real Housewives, and luckily when I present this plan to Jack, he wholeheartedly signs off.

We arrive home at the brownstone late on Christmas Eve, after spending the evening at Gem and Harley's place, stuffing our faces with Italian food and drinking a fair amount of wine. The cold night air sobered us both up quite a bit during our walk home, and as soon as the front door closes behind me, Jack has me pressed up against it, his mouth covering mine. No two of Jack's kisses are ever the same, and this one is devouring.

"Merry Christmas," he says when he finally pulls away.

I have to catch my breath before I can respond. "Merry Christmas."

He gives me a wicked grin. "Should we do presents now?"

"Um, yes. Obviously." I agonized over what to get Jack because hello, what does one buy for the nerd who has everything? But I found the perfect gift when I was pillaging a nearby antiques shop, and I'm desperately excited to see his reaction. Also slightly terrified. "I need you to open yours first, though." As cool as my gift to Jack is, I'm 99 percent sure he's going to upstage me.

He kisses me on the cheek before heading over to the living room sofa. We've set up a small tree in front of the window, and since we just got back from our main holiday gathering, only one present remains under it. "That's fine. Yours is upstairs anyway."

"Are you going to paint me like one of your French girls, Jack?" I throw a saucy wink over my shoulder.

"Well now I am, yeah."

I pick up the small wrapped package and hand it to him before sitting at the opposite end of the couch. "I'm going to hold you to that."

"Please do." He looks at me for permission, and when I nod, he rips into the paper like a little kid with no self-control.

And I wonder how long it's been since Jack received a Christmas present. I squeeze my eyes shut for just a second to hold back the sudden spring of tears. And then I force them back open, not wanting to miss the expression on his face.

Jack tosses away the paper, running his hands over the green-leather-wrapped book cover in his hands, his fingers tracing the title, *The Fellowship of the Ring*, embossed in gold. He looks up at me as if asking for confirmation.

"It's not a first edition or anything, but it's an early one, and to be honest, I had no idea what to get you, and I saw this one day when I was out and I thought you might like it. And you were wearing a *Lord of the Rings* shirt the first time we met, which, not going to lie, I seriously judged you for, but then it kind of seemed like finding this was a sign, and I really hope you like it."

"It's perfect, Sade." He flips open the cover and a small piece of paper falls out.

"I, um, wanted to give you a little note, but I figured it might be blasphemous to write in the book itself." I hold my breath as his eyes take in the two-word phrase I've written. He doesn't say anything for a really long time, and my heart drops to my stomach. "It means—"

"I know what it means."

"Oh." Now my stomach is being punched. Repeatedly. By a heavy-weight boxer. "Would now be a good time to give you shit for knowing how to speak Elvish?"

"I don't know how to speak Elvish. Just this phrase." He still won't look at me, eyes glued to the three-inch strip of paper like it contains the secret formula for eternal life. "My mom used to say it to me."

"Oh shit. Jack. I had no idea." I start to move closer to him but then think better of it since he probably wants some space. I try to scoot back to the corner, but he clasps his hand around my wrist, pulling me into him. "I'm sorry," I whisper, reaching for the paper. "Let me just throw it away."

Jack tucks the slip back into the cover of the book, setting it on the coffee table. "I love you too, Sadie."

My heart full-on stops beating in my chest. "You do?"

"Of course I do. This is the best present anyone has ever given me." He takes my hips in his hands, shifting me fully into his lap, wrapping my legs around his waist.

I dig my fingers into his curls and bring his lips to mine, this kiss soft and gentle.

"Say it, Sadie. Please." He murmurs the words into my mouth.

I put a small amount of space between us, so I can look directly in his eyes, which are darkening to the shade of the Christmas tree behind us. "I love you, Jack."

His lips find mine again, insistent and breathless. My hips roll against him; he's already hard beneath me.

"I hope you know me well enough by now to know that I'm not going to forget about my part of this present exchange." I punctuate my words with a line of kisses along his jaw.

He breaks away from me with a grin. "Yeah yeah." He stands, cupping his hands around my ass to lift me with him.

I slide down, place a quick kiss on his lips, and gesture for him to lead the way. He takes me up to BaBs. He's been spending more and more time up here lately, and I'm sure there's a part of him that will be happy to see me turn the space over to him once the store is finished.

He takes me over to the left side of the room, where his easels and supplies are set up. The three paintings he's done of my arrangements are lined up under one of the big windows. They still take my breath away every time I see them.

Jack places me directly in front of a tall easel, the entire thing covered with a large gray drop cloth. "Sorry it isn't wrapped, but I just finished it yesterday and it needed time to dry."

I wave my hands in a *Who cares* motion. Because really, who cares?

"You ready?"

I nod, clasping my hands together in anticipation.

Jack slowly and carefully pulls the cloth away from the easel.

And I just stare.

And stare.

And stare.

Dashing the heels of my hands in my eyes and blinking away the wetness blurring my vision, I take a step closer. It's a painting, obviously. And I might be biased, but it's quite possibly the most beautiful painting I've ever seen.

Which sounds really egotistical, because the subject of the painting is me. I'm standing in the middle of a typical New York street, the Brooklyn Bridge looming behind me. My body faces the bridge, and I'm looking over my shoulder at whoever is viewing the painting, a teasing smile on my face. But it's not the bridge or the street or even me that makes the painting breathtaking. It's that the dress I'm wearing is made purely of flowers. Hundreds of them, the texture so detailed I can almost feel the velvety petals. They wrap around my bare back, trailing down into a train that spills over the bottom half of the canvas.

It's absolute perfection.

"Bridge and Blooms," I breathe when I finally manage to make my voice work. I've stopped trying to stem the tears, letting them flow freely over my cheeks.

"Bridge and Blooms." Jack steps over to me, taking one of my hands in his. "Do you like it?"

I choke out a laugh. "Do I like it? Jack, this is the most beautiful thing I've ever seen. And not just because it's me. That's like the least beautiful thing about it."

He takes my other hand and pulls me into his arms. "Not sure I agree with that assessment, sweet pea."

I turn my cheek, resting it against his chest so I can stare at the painting some more. "Talk about the best gift ever."

He kisses the top of my head. "I'm glad you like it."

"I love it." I tilt my head up to kiss him. "And I love you."

"I love you too."

"Ugh. We're making me nauseated." I pull away from him a little, a wicked glint in my eye. "I did get you something else, though." I run my hands through his curls before dragging them down to his chest.

"Really?" His hands slide down to my hips, pressing them into his.

"I got tested two weeks ago. All clean." My fingers slip under the edge of his button-down shirt, traveling up his back.

His breath catches in his chest and he hardens against my belly. "Oh yeah?" The two words come out in a hoarse gasp. "Me too. I mean, it wasn't two weeks ago, but I'm clean. Also clean. Totally clean."

I bite my lip because he's adorable when he can't form a coherent sentence. "And I refilled my birth control prescription while I was there." I move my hands around to his stomach, lightly tracing his lean abs.

His hips press into mine. "Please tell me this means what I think it means."

I let my hand wander down to the front of his jeans, cupping his length in my palm. "Shall we head downstairs?"

He grabs my hand and tugs me out of the studio.

We practically fly down the stairs and into my room, Jack shutting the door behind us and pressing me up against it in a repeat of his earlier move from downstairs. The urgency is hot and desperate, but his kiss is slow and consuming. He links our hands together, bringing them above my head while his hips thrust into mine until I whimper.

I break free of his hold, my fingers rapidly working through the buttons of his shirt, pushing it down his arms and trailing my hands over his shoulders and up through his curls. He tugs my sweater over my head, pausing for a minute to admire my fanciest bra, which I donned in the hope we would end up here. He lowers his head, licking along the lace edges before sucking my nipple through the sheer fabric.

His mouth moves down farther, softly licking and nibbling the skin of my stomach, and he cups my ass in his exquisite hands before his nimble fingers unbutton my jeans and slide the fabric down my legs. His lips embark on a northward exploration, kissing me everywhere as he makes his way back to my mouth.

My hands travel to the front of his jeans, palming his hard length once again, delighting in the growl he releases, rumbling against my lips. I move to unbutton his pants, but he nudges my hand away.

"Not yet," he mutters into my neck. His arms reach around me and he unhooks my bra, his fingers teasing and pinching me as I toss it to the floor. His tongue replaces his fingers, licking and sucking until my hips thrust against him. It's frantic and breathless and hot as fuck.

He lowers himself to his knees in front of me, hooking his thumbs in my panties and dragging them down my legs, helping me step out of them. He kisses his way up until he is right where I want him most. One of my legs gets thrown over his shoulder and then his mouth is on me, licking up my center, swirling over my clit.

My head falls back against the door, and I grasp onto the knob, anything to keep me from collapsing to the ground as he devours me. The fingers of my free hand tangle themselves in his curls, and I can't seem to stop my hips from rolling against his mouth. As soon as he slips a finger inside of me, my nerves explode and I cry out my release.

Jack rises, catching me before I fold to the ground. He places soft kisses along my collarbone and up my throat, finally landing back on my mouth. This time when I move to undo his pants, he lets me, kicking them off as we stumble over to the bed.

I yank back the comforter, and we fall onto the sheets, which are cool against my heated skin. We lie facing each other, legs intertwined. Jack cups my face in his hands, kissing me like it's the first time.

And this time, the buildup, the tension, the explosion, happens inside my chest. Lying here, face-to-face with Jack, both of us completely bared to each other, is a feeling unlike anything else I have ever experienced. This man is completely burrowed deep in my heart, and I know in this moment, beyond anything else, that I will love him forever. The certainty hits me just as strongly as that mind-blowing orgasm did, and the aftershocks linger far longer. When the ripple of emotions subsides inside me, I pull Jack on top of me.

He dots kisses over my cheeks and eyelids, along the edge of my jaw and down my throat.

I reach between us, taking him in my hand and wrapping my palm around his hardness. I guide him to my entrance. "Do you still want this?"

His lips brush against mine. "More than I can put into words. Do you?"

"Abso-fucking-lutely."

He buries his face in my neck, his laughter tickling me. And then he's pushing into me, slowly, inch by inch.

Once he's fully seated inside of me, I hold him in place for a minute, bringing his lips to mine, kissing him deeply. I release my hold, and he rolls his hips, slowly, tauntingly, until my body is tight with tension.

"Fuck, Sadie. You feel so good." He drops his forehead to mine as his pace increases, his thrusts stroking me harder and faster.

I clutch on to his shoulders, wrap my legs around his waist. "I'm close," I breathe out, my hips bucking up to meet his.

Jack's fingers slip in between our bodies, caressing my sensitive spot. The combination of sensations is overwhelming, and a minute later, I'm calling out his name, tightening around him as my body explodes in release once again.

He shudders his own release a minute later, burying his face in my hair and muffling his groans. His hips continue to roll slowly, as we both come down.

Jack props himself up on his elbows as we catch our breaths. He pushes a stray strand of hair behind my ears, his fingers tracing down along my jaw. "I really fucking love you."

I laugh, pulling him down for a quick kiss. "I really fucking love you too."

We collapse, lying flat on the pillows, my leg thrown over his, our fingers interlocked.

A few minutes later, Jack rolls onto his side, tugging me onto mine so we're face-to-face. "Not to totally kill the vibe or anything, but I can't really let tonight pass without telling you how much the past month has meant to me. It probably goes without saying that the holidays haven't been the easiest time of year for me since the accident." He cups my cheek in his hand. "This is the first holiday season in a long time when I felt like I had a family."

I tilt my head up to kiss him, scooting closer into his embrace. "When I was deciding where to go to college, New York stood out among the rest for a particular reason."

He runs his fingers through my hair. "And what was that?"

"I felt like New York was where people came to make their own family. And that's what I wanted more than anything. More than money or a degree or a good job. I wanted to make my own family." I meet his gaze, a waterfall of emotion mirroring my own.

"You made a damn good one, sweet pea." He kisses my forehead, tucking my head into his chest.

"And it's yours now too, Jackpot." I wrap my arms around him, burrowing into his warmth and falling asleep.

On Christmas, we swap out the vintage Real Housewives marathon for a stay-in-bed-and-have-lots-of-sex marathon. Jack throws on a robe to grab the Chinese food delivery, but it's the only time either of us puts clothes on throughout the day.

The following day is when the real work on Bridge and Blooms will begin, and so I relish this day of so-called rest. The hours we spend cuddled under my covers, the feel of Jack thrusting inside of me, the laughter and the giggles, and eating leftover pie and drinking wine in the center of my bed like it's a picnic blanket.

It's the best Christmas I've ever had.

HARLEY: How is everything coming with the store?
I can come by this weekend to help!

ME: That'd be great!

ME: A bunch of furniture is getting delivered on
Friday so this weekend is going to be
all about layout.

HARLEY: Awesome, Nick and I will be there!

NICK: Whoa. I don't remember signing up for this.

HARLEY: We need your muscles, babe.

ME: Also, it's in your best interest to help out,
remember?

NICK: I seem to recall you placing a lot of emphasis
on the silent bit in "silent partner."

ME: Yeah, we need you to silently move stuff while
we tell you where to put it.

JACK: Nick. Please come. Save me.

NICK: Fine, but I'd like it noted for the record that
I'm showing up for Jack, and only Jack.

ME: Yeah yeah. You love each other, we know.

GEMMA: We've been back in school for two days and I already hate my life so I'll be there but only if I can drink while we work.

NICK: Yeah, that's a huge liability so that's gonna be a no.

GEMMA: What happened to silent?

⁓

JACK: I'm bringing you dinner, what do you want?

ME: You don't have to do that, I'm almost done, swear.

JACK: Yeah, I know how that goes. Almost done means two more hours.

JACK: Did you eat lunch?

ME: I had a bag of pretzels and a Gatorade, which totally hits all the main food groups.

JACK: . . .

ME: Pizza sounds amazing, thanks, babe!

JACK: I'll see you in twenty minutes.

ME: Could you also bring a level? I'm trying to hang some shelves.

JACK: You got it.

ME: And now that you mention dinner I'm kind of hungry. Could you also get a salad? And cheesy garlic bread?

ME: And maybe some cheesecake?

JACK: Already ordered all of that 😊

ME: God you're amazing. You're so getting laid tonight.

JACK: Lol. We both know you'll be asleep before your head fully hits the pillow.

ME: You're probably right. Fuck. Sorry.

ME: I'm like the worst new girlfriend ever. Sorry I'm such an asshole.

JACK: Stop talking about my amazing, determined, driven, funny-as-fuck, super-hot girlfriend like that.

ME: I love you.

JACK: I love you too. See you soon.

~

ME: Hi, friends! Sick of me yet?

ME: Don't answer that!

ME: I promise the madness is almost over. But
I could really use your help on Saturday. It
should be the final push!

HARLEY: I'm in!

HARLEY: So is Nick 😊

JACK: I'll be there, obviously.

GEMMA: If this is ACTUALLY THE LAST ONE then of
course I'll be there 😊

ME: Yay! You guys can meet Lucy, Bridge and
Blooms' first official employee!

GEMMA: What are we, MySpace?

ME: Sorry, Bridge and Blooms' first paid employee!

ME: And I promise to treat you all to dinner and
drinks when we're done!

NICK: I think you mean dinner and drinks until the
end of time.

ME: SILENT partner.

SEVENTEEN

I WRAP MY HAND around a stray weed and yank it out of the dirt, using so much force I actually fall back on my heels. Righting myself, I toss the discarded stem into my trash pile and move on to the next one. Unfortunately, I apparently take too good care of the brownstone's backyard garden, because hardly any weeds remain, and I need to take my anger out on something.

Maybe not anger. Frustration. Exhaustion. Anxiety. I'm bone-weary and full of self-doubt.

The store is mostly ready and everything is coming together, but the past couple of weeks have been the hardest of my life. I spent more time than I'd like to admit sitting on the floor in the center of the shop, head in my hands, tears pouring down my face.

I thought the recent success of Bridge and Blooms had prepared me for running my own business, but trying to open a storefront has been about a million times harder than I thought it'd be. I'm so, so tired. And I don't know if I can do it. I don't know why I ever thought I could do it.

I yank off my gardening gloves and shove my hands into the cold soil. The dirt clumps around my fingers, and the smell of earth fills my nose, grounding me. I close my eyes and force myself to take three long breaths.

Pushing up off the ground, I shake my hands clean and collapse into a patio chair. The dirt stuck under my nails is a welcome departure from the manicured perfection I felt I needed to maintain at my old job, but as the store gets closer to its official opening, I can't help but wonder if I made a mistake leaving behind a stable industry for the huge risk that is Bridge and Blooms.

It's chilly outside, but the weeding has warmed me. I know I have a to-do list as long as my arm, but I can't make myself stand and go inside, the comfort of being outside in the garden like a cozy blanket wrapping around me.

A mug appears in front of my face.

"You doing all right?" Jack drops into the chair next to me.

I take a small sip of my latte, knowing the appearance of being okay is more important right now than the coffee. "I'm fine."

"Tell me what I can do to help, Sade. Put me to work."

"It's fine. I've got it all under control." My grip on the mug tightens, my knuckles bearing the brunt of my tension.

Jack leans forward. "It's okay if you don't, you know."

"It's not, actually. I don't have time to not have everything under control because my store opens in a matter of days, and I somehow roped one of my best friends into investing a huge chunk of money into a business that hasn't been around nearly long enough to justify such a ridiculous amount of money and I'm pretty sure I'm going to be out of business in a year, and then Bridge and Blooms will be a total bust and I'll have to try to find a job in finance so I can be miserable for the rest of my life, and I knew I wasn't ready for this." I set my mug on the table and lean forward, letting my head fall between my knees and forcing myself to take deep breaths. "I was stupid to think I'd end up anywhere other than failure."

He doesn't say anything, but his warm palm lands on my back, rubbing slow, calming circles.

Eventually, I sit up and Jack's hand drifts down to take mine in his. "Can I actually do this, Jack?"

He scoots his chair closer to mine, squeezing my hand. "I can't answer that for you, sweet pea. Self-doubt is normal when you're taking on something new." He places a soft kiss on my lips. "I believe you can do this, but you have to believe too."

I nod. "I think I just need to sit out here by myself for a little bit."

"Okay." He stands and drops a kiss on the top of my head. "You know where to find me."

Once he's back inside, I wrap my hands around my mug, letting the warmth soothe me from the outside in.

It's tempting to throw in the towel now. Quit before I really have the chance to fail. Nick would lose all his money, but it's not like he doesn't have enough to fall back on.

I stare into my latte for a long time, looking for answers in the swirls of milk.

After several minutes, I look over at the garden beds. It's midwinter, so everything is dead at the moment, but even without the blooms of the flowers, I'm proud of the space I created back here, taking an overgrown monstrosity and turning it into something beautiful.

It's a little sliver of proof that I can do this. I can make something from nothing.

Bridge and Blooms can be just like this garden, only on a larger scale.

I gulp down the now-cold dregs of my latte, gather up the weeds, and toss them in the trash. Back in the house, I plant a kiss on Jack's cheek before bounding up the stairs to BaBs to get back to work.

Jack carefully unloads his paintings from one of my delivery wagons bright and early Saturday morning, one week before the launch party for Bridge and Blooms, and two days before I officially begin to operate the business from the shop. Each canvas is bubble-wrapped within an inch of its life, which I thought was a little excessive given the whole five-minute walk, but he insisted. He's generously handing over the three paintings he's completed of my arrangements to go along with my Christmas painting, which will hang centered behind the cash register.

"I really wish you'd let me pay you for these." I take each one as he unwraps it, setting them carefully on the long wooden counter where I'll be doing most of my arranging.

He gives me an eye-roll/push-the-glasses-up-his-nose combo. "Where else would these hang? They were made to go in this space."

"Yeah, but this is like hours and hours of your work, and I'm just taking it." I examine the first one he completed, still marveling at the detail he captured.

"You're not taking it, I'm giving it to you." He unwraps my Christmas gift, now officially titled *Bridge and Blooms*, as if he were handling the *Titanic* Heart of the Ocean diamond. "And I wouldn't even be painting if it weren't for you. So a couple small canvases is the least I could do."

I let him lay the canvas on the front counter before wrapping my arms around him. "I still can't quite believe this is all happening."

"It's not simply happening, sweet pea. You made it happen." He kisses my forehead.

I tilt my head up for a deeper kiss. Between my regular orders, trying to get the store ready, and squeezing in one bar shift a week, there hasn't been a lot of time for the two of us over the past few weeks. And, Jack being Jack, he never complains, never makes me feel guilty. He's waiting for me every night when I get home, on the rare nights he doesn't come to the store with me to walk me back to the brownstone. It's like I dreamed up this super-perfect boyfriend and he just popped into existence.

"Oh my god, I did not sign up for this." Gemma's voice breaks apart our kiss.

I grin at Jack, planting one more kiss on him before stepping out of his embrace. "Yeah yeah."

She holds up a bag. "I brought doughnuts and everything."

I wrap her in a tight hug, holding on for way longer than I know she wants. "You're the best."

She riffles around in the bag, handing me a maple bar and taking a sprinkled one for herself, before hopping up onto the end of the counter.

Handing Jack an old-fashioned, I lean my butt up against the counter where Gem sits. "I'm glad you got here early, actually, because I wanted to ask you something."

"No, I will not participate in a threesome. At least not with you." She gives me a wink and a grin.

"Good to know, but not what I was going to ask." I lick a drop of frosting from my doughnut. "How would you feel about catering the launch party? Nothing big, just a couple of passed apps and maybe a charcuterie display?"

She picks a sprinkle off her doughnut but doesn't say anything.

"I'd pay you, obviously, and I just thought it might be kind of a good test run, you know?" I was confident she'd jump at the chance, but she looks so miserable I can't stop myself from throwing my arm around her shoulder. "Okay, no worries, I can totally find someone else. I'm sorry I asked, Gem. I didn't mean to upset you."

She gently removes herself from my embrace. "I'm not upset with you, Sade. I'm mad at myself."

Jack gives me a worried look and slowly starts to move toward the office in the back, motioning in a very not-subtle way that he'll give us some space.

Once he's cleared the room, I move so I'm standing right in front of her. "Why are you mad at yourself?"

"How do I count the ways? I'm twenty-eight and in a job I despise and everyone in my life is happy and successful and I still can't decide what the fuck I want to do." She tosses her doughnut back in the bag, even though it's half-eaten.

"Gemma, god, where do I start? One, you say 'twenty-eight' like it's eighty, which I refuse to accept, as I'm two months older than you.

Two, hello, I was literally you less than a year ago." I throw my arms wide open. "And look where I've ended up after also hating my job and having no idea what I wanted to do."

"You did know what you wanted to do, Sade, and you did it. That's the difference."

"Cut out this pity-party bullshit right the fuck now. You can do it too. You're one of the smartest people I know, and you work your ass off, Gem. Not to brag or anything, but my launch party is going to kill it on social media, and you're going to do the catering because the worst thing that can happen is you hate it and never want to do it again and so you don't. And the best thing is everyone at the party wants to hire you to do their own party." I pull her off the counter and drag her to the other side of the room, where I left my planning note-book, opening it to the party page. "Here's your budget. I trust you to make it awesome, so I'll send you the money and you can do whatever you want."

She looks over my notes, her darting eyes doing nothing to hide her nerves. "What if I ruin your party?"

"You won't. I know you. You won't let yourself let me down." I take her face in my hands and plant a loud kiss on her cheek. "We good?"

"I could do those bacon-wrapped scallops you love, if I can find a good deal." She takes out her phone, snapping a picture of my note-book page. "And maybe some pot stickers."

"Yes. Love it. Sounds amazing." I turn toward the back. "Jack, you can come out now! Let's get these paintings hung!"

He peeks his head out of the office, half a doughnut stuck in his mouth. "I'm actually going to wait for Nick before I hang anything. It's much easier with a tall person to assist."

"You rang?" Nick pushes open the door to the shop, holding it for Harley, who's carrying a tray of coffees.

God, I love my friends.

Harley sets down the tray, then immediately moves along the counter to where Jack's paintings are lying in wait. "Holy shit." She turns to Jack, her mouth dropped open. "You painted these?"

Jack, who was in the middle of some secret-handshake bro dance with Nick, shoves his hands in his pockets. "Oh yeah. I did."

"If you think those are good, get a load of this one." I gesture for the three of them to come look at *Bridge and Blooms*.

There's a solid minute of silence as they all take it in.

"What the fuck, bro?" Nick punches Jack in the shoulder, knocking him back a step. "Why didn't you tell us you could do this?"

He shrugs, his cheeks reddening as he shrinks into himself. "I couldn't really. Not for a long time anyway."

They all three turn to stare at him, and he might as well be a turtle retreating into his shell.

I lace my fingers through his, tucking myself into his side. "Jack did a lot of painting when he was younger, but he stopped for a while after his parents died."

"Well, you should be selling this shit." Gemma doesn't do canned pity, and I've never been more grateful for it.

Jack gives her a timid smile. "It's not really about the money these days."

His word choice snags something in my brain for a minute, but I shrug it off. "And you know me, happy to capitalize on the free labor of you unfortunate souls who are stuck loving me." I rise on my toes and plant a kiss on his cheek. "Speaking of. Talk less. Work more."

Various things are thrown in my general direction, but everyone gets to work. Paintings are hung, supplies organized, décor put in place. Lucy, my new employee, joins us for a couple of hours. She's in her late thirties, and for a minute, I worry our antics will annoy her, but she fits right in, giving as good a ribbing as she gets. By the end of Saturday, Bridge and Blooms looks just about complete. You know, minus the blooms.

We all bundle up in our coats and scarves before heading out, the January weather having turned bitterly cold over the past two weeks.

I lock the front door after everyone has exited the building, then loop my arm through Jack's as we head to dinner. "I can't believe tomorrow I get to go to work in my store."

"Have I mentioned how proud I am of you?" Jack leans down and plants a kiss on the top of my head.

"Once or twice." I snuggle deeper into his side, needing the warmth and reveling in the comfort. "Have you thought any more about selling some of your paintings? I think the reaction from the gang only further cements my claim that a shit-ton of people are going to want them once they see them in the store." I tilt my head up so I can see his eyes.

And if it weren't already dark outside and limiting my visibility, I would swear there's a flash of something like panic darting through the bright green.

But Jack just shrugs. "I've never wanted to sell my paintings before. It's not about money for me."

"I'm totally happy to be your art pimp if you need me to."

He chuckles. "I think you mean my art dealer."

"No. Art pimp. That will be my official title or no deal."

We arrive at the restaurant, and Jack holds the door open for me. "You're something else, sweet pea."

"That's why you love me, Jackpot."

"That I do."

~

The final week before the launch party is a haze of activity and emotions. There's still work to be done in the store itself, namely setting up window displays and filling the place with flowers, all while fulfilling my orders for the week. But it's quite a rush to head to the store each morning, working on arrangements from the long counter in the center of the shop, making the space really feel like my own. It's going to be quite some time before the seeds currently baking in the greenhouse in BaBs will be producing actual blooms, so for now I'm sourcing everything from as many local farms as possible. I also spend a fair amount of time during the week scavenging for vessels that can be repurposed. There will be no short square clear vases in my house. Unless I happen to find one discarded on the street; then I'm totally taking it.

Lucy works with me throughout the week, learning how to arrange, but also figuring out the ordering system and working on the logistics of deliveries. I'm still not quite comfortable taking on large events, but we go ahead and schedule some consultations for smaller parties, and hopefully those will give me enough experience to grow my confidence. I find a super-cute old bistro table at a flea market, and I set it up in the back corner of the shop specifically for client design meetings.

Gemma has checked in approximately eight million times over the week, clearing menu items with me, asking if I'm totally sure I trust her, and sending me photos of her test runs. Which really is just mean, because I don't get to actually eat any of those said test runs. I know she's going to be great, and I hope the night gives her the boost she needs.

And Jack. Really, what more can I say about Jack? Have I mentioned how he's the absolute perfect boyfriend? Honestly, if I had a thought to spare, I'd probably be freaking the fuck out, because there's no way a man this good will want to stick around for the likes of me. But luckily, I don't have time for those kinds of thoughts. I just allow him to take care of me in a way no one has ever truly taken care of me before. And I'm too distracted to let myself sabotage this thing between us.

The Friday night before the party, I make myself head home early, knowing I'm going to need a full eight hours of sleep or else I'll be a monster on launch day. Who am I kidding? I'm going to be a monster no matter how much sleep I get, just to varying degrees based on restfulness and coffee consumption.

Jack has wine open and Chinese food on the way when I get home, giving me enough time to shower and change into my pajamas before we eat cross-legged on the basement sofa, hours of backlogged Bravo shows playing on the TV.

When I fall asleep during an epic Ramona/Sonja blowout, Jack knows it's time to cart my ass off to bed. He tucks us both under the covers, kisses me good night, and falls right asleep because of course he does. Seriously. Bastard.

Despite my bone-deep exhaustion, I can't seem to make my eyes stay closed, and I stare up at the ceiling, picturing all the millions of things that could go wrong tomorrow.

Finally, I force myself to turn on my side, ceiling be damned. I push myself into Jack's space, nuzzling my cheek against his bare chest.

His arms automatically encircle me, his voice sleepy and gruff. "You okay?"

"Can't sleep."

He runs his fingers through my hair, instantly calming me. "Everything's going to be perfect, sweet pea. You've planned every last detail."

"What if no one shows up?" I trace light circles along his stomach, needing my fingers to do something.

"I'll be there. And so will your friends. And so will lots of other people." He cups my cheek in his hand and pulls my lips up to his. "It's going to be amazing, Sade," he murmurs against my mouth, before deepening the kiss, pulling me into him.

I sigh into him, his mouth providing a wondrous distraction. "Hey." I break the kiss. "I know what you're doing, mister."

He moves his lips down to my jaw, nibbling until I expose my neck for him. "I'm just trying to take your mind off things."

"You think you can sex me into not worrying about tomorrow?" I wedge my leg in between his, delighting as he hardens against me.

"No, but I think we might as well try." He wraps his arms around my waist, rolling me over so I'm on top of him.

He releases me, giving me just enough space to shuck my shirt, leaving me in a tiny pair of cotton panties. Jack's fingers trace over the curve of my breasts before he sits up, me in his lap straddling him. His tongue flickers over one nipple and then the other, before he takes it in his mouth, sucking and nipping until my hips are rocking over his cock, hard beneath me.

His hands cup my ass, raising me up until I'm standing on the bed. He slides my panties down my legs, holding me steady while I step out of them. Once my feet are firmly planted on the mattress, his hands slide back to my ass, guiding me closer to his mouth. He gives me a wicked smile before his tongue darts out to tease me, licking softly and slowly.

I look down, watching as his mouth devours me, and it's quite possibly the hottest thing I've ever seen. My first orgasm rocks through me a minute later, and Jack eases me down to his lap. He falls back on the pillows, lifting his hips so I can remove his pajama pants. I run my tongue over his hard length, licking him from base to tip, but he hooks his hands under my arms and pulls me up, settling himself at my entrance and slowly pushing into me.

Once I'm fully seated, Jack tucks his hands behind his head, giving me a very un-Jack-like cocky grin. "Ride me, sweet pea."

"Fuck, Jack. Why is that so hot?" My hands dig into his chest, leveraging my weight as I slowly rock over him.

"You like being in charge, Sade. This is not new information." He grins teasingly, but his eyes darken as he watches me roll and swivel my hips, and I know he's enjoying this just as much as I am.

And he can't keep his hands off me for long. One travels to my breasts, caressing and pinching my nipples, while the other slides between our bodies, stroking me until I'm so tight with tension I can barely move. But with a few more thrusts, that tension boils over and I tighten around him as I cry out.

He sits up then, his arms wrapping around me, his lips finding mine as he pumps into me several more times before finally grunting out his own release.

He kisses me softly until we both fully come down, his hands stroking my bare back until I'm 100 percent zombie-brained, gummy-limbs relaxed.

Jack lowers me onto the pillows, bringing the covers up under my chin. He tucks himself behind me, his front spooning my back, his arm draped around my waist. "No matter what happens tomorrow or next week or in a month or in a year, you are the best thing that's ever happened to me, Sadie Green." He places a soft kiss on my bare shoulder.

I turn around to return the sentiment, but he's already fallen asleep.

Bastard.

EIGHTEEN

SURPRISINGLY, OR MAYBE not, since as Jack said, I planned out every second of launch-party day, everything goes smoothly. Lucy and I complete all of the arrangements for the party in the morning hours, storing them in the coolers until it's closer to go time. The rentals get delivered on time, just a few high-top cocktail tables placed randomly around the room so people have a place to set their drinks and snacks. We set up a mini bar at the work counter and bring in an extra-long table for Gemma to display all her yummy food. I hired a bartender and two servers to handle all the drink-making and food-passing and, most important, the cleaning up.

I head back to the brownstone two hours before guests are due to arrive for a quick shower and brief gussying-up stint. I've worn only the barest of makeup for much of the last few months, but for tonight, I go for a subtle golden smoky eye, dark lashes, and bright pink lips. My dress for the evening is tight and black, and when I walk down the stairs, Jack literally stops in his tracks.

My heart flutters in my chest as he watches me descend, and I feel like a fucking queen. A boss-ass queen.

He kisses my cheek when I reach him at the bottom of the stairs. "You look fucking fantastic."

"Thanks, Jackpot." I tug on the lapel of his blazer, worn over dark jeans and a white button-down shirt. "You don't look so bad yourself."

He runs a hand through his hair, smoothing back curls that have grown a little long. "I can't remember the last time I wore an actual collared shirt/jacket combo."

"Well, it looks good on you." I plant a kiss on his cheek, wiping away the faint smudge of pink I leave behind.

He helps me into my coat, and I wrap a scarf around my neck, thankful the walk to the store is short.

It's a quick and quiet stroll through the bitter January cold, and I start to run through all the last-minute tasks I'll need to finish before people start arriving for the party.

Jack squeezes my hand before reaching out to open the door for me. "You're going to do great, sweet pea."

Determined to stay busy so my internal freak-out doesn't take over my brain and shut me down completely, I toss all my outerwear in my office, put Jack in charge of my phone, and then get to work, placing arrangements, checking in with the staff, and helping Gemma set up the food.

Inhaling a deep whiff of bacon, I can't help but snatch a wrapped scallop from one of the platters. "Good lord, Gem. These are amazing."

She smacks my hand away as I reach for a second. "Save them for the paying customers, lady."

Standing back, I take in the spread. Not only does the food smell amazing, but her presentation is stunning. "I hope you're ready to be inundated with catering requests after tonight."

She shrugs off the compliment, but there's an unmistakable gleam of pride in her eyes. "Thank you for this, Sade. Truly. It means everything to me that you trusted me to do this for you."

I pull her into a quick side hug. "Mostly I just wanted top-notch food at a killer price."

She loops her arm around my waist. "Don't do that."

"Do what?"

"Write off your generosity like you have ulterior motives."

Rolling my eyes, I gently push her away. "Come on, Gem, we all know my motives are self-motivated."

She shakes her head and gives me a sad smile. "You couldn't be more wrong."

I open my mouth to retort, sarcastically of course, but nothing comes out.

"I'm going to take some stuff out to the trash." And she leaves me there alone in the middle of the store, wondering for a half second if she's right. But she's not, obviously, and soon enough my attention is pulled elsewhere.

Twenty minutes after the party's official start time, my nerves have fully taken over. All of my crew is here, and a couple of other invitees, but the space looks scarily empty. I invited a bunch of Brooklyn-based influencers, along with all the other florists located in the general area, looking to build relationships and hopefully a referral network. I was relying on the influencers to help spread the word about the shop's opening, but so far, none of them have stepped through the door.

"I told you no one was going to come," I whisper to Jack, trying to keep from actually wringing my hands with worry.

He places a calming kiss at my temple. "It's early. How about some wine?"

I happily accept a glass and attempt to force myself to look anywhere but the front door.

But thankfully, fifteen minutes later, the store starts to fill up. A slow trickle of people continues to come through the door, and when I'm not flitting around and saying hi to everyone, I try to catch their reactions when they see the space for the first time. There's lots of oohs and aahs, and every smile makes my heart flutter. This might be better than sex.

Jack hangs mostly with Nick and Harley while I run around introducing myself to the guests, and Gemma stands guard at the food table, restocking and tidying with an effort bordering on overzealous.

I chat with probably fifty people I've never met before tonight, all of them raving about how awesome Bridge and Blooms looks. The influencers are live-streaming and posting up a storm, and I'm itching to check my phone and see how our stats look, but I know it's more important to make face-to-face contact at this moment, while I have them all here.

The florists are my favorite people I meet throughout the evening, because they all really get it. How it feels to watch something grow and then turn it into a work of art, guaranteed to bring a smile to someone's face.

And speaking of art, jaws drop when people first take in Jack's paintings. All of them really, but especially *Bridge and Blooms*, hung in its spot of honor behind the main counter. Jack specifically asked me not to direct anyone his way, should they inquire, but you can bet your ass I'll be posting some of his paintings on Instagram. I don't want to push him into selling his art if he really doesn't want to, but something tells me he could be raking in commissions left and right.

I approach an older woman, probably in her early sixties, as she's taking in *Bridge and Blooms*, her eyes locked on the painting. "Hi, thank you so much for coming. I'm Sadie."

She pulls her eyes from the artwork and gives me a warm smile. "Sadie. So nice to meet you. The shop is lovely."

"Thank you so much . . ." I trail off my sentence since she hasn't introduced herself to me yet.

"Oh yes, so sorry. I'm Judy Taylor from *City Life* magazine." She holds out her hand and gives me a firm shake. "Sorry, I guess I got distracted by this stunning piece of art up here."

I beam with as much pride as if I painted it myself. "Isn't it beautiful?"

Judy takes a step closer, studying the canvas with squinted eyes. "If I didn't know any better, I'd swear that was a Jackson Bennett."

"A what?" I try to find Jack in the crowd. I know he said he didn't want to meet anyone, but this woman works for an actual magazine and she might be too good a contact to pass up.

"Jackson Bennett. You might be too young to remember. He was big about ten, fifteen years ago. Sold his paintings for millions, but was a total recluse and no one ever saw his face."

"Oh, well, this is definitely not a Jackson Bennett. I couldn't afford millions." Rising up on my toes, I search for Jack's dark curls in the crowd.

"Wouldn't matter if you could. He disappeared about seven years ago. Practically dropped off the face of the earth overnight."

Suddenly I don't care too much about finding Jack. "I'm sorry, did you say he stopped painting seven years ago?"

"Thereabouts." She gives the painting one final appraising look before patting me on the shoulder. "Congrats on the opening, I'll make sure to mention it in the next issue. Now if you'll excuse me, I must get another one of those pot stickers."

I wave her toward the food table as those same pot stickers start to churn inside my stomach. A zillion thoughts ping around in my brain, but before I can even start to puzzle them out, I'm approached by an influencer for a selfie. We pose, and I plaster a fake smile on my face because I can't get the woman's words out of my head.

Jackson Bennett.

Seven years.

Millions.

There's no fucking way.

Harley, emotions wizard that she is, glides across the room, taking my elbow in her hand and dragging me to the back of the store. "You okay? You look like you might throw up." She places a hand to my forehead.

I shake my head, knowing I can't get into this now. "I'm fine. I think I just need some air." I pull away from her, ducking out back into the freezing night. The air chills my lungs but does nothing to numb my racing thoughts. It couldn't be possible. There's no way my perfect boyfriend is a total fraud. But it would explain everything. The logistics— his money, his seclusion, his lack of friends. And more important, it'd explain how a man like him ended up with me. The whole thing was a lie. Is a lie.

The door opens behind me and I know who it is before he says a single word. And without making a conscious decision, I spin around to face him. "Are you Jackson Bennett?"

He stops three feet away from me, the color draining from his face. He's caught off guard and doesn't have time to hide his reaction, his wide eyes giving it all away.

"Give me my phone." I hold out my hand, needing to search for the truth and see it myself.

He clears his throat, his voice low and rumbly with something like pain. "I'll tell you whatever you want to know, Sadie."

I cross my arms over my chest, because it really is fucking freezing and I didn't bring my coat. "Why did you lie to me?"

"I didn't lie. I haven't been Jackson Bennett in a long time. Jack Thomas is who I am now." He starts to remove his coat.

I hold up my hand to stop him. "I don't want your jacket. I don't want you to hide behind your chivalrous, meaningless gestures, Jack. I want you to tell me the fucking truth."

He stares at me for a minute, but he knows me well enough by now to know I'm not backing down. Sighing, he pushes his glasses up on his nose and starts talking. "I sold my first painting when I was eleven. Not for much, couple hundred bucks I think, and just to a family friend. They hung it in their living room, where all their rich friends could see, and seemingly overnight, everyone wanted a painting from the art-world wonder kid. I made my first million by fifteen. My parents were supportive but protective. They wouldn't allow anyone to photograph me, and they never let me make appearances in person, so I essentially stayed hidden the entire time I was 'famous.' Kept going to school, kept living a regular life, painting on the weekends and during school breaks, just making millions in my spare time." He shrugs like it's no big deal, but his eyes fall. "By the time they died, I'd already moved into the brownstone, and was no longer a minor, obviously, but I still did the whole never-show-my-face routine because it had worked for me so far. No one ever saw Jackson Bennett. And the money I made combined with my parents' estate set me up financially for life."

It's like he's telling me the story of someone else. He sounds so detached from the whole experience, like he's reading from a Wikipedia page.

"Is Jackson Bennett your real name?" I latch on to the small details, still struggling to connect the dots and paint the full picture.

He shakes his head. "Not fully. My legal name is Jackson Bennett Thomas. As things took off, my parents didn't want me to use my real last name, so we went with my middle name instead." He takes a step closer to me.

I take an equal step, farther away. Because I can't believe this is happening tonight. I knew it was coming, I knew something would eventually blow us up, but I wasn't ready for it to be tonight.

"Sadie, I didn't mean to lie. Truly, Jackson Bennett died in that car with my parents. I'm not that person anymore, and I won't be ever again." His eyes are pleading, and he reaches out for me.

And I want to go to him. To tell him I understand. I'm tempted to forgive him, because even with this betrayal, he's still the best man I could ever hope for.

But I can't let myself have this, this happiness and this success. It's too much. And I am still not enough.

"I can appreciate that, Jack, but it doesn't change the fact that you kept this huge part of yourself, your life, your childhood, secret from me." I hug myself a little tighter. "I told you things. Real things. When you asked about my parents, I told you the whole truth."

"Did you?" His question cuts through the air, though there is no malice in his tone. "Did you tell me everything about them? About your relationship? About the things that were said to you? Or just what you were comfortable sharing?" He tugs on the curls at the nape of his neck. "I told you things, Sadie. Things I haven't shared with anyone else."

He's right. And the worst part is I know he's right. The slivers Jack and I have revealed to each other have come in slow pieces, little bits of memories and experiences and small shards of our souls. But I haven't told him everything. Not even close. I certainly haven't told him how I do my best to push all the good things in my life away, before they can hurt me.

And so, I push. "I'm going to go inside now, but I think you should go. I can't deal with all of this, not tonight." I walk back toward the door, giving Jack a wide berth so I don't take his proffered hand.

"Don't walk away from me because you don't think you deserve to be happy, Sade."

I spin around, his condescending tone just enough to push my buttons. "How dare you put this on me. I'm walking away because tonight is huge for me, and I'm not going to let you ruin it. And you don't get to tell me how to react when you're the one who fucked up. You fucked up, Jack. Not me. And trust me, no one is more surprised by that fact than I am. I spent all this time thinking how much I don't deserve you, and turns out, you're the one lying to my face." A small river of relief trickles through me. He's presented me with something I never thought I would get from him: a justifiable reason to leave.

"That's a cop-out and you know it." He crosses over to me, backing me up against the door. "Maybe I did fuck up, and I'm sorry I hurt you, but you don't get to tell me how I manage my grief."

"Wow, you're really going to hide behind your dead parents?"

Jack jerks away from me as violently as if I'd slapped him.

I hate myself the second the words are out of my mouth, wanting to take them back and beg for his forgiveness, the look of absolute pain in his eyes a knife in my heart.

But I don't get a chance. Because Jack turns and walks away without another word.

NINETEEN

*H*ARLEY TAKES ONE look at me when I walk back into the shop and gives Nick and Gemma the time-to-wrap-it-up signal. I duck into my office, unable to even say my goodbyes as everyone leaves, shouting congrats and promising to share their photos and tell their friends.

Gemma and Lucy stay behind to manage cleanup with the hired staff while Nick and Harley walk me back to the brownstone. The closer we get, the more my stomach threatens to heave its contents all over the frozen sidewalk. I can't believe what I said to him, the words and the hurt in his eyes looping in my mind like a GIF on repeat.

"Do you want us to come in?" Harley walks me right to the front door, holding on tightly to both of my forearms, as if she can tell I'm on the verge of collapse.

I shake my head, unable to make any words come out of my mouth.

"Call me tomorrow." She jogs back down the steps to where Nick waits for her.

They both stand there until I get inside the house. As soon as the door closes behind me, I beeline upstairs and to my room, not wanting to chance a run-in with Jack. I think we both need to sleep on the events of the night, which is, you know, a huge downside to living with your boyfriend, when you find out he's a liar and your response is to say the worst possible thing right to his face. Too much has happened, too much has been said, for anything productive to come of more conversation tonight.

Turns out, I didn't need to worry. There's a folded piece of paper, along with my phone, on my pillow.

Going to Connecticut for a while. —Jack

I flip the paper over in my hand because surely that can't be all he has to say. But it is.

I head to the bathroom and turn the shower as hot as it will go. As it scalds me, turning my skin lobster red, I replay the conversation, over and over and over, until I'm not sure who to be more mad at, me or Jack.

You, of course.

How could you say something like that?

Cut so deep and go so low.

You never deserved him.

Shutting my eyes, I attempt to drown out the voice. But this time, the voice is right.

Back in my bed, tucked under a comforter that smells like Jack, I open up my laptop and get to googling.

I don't find out much more than what I gathered from the woman at the party and from Jack himself. Jackson Bennett rose to an insane level of popularity in a ridiculously short amount of time. And while there were multiple blog posts and articles written after his disappearance, speculating on his true identity and why he vanished, no one seems to know what really happened to the elusive painter.

But I do. Because despite this lie, this omission really, he let me know him. All for me to turn his pain into a weapon against him.

I spend most of my search time looking through images of his paintings. There are a ton of them, all of them gorgeous. I might be biased, but none of them come close to *Bridge and Blooms*.

When my eyeballs feel like they might burn out of my skull, I close the computer and hunker down for another sleepless night. And as I suspect, my eyes never once manage to stay closed.

$\sim$

Lucy is waiting for me at the shop the next morning, furiously typing away, looking scarily harried, and honestly, I couldn't be more grateful for the distraction. I haven't slept at all, and I'm sure my look this morning is zombie chic, minus the chic. Right now, nothing sounds more appealing than a day absorbed in work, avoiding all thoughts of the previous night.

I hand Lucy a cup of coffee. "Everything okay?"

She spins the computer screen around so I can see our completely booked-up calendar for the next two weeks. "Sadie, you must have some kind of luck, because I'm still going through emails and website orders, and look at how many arrangements we're going to have to make and deliver this week."

My first reaction is total elation. My second is, *Holy fuck, what have I done.* "Oh my god, we're never going to be able to get all of these out on time." I pull out my phone to text Jack an SOS. I have my messages pulled up before I remember I can't exactly turn to him for help right now. It's a sucker punch to the gut. "Fuck."

"I mean, this is a good problem to have, right?" She raises her perfectly arched eyebrows, turning her attention back to the screen.

"It is, but I don't think any of my crew are going to be around this week to help. Do you know anyone who could pick up some delivery shifts?" I punch over to my contacts list, scrolling through as if some qualified rando is going to pop out at me.

Lucy's tapping fingers pause. "Um, I might know someone."

I shove my phone in my back pocket. "Thank god. Think they could come in and meet me today? Fill out some paperwork?"

She nods, biting her lip. "Sure. It's my brother, actually."

"Awesome. He's over eighteen, yeah?" Heading back to the office to dump my stuff, I continue the conversation in a raised voice thrown over my shoulder.

"He's thirty actually."

"Great. Can you call him now?" Back at the worktop, I start pulling out bottles, laying everything out on the counter so I can see what we have on hand.

"Sure." She gives me a long look. "But I should probably let you know up front that he's got a record, convicted felon."

"Oh shit." True to my fashion, the words fly out before I can stop them. "I'm sorry. That was insensitive. Can I ask what he was convicted for?"

"Marijuana possession." She purses her lips like there's more to the story.

"Was this like fifteen years ago or something?" I realize New York is way behind the times and still adjusting to the whole legalization bid, but I can't imagine anyone ever being convicted of a felony for pot.

"Try five."

My eyebrows shoot to the top of my forehead. "What the actual fuck."

"I know."

"That's a story I'd really like to hear, but honestly, my brain can't handle any more new information at the moment. Ask him to come in. And if he can start tomorrow."

She gives me a small smile. "Will do."

I stop randomly grabbing bottles as soon as I realize I don't even know how many arrangements I need to assemble. Pulling up the schedule Lucy has neatly organized, I start to make sense of what needs to get done. We're so busy prepping for the week and chatting with the handful of customers who pop in to check out the shop that I don't have time to think. Which is a welcome blessing since I know once I open the door to any thoughts of Jack, I'm going to fall down the rabbit hole, and quite frankly, I can't afford to do that at the moment. I don't see him forgiving me, because why would he, and I'm going to need the shop to flourish so I can actually afford a place to live.

It's late evening by the time I have all the vessels and blooms for tomorrow's orders ready to go. Lucy's brother, Jason, came in right after lunch, charming me instantly with his easy smile and warm brown eyes. We get his tax forms filled out and run him through the basics of delivery protocol, and he promises to be in the shop tomorrow afternoon.

I lock the front door, give Lucy a quick wave, and head to the brownstone. I haven't made it two steps before reality comes crashing back down on my brain. And my heart. The events from the party flip through my mind, and while the tears come immediately, I manage to blink them away, low-key afraid they might freeze on my cheeks in the biting late January night air.

But when I turn the corner and see three people lounging on my front stoop, the tears spill over. I press my hands to my eyeballs, but all that does is soak my mittens.

Harley takes my keys from me, opening the door and guiding me into the dining room. We all shuck our winter gear before collapsing at the farm table. Well, I collapse; they all sit like normal human beings.

"Is this some sort of intervention?" I rub my temples, hoping to ease some of the tension brought on by my sudden crying jag.

"Yes," says Gemma from the seat on my right.

"No." Harley puts her arm around me from the spot on my left. "This is not an intervention. We just want to make sure you're okay."

"It's also kind of an intervention." Gemma gives Harley a fierce look.

I turn my attention to Nick. "Did he tell you what I said?"

"No. Not for lack of my trying. All he told me was you guys had a fight and he was going to get some space at his parents' house."

Leave it to Jack to protect me even after I was a monster.

"Did he tell you how he lied to me?" I clearly do not feel the need to reciprocate said protection. Because hello, monster.

"He did tell me that, yes. And I told Gem and Harley, so we're all caught up there." Nick crosses his arms, leaning on the table.

"But we'd kind of prefer to stay out of that aspect of this whole thing," Harley says quietly. "Jack lied, and he has his reasons, and whatever you're feeling about it is justified. But that's between the two of you."

The intervention starts making more sense. "Ah. So you guys are here to take me to task for the truly disgusting thing I said to him. Even not knowing what I said, you know me well enough to know it was bottom-level shit. Because of course, Jack's the perfect boyfriend, and I'm a garbage human and I totally fucked it all up because that's what I do."

All three of them stare at me silently. Gemma glares like she's angry. Nick's mouth hangs slightly open in shock. Harley has a light sheen of tears in her eyes.

"You don't need to tell me how truly awful I am, guys. I already know." The words come out, but just barely.

Gemma clears her throat. "We know nothing of the sort. And quite frankly, we could refute your totally bananas, couldn't-be-more-wrong opinions of yourself. We could list all the ways you help us and care for us, we can sing your praises until the cows come home, but it'll never be enough."

I open my mouth, but Harley cuts me off. "We love you, Sadie. And we think you're kind, and thoughtful, and caring, and generous. But nothing we say can undo years and years of abuse, hon."

Her words are stark and honest and they punch me in the gut. I struggle to catch my breath, even as the tears build back up.

"What she's saying is, it's time to go back to therapy." Gemma reaches out and takes my hand in hers.

And this voluntary physical touch, this show of comfort from her, clicks together a lot of pieces in my brain. "I thought I was healed." I squeeze Gemma's hand, staring at our clasped fingers so I don't have to look any of them in the eye. "I did the work and shared my feelings and got a degree and a job and made some money, and none of you abandoned me, and I thought I was all better."

Harley scoots closer to me, wrapping me in her arms as I break down completely. She strokes my hair as I soak her sweater, never once letting go of Gemma's hand. When I feel a large hand rubbing slow circles on my back, I know Nick is behind me as well.

My sobs subside, slowly, but they kick up again when three sets of arms fully engulf me. Eventually, I've drained myself of tears. Without a word, Gemma moves into the kitchen while Harley guides me upstairs and into the shower. When I step out of the steaming water, I find a clean pair of pajamas sitting on the counter. I dress and duck into my room before heading downstairs, pulling on the Captain America hoodie as I walk.

Gemma hands me a bowl of macaroni and cheese, Nick pours me a glass of wine, and we all sit and eat together. Nick does the dishes after dinner while the girls head down to the basement for some Real Housewives. Harley and Nick head home shortly after, both of them with early wake-up times on Monday. But Gem stays with me, telling me she already called for a sub and is going to hang with me at the shop the following day.

She and I curl up in my bed, me with the hoodie still wrapped around me, and with my best friend next to me, I sleep better than I have in weeks.

~

I schedule my therapy appointment for Tuesday in the late-afternoon hours, when deliveries will be mostly done and Lucy can handle any problems that might come up at the shop. I don't let myself contact Jack until after my hour is up, even though I'm desperate to hear his voice. To apologize. And to let him explain himself, and actually listen this time.

My phone is pressed to my ear the second I enter the brownstone, but he doesn't answer. It rings twice and goes to voicemail, so his phone is on, he just doesn't want to talk to me. Which is fair. I don't know if I'd want to talk to me either. But I can't just not say anything, so I text instead.

> **ME:** Hi. So, totally cool that you're not ready to talk.
> I get it, and I certainly don't blame you.

> **ME:** Ugh. I'm just going to put this in one giant paragraph, otherwise your phone is going to be beeping every two seconds and you'll hate me even more than you already do. Because I know you hate me, and that's totally justified because I said a horrible thing to you. Like the worst thing. And I'm so sorry, Jackpot. Yes, I was mad because you sort of lied (which is like a whole other thing, but let's just focus on me for now, yeah?), but that doesn't excuse what I said. Anyway. I'm sorry. So so so sorry. I want to talk to you. And I want you to come home. And I can move out, of course, but I really hope you'll find a way to forgive me because I miss you, Jackpot. And I love you. So much.

> **ME:** And I'm sorry. Did I mention that yet?

JACK: I could never hate you, sweet pea. And I'm sorry I wasn't honest with you. But I need some space. Some time to get my head straight and figure some stuff out.

ME: Of course. Take all the time you need.

ME: Is it okay if I text every once in a while?

JACK: Of course. I might not respond, but I'm here. Always.

ME: Therapy was really good today. Did I mention I'm back in therapy? Clearly I needed it. Need it. And today's session was good. By that I mean I cried my face off. Apparently in professional terms that's known as a breakthrough. In Sadie terms it means I'll be drinking lots of wine tonight. Some might consider that an unhealthy coping mechanism, but I prefer to think of it as a reward for good behavior. I'm not telling you this so you'll feel sorry for me because I definitely don't need or want that. I just really wanted to tell you about my day. I wish I could hear about yours too. I miss you. Like a lot. I love you. Also a lot.

JACK: I'm proud of you, sweet pea. And I love you too.

⌒

ME: So I fucked up at the store today. Totally got wires crossed and ended up missing a delivery for someone's anniversary. I felt terrible. The guy ripped me a new one, which I fully deserved because it was definitely my bad. But when he left the store with a refund and a bomb-ass arrangement, Lucy hugged me and told me shit happens. And I definitely felt bad for the whole rest of the day, but I also kind of moved on. When my internal voice (I named it Chad) started going in on me, I told that asshole to shut the fuck up. Because everyone makes mistakes, and one missed order isn't going to sink the business. Baby steps.

ME: Also, miss and love you.

⌒

ME: So this week is Valentine's Day, aka the Super Bowl of floristry, and I'm super excited but also scared shitless. I don't know if I can do it, but I'm going to. Everyone is taking the day off work to

come help out with deliveries and I don't know
what I did to deserve all these amazing people in
my life but I'm so grateful for them. You're included
in that group, of course. Even if I haven't seen your
face in two weeks. God I miss your face. I never
really had a Valentine before because honestly I
think the whole thing is dumb (except now it's not
dumb because I'm going to make bank this week),
but if I were going to have a Valentine, I'd want it to
be you. Only you, Jackpot.

ME: Also, once the rush of this week is over, I'll start
looking for an apartment.

ME: Also, I love you. So much.

JACK: Don't even think about moving out.

JACK: I love you too.

⁓

I wake up the day after Valentine's Day, warm and cozy in my bed. My muscles ache and I have blisters on both heels, but I also feel better than I have in, oh, say, two weeks or so. Thankfully, I already decided to keep the shop closed today. If I hadn't, I'd be calling in sick. If you can call in sick to your own business.

I loll around under the covers for way longer than I should, relishing these moments of doing nothing. It's been a while since I just did nothing. Eventually my full bladder forces me out of bed, and my caffeine addiction forces me downstairs.

Where there's a very rumpled, very bedraggled-looking man sitting at the kitchen peninsula. With a large latte and a bagel.

He stands up when he sees me, and my heart absolutely shatters. Jack looks terrible. Worse than I feel even.

I tuck my hands under my arms, crossing them over my chest as if I can hide the shield blazoned across his hoodie. A hoodie I've been wearing every day at home and haven't yet washed. "Hi," I finally manage to say after we've stared at each other for at least two silent minutes.

"Hi." He gestures to the counter. "I brought breakfast."

"You didn't have to do that." I hate this. I hate this so hard. Standing here and staring silently like we're total strangers. Worse than strangers. We're not even able to make small talk. It's worse than when I first moved in, both of us stilted and awkward.

He clears his throat. "Well, I missed Valentine's Day, so breakfast was the least I could do." He gestures again, this time to the bar stools.

I sit, taking a long sip of my latte, hoping it'll magically make my brain function again. "Jack, I'm so—"

"Stop."

I purse my lips, studying the lid of my coffee cup, unable to look at him without bursting into tears.

"Will you please look at me, Sadie?"

I shake my head, lips still tightly sealed.

He sighs, and I feel more than see him move around to my side. "Come on, let's go sit on the couch."

I follow him wordlessly, sinking onto the opposite end of the sofa. It's a little easier to meet his gaze here, with more space between us. Still feels like a throat punch though, seeing the dark circles bruising the skin under his eyes.

He leans forward a little, resting his elbows on his knees. "I should've told you everything, Sade. There's absolutely no excuse for me hiding myself from you, not once it became clear this was something much bigger than just roommates who happened to be friends. You trusted me, and I should've given you that same trust in return, but honestly, I was terrified of losing you. And I'm sorry. So sorry."

My heart clenches. I'm terrified of losing him too. "I wasn't exactly always a totally open book with you either." I hide my gaze in my coffee cup. "But why didn't you trust me?"

He lets out a long breath. "I don't think I have a good answer for that. I'm sure some part of me feared opening myself up to caring for another person. I know what it feels like to lose the people you love most in the world, and I can't imagine going through that again. In a lot of ways it felt easier to just wall off that part of my life and pretend it didn't happen."

"I forgive you."

In truth, I forgave him the day after I found out. Because I don't know what Jack has been through, and I never will. He lost two loving and supportive parents and everything he thought his life was going to be, and I'll never be able to fathom the depth of that loss, especially at a young age. I don't love that he kept secrets from me, but I understand why he did it.

And even just in the few sessions I've had with my therapist, I've realized my tendency to run when things get hard, to push people away rather than deal with the slightest of conflicts. Jack presented me with a chance to escape before he could leave me, and I tried to take it.

His eyes widen. "You forgive me?"

"Of course I do." I pull my shoulders back, working up my nerve. "But I have to ask, Jack: why did you stay away for so long?" I force myself to ask the question, even though it'd be so much easier to just accept his apology and move on. But I deserve an answer. He bailed when things got shitty, which honestly felt worse than his original offense. And I don't know if I can handle his leaving again.

"I put my parents' house on the market."

My breath catches and I automatically scoot closer to him. "Jack. Why didn't you tell me? I would've come out to be with you."

He picks up my hand and laces our fingers together. "I know you would've. And honestly, it would've been nice to have you there. It wasn't easy. But this was something I needed to do all on my own."

"Are you sure?" I can only imagine what it must feel like to cut this final tie. Sever the last tangible link to his parents, his family, his childhood. The last link to Jackson Bennett and the person he was before.

He kisses my hand and nods. "It was time. I want to focus on the future, and there's no reason to hold on to an empty house when I have a full one right here."

My heart melts into a puddle of goo. "I love you. And I know I have no experience where all this relationship stuff is concerned, but I imagine we're going to fuck it up from time to time." I pause. "It'll be me most of the time, I'm sure. Like probably all the time. Assuming you can forgive me for the heinous thing I said to you. Which is a big assumption. But if you can, I'd love nothing more than to be a part of that future you mentioned."

"I forgive you."

"You do?"

"Of course I do." He closes the final distance between us. "We've both dealt with some shit, Sadie. Traumatic shit that doesn't just go away. But I want to be with you. I love you." He cups my cheek with his free hand.

I turn my head, placing a soft kiss on his palm, before leaning in and pressing my lips to his. "I feel like this was too easy. Shouldn't I've had to write out an apology with a skywriter or put up a message on the scoreboard at Yankee Stadium or something?"

"Please don't ever do either one of those." His mouth moves to the side of my neck. "But if you need a grand gesture, I'm happy to comply."

"How about Chinese food and Bravo?" I turn my head once again, this time capturing his mouth with mine.

"You drive a hard bargain, sweet pea."

"But there's something I want to do first." I gently push him away.

"Name it."

"Let's go for a walk. We can grab food on our way home." I stand, heading upstairs to change quickly. I reheat my coffee before we head out but end up grabbing a second latte at a café we stroll by, one I haven't been to before.

We wander for the better part of the afternoon, raiding small vintage shops and a couple of sidewalk sales for stuff I can use in the shop. The shop I have to at least peek my head into, even though we're officially closed, almost to remind myself it's still there and will be for quite some time. We have margaritas during happy hour and ice cream before dinner. On our way back to the brownstone, we pick up Chinese food to go.

I tuck myself into Jack's side embrace as we head back. "Today's been perfect, but not gonna lie, I'm excited to get home."

Jack leans down, planting a kiss on the top of my head. "I've been home all day."

I tilt my head up to meet his gorgeous green-eyed gaze.

He grins. "My home is you."

EPILOGUE

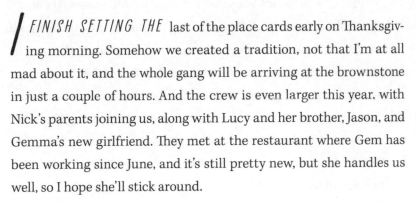

I *FINISH SETTING THE* last of the place cards early on Thanksgiving morning. Somehow we created a tradition, not that I'm at all mad about it, and the whole gang will be arriving at the brownstone in just a couple of hours. And the crew is even larger this year, with Nick's parents joining us, along with Lucy and her brother, Jason, and Gemma's new girlfriend. They met at the restaurant where Gem has been working since June, and it's still pretty new, but she handles us well, so I hope she'll stick around.

"Table looks great, sweet pea." Jack wraps his arms around my waist from behind me, nuzzling into my neck.

My head falls back against his shoulder, but I only give in for a second before I bump him away from me with my hip. "We don't have time for that, Jackpot."

He spins me around, capturing me in a searing kiss. "Do you remember what happened on Thanksgiving last year?"

I roll my eyes, but it doesn't detract from my wide smile. "Duh."

He kisses me again, this one soft and serious. "This has been the best year of my life, Sadie Jane."

"Ditto." I reach up for one final kiss before stepping out of his embrace. "But really, we got shit to do."

Gemma and Taylor, the new girlfriend, arrive a few minutes later, heading straight for the kitchen with barely a hello. Thanks to Taylor I'm free of sous chef duties this year, so I take my time finalizing décor before sneaking up to BaBs to answer a few emails and post on Instagram.

The studio is currently filled with paintings, and while I'm up there, I check out some of Jack's most recent work. He's started taking on a few commissions, though he doesn't use the name Jackson Bennett. A couple of people in the art world have started to sniff around the story, but Jack talks only to his clients, refusing to confirm any theories. All the money he makes from his paintings is funneled directly into the foundation he set up with the profits from the sale of the Connecticut house. It's a scholarship fund for people in their late twenties and older who want to go back to school or start a new career but don't have the means. Jason was the first recipient, and Gemma the second.

When I hear a knock on the front door, I dash into my room to change before bounding down the stairs to greet our guests. Soon the house is filled with laughter and clinking glasses, the smells so tempting I consider sneaking bites of everything before Gemma plates it all. But she'd kill me, so I don't.

I help Gemma and Taylor set up the buffet on the kitchen peninsula. Everyone fills their plates and finds their seats, and that silent hush falls over the room as we all dig in.

This year, it's Jack who makes the first interruption. "At the risk of sounding like a total sap, this was my favorite part of last year's meal—though the mac and cheese gave it a run for its money—and so I'm hoping to start off this year, if you don't mind." He reaches over and takes my hand. "Once again, I'm so thankful for everyone at this table. You'll never know what it means to me to have a house full of love and laughter during the holidays, and I'm not exaggerating when I say you all have changed my life." He turns to me and gives me a quick wink. "Mostly this one over here, but you've all certainly helped. So thank you."

We move around the table, everyone giving thanks for friends and family and opportunities and love. Finally, we come to Nick, having purposefully maneuvered around the table, saving him for last.

Nick clears his throat, taking a minute to look at the faces in the room before he speaks. "I don't think it's any secret that I have a lot to be thankful for in life. I have loving parents and the best friends a guy could ever ask for. I've never wanted for anything, and I am, and always have been, thankful for that." He turns to Harley, sitting next to him, watching him speak with nothing but pure love in her eyes. "But even with everything I've had, I never knew what I was missing until you came along, Harley. I'm so thankful for you. Your love and support, your kindness and compassion. You're the most incredible woman I've ever met, and we're sitting in a room with some pretty incredible women."

"Hear hear!" Gemma calls, sending a ripple of laughter through the room.

Nick pushes his chair back, rising from his seat before falling to one knee. He reaches into his pocket and pulls out a small black box, and the room takes in a collective gasp. Harley's hands fly up to cover her mouth, and I know by the look in her eyes that she's truly surprised.

Jack squeezes my hand and we share a quick glance. We both knew this was coming, and yet, there's a sheen of tears in both pairs of our eyes.

Nick opens the box and the ring catches the light, sparkling even from across the room. "Harley, I love you more than anything, and I want to spend the rest of my life making you as happy as you've made me. Will you marry me?"

The room explodes before she's even fully accepted, everyone pushing out of their chairs and rushing in for hugs. Gemma and Taylor pop two bottles of champagne and everyone toasts.

When we finally make it over to the happy couple, I wrap Harley in my arms. "I'm so happy for you. I can't think of a single person more deserving."

She squeezes back. "Thank you, Sade." She wiggles her ring finger at me. "And thank you."

I give her a wink. "You know I got you."

Nick pulls Jack into a bro hug, slapping him on the back. "Sorry to steal your Thanksgiving thunder, man. Best of luck topping that speech."

Jack catches my eye over Nick's shoulder, giving me a slight eyebrow raise. I grin and nod, not needing to hear his question; he already knows my answer.

I already can't wait for next year.

ACKNOWLEDGMENTS

It might sound hyperbolic, but *Lease on Love* saved me during some of the roughest months of the pandemic. I would sit down to write every night after a long twelve hours with my then six-year-old, relishing the tiny bit of peace and quiet I was able to find at only the latest hours of the day. Diving into the writing, traveling vicariously to one of my favorite cities, living through these characters, was the escape I so desperately needed during the worst of it all, and for this story to have resonated with others is basically a dream come true. A dream I certainly didn't accomplish all on my own.

Thank you so so so much to my agent, Kimberly Whalen. When the pandemic first started, I asked you what I should be working on and you told me to write whatever I wanted, whatever spoke to me. Thank you for giving me that space and encouragement, because from it this book was born. Thank you for always having my back and for fighting so hard to find the perfect home for *Lease on Love.*

To my editor, Gaby Mongelli, I feel so damn lucky to have landed in your extremely capable hands. Thank you for taking this book across the finish line with me. I am so grateful for your insight, and working with you has been an absolute dream. Thank you for loving these characters as much as I do.

Thank you to everyone at G. P. Putnam's Sons, especially Sally Kim, Aja Pollock, Alison Cnockaert, and the entire marketing team. Sanny Chiu, thank you for the most gorgeous cover I've ever seen.

Alexa Martin and Suzanne Park, you picked me out of your Pitch Wars submissions pile and literally changed my life. I could not be more grateful for the guidance and support you both have given me the past couple of years. You signed up to mentor me for a few months, but little did you know you would be stuck with me for life! I won the mentor lottery, and I owe you both a drink (or ten). Thank you to the entire Pitch Wars crew for all the hard work you do, it is much appreciated.

Corey Planer, my Pitch Wars bestie and CP extraordinaire. This book would not be the same without your thoughtful and honest critiques. Thank you for always pushing me to be a little bit mean to my characters. You will always be the first person to ever purchase one of my books, and I can't wait to do the same for you. I'll meet you in Palm Springs!

Allison Ashley and Eagan Daniels, thank you so much for reading early drafts of this book. Your comments were both uplifting and insightful and exactly what I needed to keep pushing.

Haley Kral, thanks for being my longest Twitter writing friend! I have loved getting to share this experience with you.

Katie Golding, you offered me a positivity pass when I needed it most. Thank you for being a bright light in the romance community.

Rachel Lynn Solomon, Sarah Hogle, Melonie Johnson, Denise Williams, and Rosie Danan, thank you for your enthusiasm for *Lease on Love*. I admire all of you so much; your support means the world!

To the Write Squad, Kickass Writer Moms, #writingcommunity, and #22Debuts, thank you for all your continuous support.

Endless thank-yous to the bloggers, bookstagrammers, reviewers, librarians, and bookish community. Your support has been overwhelming, and I'm so grateful. The endless hours you put in to lift up books and writers do not go unnoticed, thank you thank you thank you!

To all my IRL friends, thanks for all the love, even if I get to see your pretty faces less than I would like! Brianna, thanks for always talking plot with me in line at Disneyland (and thanks for the author photos!). Ashley, thanks for the endless encouragement any time I needed an ego boost (which was often), and thanks for always being there to pop the champagne with me (literally and figuratively).

I have literally the world's best in-laws, and I couldn't have done this without them. Thank you for everything, from taking the kid for sleepovers to coming up with custom *Lease on Love* cocktails.

My mom has encouraged my writing from the time I could first hold a pen. If you let her, she'll tell you all about that play I wrote that one time in third grade (please don't let her). Mom, thank you for always having my back and supporting me and my wild dreams.

Canonball, I really hope you don't ever read this book (though when you are old enough, I will happily point you in the direction of the many romances you should read), but I do hope I make you proud. Thanks for being the best kid ever. I love you, goob!

Matt. One of my favorite writers (Sarah Hogle) said it best: "We take turns being brave." Thank you for always giving me the space to be brave. You have never once balked when I came up with an outrageous new life plan, never once discouraged me from absolutely going for it, even when it made life stuff more difficult for you. You offer support in whatever form I need it, whether that's making dinner or pouring me a glass of wine or giving me an extra-long hug or taking the kid and leaving me alone for a few hours of quiet work time. I *literally* couldn't have done this without you. I love you the most.

DISCUSSION GUIDE

1. What were your first impressions of Sadie and Jack? It's clear from the beginning that they are very different people, but they end up living surprisingly well with each other. Why do you think that is?

2. Sadie has a great found family in Harley, Nick, and Gemma. Discuss how her friends played roles in her and Jack's love story. What about their own individual journeys? Did you have a favorite out of the friends?

3. Jack lost his parents several years before the start of the novel. Talk about the ways in which he internalized and processed his grief. How did the death of his parents shape the man he is today?

4. Starting Bridge and Blooms is a major risk for Sadie. What did she learn from the experience? Have you ever taken a similar leap of faith? If so, what kind of support system did you lean on?

5. The brownstone is almost a character in itself. Did you have a favorite feature or element of the house?

6. Sadie had a difficult upbringing, with her parents significantly impacting her sense of self. What work does Sadie do throughout the novel to overcome this? How are her own views of herself challenged by her friends and by Jack?

7. Do you think it was a good idea that Sadie and Jack waited to take their relationship to the next level? Did the slow-burn elements pay off for you?

8. Were you surprised by Jack's secret? How do you think you would have reacted if you were in Sadie's position when she learned the truth?

9. Would you want to live with either Sadie or Jack as a roommate? Why or why not?

10. We get a glimpse of the gang's futures in the epilogue, but what do you think is next for these characters?

ABOUT THE AUTHOR

Photograph of the author © Brianna Mowry

FALON BALLARD loves to write about love! She also has an undying affection for exclamation points and isn't ashamed to admit it! When she's not writing fictional love stories, she's helping real-life couples celebrate, working as a wedding planner in Southern California. She has a deep ~~obsession~~ appreciation for the Marvel Cinematic Universe, is a Disneyland devotee, and is a reality TV aficionado. If she's not busy wrangling her seven-year-old, you can probably find her drinking wine and posting a pic on Instagram while simultaneously snarking on Twitter, because multitasking!

VISIT FALON BALLARD ONLINE

FalonBallard.com

 falonballard

falonballard